Secrets

This was an intriguing book. I was drawn to the descriptive beauty of Bullard's North Florida, contrasted by the lives of the characters and their story of struggle and triumph. I began reading and couldn't put it down until I finished! There were some passages that had me laughing out loud. Johnny Bullard is a wonderful storyteller and has woven a story that will both hold your

interest and put you in the lives of his characters. I so look forward to his second book, "Secrets". Congratulations on a unique and beautiful novel.
Laura R.

Great story, well told. Johnny Bullard has three loves: living in the south, singing gospel songs with the Bullards, and telling stories. He has finally brought his storytelling skills to print. Nightshade has a good storyline with colorful narratives that quickly draws the reader into the customs and mores of southern living. The characters are believable and true to life. By story's end, you'll find yourself wanting to move to Seraph Springs to meet Wanda Faye, Nadine and Destini.
Lesleigh

Truly Southern! A very good read and written by a talented and eloquent writer. I love books about the Deep South and am looking forward to the next one.
Dianne Banks

Old school Southern writing. A fantastic take set in the Deep South by a talented writer. A real treat. I can't wait until he publishes something else!
Charles B. Pennington

Dark water: From the very first chapter, I personally identified with the setting and characters. The mystery, intrigue, redemption and "dirty deeds" are spot on; kept me wanting more. Johnny Bullard is an excellent writer and has a way of bringing you right into the story. Can't wait for the next one.
Monica Chambers

I loved this book! It was like reading about old friends! I do believe that Johnny Bullard has just become one of my favorite Southern writers! Can't wait until his next book!
Sharron Handley

This book will keep you turning the pages, as you anxiously await what will happen next! Wonderfully written by our own Johnny Bullard! I am patiently awaiting the sequel, "Secrets"!
Cathy F.

I loved this book and can't wait for the sequel to come out. I live in this area, the great Suwannee River, and know the author. What a great book and great man.
Amazon Customer

A marvelous story of hope, survival and triumph set in a South that is often overlooked and seldom known.
Amazon Customer

Johnny is a great storyteller. This is a great story about those who live along the Suwannee River in a quiet North Florida town. A great storyline with real life situations, struggle and hope. I read this book in one day and thoroughly enjoyed it.
Amazon Customer

A glimpse of what life around the Suwannee River might be: If you love the South, you will enjoy this book. Written by a true southern gentleman, Johnny just makes the characters come to life. I can't wait until the sequel "Secrets" hits the shelves. I hope Chester gets a little more punishment. And Destini? What else could she be hiding?
Amazon Customer

Secrets

Johnny Bullard
White Springs, Fla.

Editor's note:

When Johnny first told me he was writing a book, it didn't surprise me. After all, he loves to write and he is a skilled storyteller. He asked for my opinion of his rough draft, and after quickly skimming through it, I thought, wow, this is really good.

I edited the first chapter and showed it to him. He seemed impressed with my efforts, so I continued. By the time I finished chapter three, I was hooked on the storyline.

The original manuscript was over 100,000 words, so we decided to turn it into two books. About three weeks later, I finished my first draft of Book One. After some minor changes, we had what we both felt was Johnny's first masterpiece novel, "Nightshade".

During the editing process, there were many times I was bowled over in laughter and other times my eyes welled up with tears. Johnny certainly has a knack for expressing deep emotions from one end of the spectrum to the other.

He experienced record sales within one hour after launching "Nightshade" on his Facebook page and the sales are ongoing. "Secrets" is the second part of this fascinating duology, and both novels are available in paperback and digitally on Kindle.

Book reviews, especially positive ones, are like pure gold to an author. If you enjoyed reading "Nightshade" and "Secrets", please consider rating and reviewing them at Amazon.com.

Joyce Marie Taylor, Editor

ॐ ॐ ॐ ॐ ॐ

Dedication

For all the joy brought to my life by the residents of my beloved home "Around the Banks of the Suwannee" who have encouraged me and supported me, and to my beloved niece, Laura Leigh Bullard, who shall forever be the love of my life, and that is no "Secret."

Chapter 1

Dink a daddy

Drayfuss Lowell, otherwise known as Dink by friends and family, was the happiest man in the world, or at the very least, the happiest man in the small, rural town of Seraph Springs where he, his wife and her four children lived.

Marrying into a large, ready-made family seemed to suit him perfectly since he wasn't able to have children of his own. Besides, he was now betrothed to the woman he had been in love with since he was fourteen years old.

His new bride, Wanda Faye Easley Lowell, and her four children had moved from the small government subsidized apartment they were living in out to Dink's house on the edge of town about two weeks after the nuptials.

It was an old clapboard farmhouse on twenty acres that had been in the family for several generations, and it was huge. There were six bedrooms, so each of the kids had their own room, which was a first for them.

What they really enjoyed was playing in the backyard and venturing into the nearby woods where oftentimes they'd see deer, foxes, turtles and any number of other wildlife species indigenous to north central Florida.

Yes, Dink was in his glory with his new family and his new job. He loved his brand new 18-wheeler, an investment he and Wanda Faye had agreed upon after receiving reward money for turning in close to one million dollars of drug money they discovered in her mama's old tobacco pack house. Wanda Faye's ex husband, Chester Easley, had hidden the money there and it was pure dumb luck, along with Dink's overwhelmingly curious nature, that they happened upon the money, which was neatly packed inside four cardboard boxes marked "Junk" that were taped shut. The reward money was substantial enough that the Lowell's were able to put a large down payment on Dink's new 18-wheeler.

Dink was already making runs from Florida to Georgia and back for the Fernandez Transport Company in his new truck and he stayed busy every week. Usually, his trips took him north of Atlanta to the transfer station the company had near Hiawassee.

On Mondays and Tuesdays, his days were spent doing paperwork for the company and working with other drivers. On Wednesdays, he drove his truck up to Atlanta to be loaded with produce, and then he drove straight through to Miami. He was usually home no later than four o'clock on Friday afternoons. His weekends were always free to spend quality time with his family.

As for Wanda Faye, moving from her small apartment to such a large house was an adjustment, but she was determined to work hard to keep the place spic and span. On Fridays, when Dink would be coming home, she made certain a home-cooked meal was ready and waiting for him.

Her mama, Miss Jewell, had given her some valuable advice not long after the wedding.

"Wanda Faye," she said. "You know I ain't one for makeup, and paint and powder, but you ain't been married in a while. I want you to know that a man don't want to look at a woman who ain't fixed up. After you prepare Dink a good supper on Fridays, you go in and fix yourself up, girl. Fix your hair, put on a nice outfit, and look good when your man comes in from the road. No man wants to come home to a woman who is haggard and looks like ten miles of bad north Florida road."

Wanda Faye couldn't believe her mama was giving her such intimate advice at first, until she reminded her about her marriage to her father, Lucius Lee.

"Even though you and Nadine only saw me as Mama, I experienced great love with your daddy. I have known the passion that a woman feels for the man she loves," her mama told her. "There's nothing in the world more precious and worth fighting for than to feel that love returned to you by your husband."

Meanwhile, Dink seemed utterly happy and content driving for the Fernandez Company, as well as spending time with his new family on weekends. He never complained about being tired when he came home on Friday afternoons, and he never seemed to mind how much the children clamored for his attention when he walked through the front door.

Each Friday afternoon it was as if Santa Claus had just arrived. Dink may not have had huge, expensive presents for the children, but there was, each time, some kind of treat he brought for them, and they looked forward to the surprise.

He played with the children, let them bang on his old guitar and put a goofy Mexican hat on his head, and they sang a lot together. He made up crazy songs and the kids would even add their own silly lyrics. He'd even play hide-and-go-seek with the younger ones. He seemed to love their moments of childhood as much as the children did. Once in a while, Wanda Faye wondered who he loved more, her or the children.

That question, though, was only a passing one that made her smile, for when Dink held her in his arms at night and they made love, she knew that he loved her very much.

One afternoon, just days before Thanksgiving, the children were outdoors playing, while Wanda Faye and Dink were busy shelling and picking out pecans at the kitchen table.

Wanda Faye turned to her husband and calmly said, "Dink, I don't want us to have secrets from one another, so I'm gonna tell you something, and I think it might surprise you."

"What is it, Wanda Faye? Have you been secretly buying lottery tickets and you've hit the Powerball?"

"No, Dink, you silly ol' boy," she said. "You know

I don't buy them things. Money's too hard to come by, and I wish you'd quit spending ten dollars a week on that mess, but I ain't gonna hound you. You quit smoking, and I did, too, so that saves us far more than ten dollars a week, and if it brings you a little pleasure, then go ahead, but, no, Dink, that ain't the secret."

"Well, go ahead, Wanda Faye, what is it?"

"Remember when I took Little Chet to the doctor about a month ago when you came home early on Friday?"

"Yeah, I remember," he said.

"Do you remember when the nurse came out and took us all to the examination room and swabbed the insides of our mouths, and you asked why, and she said she just wanted to determine if the frequency of strep at our house was in any way related to us?"

"Yes, I remember, but I thought that was a little odd, and I never quite understood it."

"Well, it wasn't about strep throat, and it wasn't about infection. It was about something I've known for nearly ten years, but I wanted to make sure it was true."

"Go ahead, Wanda Faye. Gosh, you're as slow as cream rising. Quit hemmin' and hawin' around. Christmas is a comin', girl."

"Dink… Little Chet is your son. He's your boy," she said.

"Well, goodness gracious, I know that," Dink said, shaking his head. "All the children are mine… and yours. We love them."

"No, Dink, Little Chet is your biological son. He's yours. That stuff your mama told you about the mumps must not have been a hundred percent true because Little Chet is your child."

"Oh, go on," he scoffed at her. "Have you been drinkin' today?"

"I'm totally sober, Dink. Remember that Saturday afternoon at the revival when we were teenagers and me and you snuck out of the House of Prayer and went down by the river?"

"Well, of course, I do. I'll never forget that afternoon."

"I won't either, Dink, and after three times of making love to you that afternoon, something must have took, because that boy is yours. Can't you look at him and tell?"

Dink sat silently at the table for a few moments and just stared at her in disbelief. Then, he put his head in his hands with his elbows on the table, as if he was in deep thought. When he looked up again there were tears in his eyes and he turned to Wanda Faye.

"But you left from here and you went up to Georgia to go to high school," he said to her.

"I went to Georgia because I was pregnant, Dink" Wanda Faye said. "You were fourteen years old and so was I. What were we gonna do about things? Your mama wasn't gonna let you marry at fourteen and my mama would have sent me off to some home for unwed mothers. I went to Georgia and I married Chester. He was awful to me, but he did give that child, as well as my other children a name. I have to say, for what I suffered at his hands, and it was a lot, I have to say that I used Chester Easley. Just as sure as grits are groceries, I used that man."

Wanda Faye got up from the table and went over to the kitchen counter. She opened a drawer, pulled out an envelope, and then handed it to Dink.

"Go ahead," she urged him. "Read what it says."

It took him about a minute to read through the lab report from the doctor's office, which stated there was a 99.9 percent chance that Chester Easley Jr. was his son.

"Read the next page," Wanda Faye told him.

Dink flipped to the second page and saw that there was no way possible that Chester Easley could be the boy's father. Wanda Faye explained that Carl Alvin had helped her get Chester's DNA report from the prison because she wanted Dink to know for certain Little Chet really was his biological son.

Dink looked at Wanda Faye and held out his arms. Tears were streaming down his face now.

"This is the best news I think I've ever gotten in my entire life," he said, wrapping his arms around Wanda Faye, as he choked back sobs. "If I ever doubted you loved me, Wanda Faye, I'll never doubt it again, honey. I love you so much."

"I love you, too, Dink," she said, as she shed her own tears of joy.

"Are we gonna tell Little Chet?" Dink asked.

"Well, I been wonderin' the same thing and I'm thinkin', not just yet. I think we should wait a little while and talk things over some more. Then, together we'll tell him. It won't be easy, but I really think we need time to put together the right words."

"Does anybody else know?" Dink asked.

"Well, my sister, Nadine, of course, and our best friend, Destini, both know."

"Does your mama know?" he asked.

"Oh, yeah, and Destini's grandma, Mama Tee, knew it the first time she put her hands over Little Chet's face when he was a baby. She knew it, and she told me so. Sometimes the blind can see things we can't see."

"Well, she sees a lot more than I can, that's for sure. God bless her. I just thought after what the doctor said... you know, he told my mama, maybe, maybe one chance in a million."

"Well, Dink, I must have been that millionth chance, 'cause it worked with me," Wanda Faye said, and then she pointed toward the window. "Out there in that yard, running around with that pair of faded jeans and that Atlanta Braves sweatshirt you bought for him... well, he's a part of you and me."

"Thanksgiving ain't till Thursday, and I got the rest of the week off, but for me, Thanksgiving is right here, right now, Wanda Faye," Dink said, still with tears streaming down his face. "There won't ever be a Thanksgiving as wonderful as this one."

Wanda Faye kissed Dink on the forehead and put her arms around his neck, cradling him to her bosom.

"For me, neither, sugar, for me, neither," she said, crying along with him.

Chapter 2

Wanda Faye and her entire family, including Nadine and Louie and their three kids, as well as Miss Jewell, Brother Linton, Miss Velma and their daughter, Jerri Faye, were all looking forward to spending Thanksgiving out at Camp EZ. The owner, Mr. Hamp, invited all of his friends to come out to the lodge because he was throwing a huge party.

He even told Dink to invite the folks from Fernandez Trucking Company. It seemed everyone loved being around Mr. and Mrs. Fernandez, as well as their son, Justo Jr. and his wife Carolina, and their two kids, Justo III and Ricardo.

Mr. Hamp told everyone he invited to bring whatever they wanted to eat. He never put any limits on what someone could bring to the Thanksgiving feasts at the camp. It was his favorite holiday of the year.

That morning, both Wanda Faye and Nadine were up well before sunrise getting everything ready for a fun and enjoyable day at the camp. Dink and Louie took the boys out to the camp just as dawn broke to go still hunting in the woods on the property for white tailed deer, which was one of Mr. Hamp's favorite Thanksgiving traditions.

Once Nadine and Wanda Faye loaded all their covered dishes in the van, they drove out to the camp with their three girls. On the way, they spotted their mama's vehicle just ahead of them. Miss Jewell was chattering away with Brother Linton who was sitting up front, while Sister Velma and Jerri Faye sat side by side in the back seat.

"Now, you know Mama's got that trunk loaded with her own special turkey and dressing, even though there's gonna be plenty of smoked and fried turkey at the party," Wanda Faye said, laughing.

"Well, you know Mama Tee," Nadine said. "She insists nobody makes dressing like Mama. Mama told me the other day that since Mama Tee's gonna be there, she wanted to make sure she made enough dressing for her."

Also joining them at the camp for the Thanksgiving feast was Mr. Hamp's nephew, Carl Alvin Brayerford Campbell, Miss Hattie Campbell and her sister, Francis Katherine, otherwise known as Miss Nanny, and Mr. Hamp's niece, the flamboyant and always fun, Dee Dee Wilson.

Dee Dee's arrival, no matter where she went, signaled excitement among both the children and the adults. Dee Dee loved kids about as much as she loved dressing in the latest styles. Usually, the more jewels she had on a sweater or a dress, the better.

Today, however, she arrived a bit more toned

down in a pair of straight-legged, black jeans and black boots, but her sweater was a different story. It was festooned with what looked like Indian beading that, more likely than not, cost her a small fortune. Dangling from her ears were beaded earrings that matched the beads on her sweater.

Wanda Faye, Nadine and Destini all went out to greet her to wish her a happy birthday, since she shared her joyous birth with the holiday.

After all the hugs and kisses, Dee Dee directed the girls and all the children around to the back seat of her Range Rover. When she opened the door, a beautiful white standard poodle came bounding out. The dog immediately started barking and licking all the kids' faces.

"Goodness, Dee Dee! What in the world?" Nadine gasped.

"Isn't she wonderful? Carl Alvin bought her for me for my birthday," Dee Dee said, all smiles. "Since I took that apartment over in Jacksonville, I've been a little frightened of staying by myself. She's a fabulous watchdog and she's completely house-broken."

"What's her name?" Destini's daughter, Bunnye, wanted to know.

"Her name is Chanel. I named her after my favorite fashion designer. Don't you love it?"

"Lord have mercy, Dee Dee," Nadine said. "You got a big baby on your hands now, girl. One you're gonna take to the vet, the groomers, and see to it that this high falutin' gal is kept up. She ain't one of them pencil-tailed bird dogs like your daddy used to keep out there on the farm for hunting quail. This gal is high maintenance."

"That's the reason I identify with her so well," Dee Dee said, holding out her perfectly manicured nails. "In that respect, she and I are a lot alike."

As Charlene and Darlene were putting Chanel's leash on, Charlene noticed her collar was beaded almost identically to the beads on Dee Dee's sweater.

"Oh, look!" Charlene squealed. "Her toenails are painted the same color as your nails, Dee Dee!"

"Isn't it great?" Dee Dee squealed along with her, and then she leaned down and hugged Chanel. "She's Mommy's precious baby. Mommy loves her Chanel. Yes, she does, yes, she does."

By this time, Mr. Hamp had come over to see what all the commotion was about.

"My God, Dee Dee, where in the world did you get that fuzzy thing?" he asked her. "Lord have mercy. I ain't seen a standard poodle like that since I was a young boy. There used to be a Yankee lady who came to stay at one of the old resort hotels in town and she had poodle just like this one. I think his name was Pierre."

"Pierre?" Nadine asked, raising her eyebrows.

"Yep, ol' Pierre used to sashay around the springs and he loved to get in the water and swim. You better watch that dog around the river, Dee Dee."

"Oh, I'm not worried," Dee Dee said.

"Well, one day, Pierre got loose from that Yankee woman, and just like my Florida Gators are gonna do the day after tomorrow, Pierre became gator bait."

"Oh, no!" Dee Dee shrieked.

"They killed the alligator," Mr. Hamp said. "He was a big one, about fourteen feet long. When they cut him open, they found Pierre's gold plated dog tag. Old man Baker mailed it to the lady and she wrote the man a thank you note and sent him twenty bucks. She told him it was all she had left of her beloved Pierre, and she would cherish it forever. If you ask me, it's silly as hell goin' on over a damned dog that way, but some people do."

"Now, listen to you, Uncle Hamp," Dee Dee said. "I seem to remember about four or five Christmases ago, sitting up with someone out here at the camp and going with that someone over to Pittstown to the vet's office, I can't tell you how many times, to get your old bird dog Sheba over pneumonia. Do you remember that, Uncle Hamp?"

"Dee Dee, that's entirely different," he said, as his face turned a bright shade of pink. "Sheba was the best bird dog there ever was. If your daddy was living, God rest his soul, he'd tell you the same thing. If I had all the quail that me and your daddy killed hunting with that ol' dog, I couldn't stack 'em in that lodge. She earned her keep."

"I suppose you're right," Dee Dee said.

"You see her over there on the rug by the door?" he asked her, pointing over toward the lodge. "She's nearly blind and lost all her teeth, but she'll still follow me out in the fields. Bless her heart, she's like me. She still wants to hunt, but she's not able. Even last year, in her shape, she pointed a number of coveys of quail when we were out just walking around. Now, when that cotton ball of yours can hunt birds or do anything useful, you let me know."

"Why, Uncle Hamp, she's protecting me," Dee Dee said, frowning. "I'm taking her to that school in Jacksonville to teach her more about how to be a guard dog."

"Well, you better have her fixed," he told her. "If she ain't fixed and she comes in heat, one of them big shepherds will be on her fluffy behind like white on rice, and then you'll have something. If she's like most of the really high classed ones I've known, they pretend like they don't want you to advance on them and take it, but they do, and once they give in, they're hot as a match."

"Uncle Hamp!" Dee Dee gasped. "Not in front of the children!"

The old man just waved his hands, like it was no big deal.

"Hell, honey, they know more now at eight than I did at twenty-eight," he said. "If you want to take Fluffball inside the lodge, you can. I don't care. Take her in the side door, though. I don't want Sheba upset by her."

"We won't upset, Sheba. I promise," Dee Dee said, and she kissed the old man on the cheek. "You are a sweetheart, Uncle Hamp," she said. "Happy Thanksgiving."

"Ahem," the old man uttered, as he cleared his throat and flushed red this time. "Happy Thanksgiving to you, too, honey. Oh, and happy birthday. Go take a look in the front hall closet of the lodge. There's a wrapped box in there. I bought you a little something. Hattie and Nanny said you'd been wantin' something like it, so I had them pick it out."

Within seconds, Dee Dee was inside the lodge. When she opened the closet, she found a beautifully wrapped box in silver and gold foil.

"Can I open it now?" she asked her uncle, who trailed in right behind her.

"You can open it whenever you want," he told her.

Dee Dee was like a five-year-old opening a Christmas present, smiling and giggling as she tore into the box. Her eyes gaped wide and her mouth even wider when she saw what was inside.

"Oh, this is the most gorgeous mink vest I've ever seen!" she said.

She immediately put it on and rushed over to hug Mr. Hamp.

"Oh, thank you, Uncle Hamp," she said, as she ran her hands across the soft fur. "I can't believe it. This is so beautiful."

"Well, believe it," he said. "That's your birthday and Christmas present all wrapped into one. Mind you, don't wear that thing too often when you're around that cotton ball. She might think it's another dog and try to hump it or something."

Dee Dee burst out laughing, as did everyone who was standing nearby.

Chapter 3

Mr. Hamp spent a good bit of time taking Mr. and Mrs. Fernandez around the lodge and showing them his vast collection of wild turkey prints, porcelain turkeys, bronze turkeys, and every kind of turkey one could imagine.

Meanwhile, all the young boys were having a ball putting on camouflage outfits and running around the campgrounds, while the girls played one game after the next, many of which were made up by the hour.

It had taken Destini and Wanda Faye a good two weeks working off and on, to unpack his extensive collection each year before the big day and get them all placed around at various vantage points in the camp. They made sure the rare, breakable ones were put in a display case away from the children, but had they broken the most expensive one, the old man would have laughed and said nothing. That's just the way he was. The joys of having the children around were more important to him than any material item.

Mr. Hamp had purchased each one of the children an Indian headdress to wear during dinner, which was usually served around four in the afternoon.

In the interim, waiting for all the hungry pilgrims and Indians was a veritable cornucopia of brunch dishes, including Destini's buttermilk biscuits, a huge bowl of fresh citrus fruits, Mr. Hamp's famous venison sausage, bacon and ham, and a huge pot of cheese grits, which would tide them over until dinner.

There would also be every jam, jelly and preserve imaginable to go on the biscuits, as well as slices of Miss Jewell and Sister Velma's banana nut and cranberry nut breads.

All of this was washed down with gallons of coffee, fresh squeezed orange juice, and for some of the adults, Bloody Marys. Even Brother Linton had a virgin Bloody Mary, as he loved the taste of the spicy tomato juice mixture.

Destini never told him or Sister Velma, but right before she served it to them, she added about a jigger of the good Grey Goose Vodka. They never picked up on it, and since they only had a couple, it relaxed them and made for a more pleasant Thanksgiving. She knew the Lord would understand. Neither of them were alcoholics, so she wasn't sending them back to rehab. She figured an ounce was no more than they would take in a cupful of cough medicine.

About the time all the brunch items were ready to be served, a private medical transport van came into the yard. Mr. Hamp had the company bring Mama Tee out to the celebration. Carefully and tenderly, Mama Tee was carried into Camp EZ where she was placed in a leather Barca Lounger, similar to the one she had at home.

On the way in, Mama Tee said to the young men who were carrying her, "Be careful with the old lady. She ain't what she used to be, but she's thankful to be here."

Mr. Hamp was standing nearby and he laughed quietly to himself.

"That's the truth, Mama Tee," he said. "I'm with you," he added, but Mama Tee didn't hear him.

Once she was seated before the fireplace and an afghan was placed over her lap, Mama Tee made herself known.

"Mr. Hamp!" she called out. "Hamp Brayerford, I know you in this room. I can smell you. Smells kinda like wood smoke and pine needles. Where you is? Come over here."

Mr. Hamp smiled and went over to her, with Destini on his heels.

"I'm here, Mama Tee. What can I do for you?"

"For starters, you can tell Destini to get my coffee can and set it over here by me."

"Now, Mama Tee, we talked about that," Destini said. "You know you can't be dippin' on snuff up here at the lodge."

"Aw, go get her the damned can," Mr. Hamp said. "She can spit all over this gosh darned floor. It's mine. She's at home here. Get her the can, Destini, and whatever else she wants. You want some juice, Mama Tee? Some coffee?"

"A little coffee would be nice, it sure would, and a bowl of that fruit I smell," Mama Tee said. "I want mostly oranges and grapefruit in mine, maybe a few bananas. I wish this sugar was where I could have me a little drink. Hamp, will you get Destini to give me a shot after awhile and later on pour me just a little of that shine. I know you got some out there in that woodshed. I know you got it."

"You know me, Mama Tee, and you've always known me, and, yes, ma'am, I will see to it."

"Put them big footsies up here. I want to feel them boots," the old woman said.

Mr. Hamp smiled, knowing what Mama Tee was about to do. With some effort, he raised one of his feet up to the ottoman. Feeling around, Mama Tee untied his Brougham shoe and removed it. Then, she lifted his foot and felt his heel.

"First time I felt these feets, the day you came out of Miz Lillian," Mama Tee said. "I was a young miss then, only about thirteen years old, but when I saw them foots I laughed 'cause they was so big. Mama was helpin' old Doc Campbell, and she turned to me and said, this boy goin' have a good foundation, a good understandin', and we all laughed. Foot's a little more wrinkled now, Hamp, but it's the same foot. I sho' wish you'd wear some socks. It sho' ain't gentlemanly for you not to wear no socks, and you can still braid briars with the bottoms of these foots. You still love goin' barefooted, don't you, boy?"

"Mama Tee, ain't nobody called me a boy since last year when you was here," Mr. Hamp said, laughing. "You are a mess."

"Ain't nobody old enough to call you one but me,"

she countered. "I lived a long time, Hamp, a long, long time. I cain't see and yet I can. I sho' is thankful to be in the number one more time. You like my shirt?"

Mr. Hamp laughed when he saw Mama Tee had on a sweat shirt with a turkey on the front of it. Underneath the turkey was written, "I ain't a young chick, but I can still shake a tail feather."

"I love your shirt," he said, still laughing. "Mama Tee, if you need anything, you let me know, anything at all."

"Before you go, boy, I want to tell you somethin', somethin' I been holdin' in a long time. That foot of yours... I know that foot real well. I know of two living peoples with that foot. You make sure you take care of them footsies. Take care of them. They precious."

Mr. Hamp rarely showed emotions, at least in public, but now his clear blue eyes were filled with tears.

"I promise, Mama Tee," he said. "I promise you I will. I will look after them always."

"That's good, boy, that's good," she said. "Now, hand me my coffee and my bowl of fruit and go on and see to these other peoples. It's a Happy Thanksgiving Day. It sho' is."

The rest of the day was filled with praise and laughter, and plenty of eating and drinking. Before the big meal, Brother Linton read Psalm 100 and everyone held hands in a big circle. Before he started, Mama Tee interrupted him.

"Reverend, I'm gettin' old now," she said. "I don't wanna die before this blessin' is over, and the Lord don't want the food gettin' cold, neither. So, do as the old folks used to say. Stand up, speak up, and sit down. The Lord will understand and be just as thankful for you sayin' thank you as he will for you to string a sermon into a blessin'."

Brother Linton smiled at Mama Tee and took her advice.

"Lord, for what we are about to receive, we are truly thankful. Bless this food, bless the hands that prepared it, and Lord, we truly offer thanksgiving to you. In Jesus' name, Amen."

"Amen," Mama Tee shouted, almost as loud as Mr. Hamp shouted.

"Preacher," Mr. Hamp said. "That's as good a blessing as I've ever heard. God Bless you and thank you for being here. I want Destini to come and get Mama Tee a plate first. Behind her, our south Florida guests, and then Brother Linton, Sister Velma, Miss Jewell, Jerri Faye and Jewell Lee, y'all can get in line. Then, the rest of us will follow. There's plenty for everybody."

છે-છે-છે-છે-છે-છે-છે-છે-છે

Nadine and Wanda Faye sat close to Jerri Faye during supper and encouraged her to eat a healthy meal, and at least taste a little bit of everything.

"Did you notice how much weight Jerri Faye has lost since the last time we saw her?" Wanda Faye asked Nadine later. "She just didn't seem to have that vibrant glow like she used to."

"Yeah, I noticed, all right," Nadine said. "It can't be a good thing, either."

Throughout the day, Jerri Faye mostly sat on the couch and often nodded off to sleep. When she awakened from her little cat naps, she seemed frustrated if Sister Velma wasn't sitting right beside her.

Jerri Faye was everyone's little angel and it was clear they all loved her very much. Wanda Faye, Nadine, Destini and Dee Dee all made special efforts to do all they could for her to make her feel comfortable.

Dee Dee even let her wear her new mink vest for most of the day. She laughed when Dee Dee first put it on her.

"Look, Mama," she said. "I'm a movie star."

"You've always been my movie star, precious," Miss Velma told her.

She also enjoyed wearing the Indian headdress, which hadn't come off since Mr. Hamp placed it on her head. Chanel even picked up on how special Jerri Faye was. The poodle with a pedigree as long as the River Nile seemed to sense, as animals often do, that she had special needs. She lay close to her for most of the day, and Jerri Faye took delight in petting her.

"Her fur is so soft and she smells like perfume," Jerri Faye said.

Dee Dee, ever kind and open-hearted, stood at the counter between the kitchen and the great room of the lodge and she winked at Wanda Faye and Nadine, as Jerri Faye played with Chanel.

"Miss Dee Dee, you reckon you ought to let that

child keep wearing that expensive fur vest," Sister Velma asked. "She's liable to mess it up."

Just then, Mr. Hamp walked over to them and Dee Dee whispered something in his ear. Mr. Hamp smiled and nodded, and then walked to the other side of the room.

"Sister Velma, that vest was a gift from Uncle Hamp. He said I could do with it whatever I wanted, so, I'm gonna give it to Jerri Faye."

"Oh, Lord, no, Miss Dee Dee," Sister Velma gasped.

Dee Dee paid her no mind and went over to the couch where Jerri Faye was sitting. She sat down next to her and took her hands in her own.

"Jerri Faye, this fur vest is yours," Dee Dee told her. "It's my Thanksgiving present to you, baby. You can be a movie star forever now. It's your vest, and you wear it anytime you want, because you're our movie star."

"You giving it to me? Forever? It's mine?" Jerri Faye asked, as she felt the softness of the luxurious fur.

"It's yours, honey, yours from me and Mr. Hamp. It's yours to keep. You will always be our movie star. Can I get a hug and a kiss from my favorite movie star?"

Jerri Faye looked as happy as she had looked all day, other than when she was playing with Chanel. She wrapped her arms around Dee Dee's neck and squeezed her hard.

"Okay, honey, I'm sure, Destini, Wanda Faye and Nadine are all gonna want hugs and kisses, too," Dee

Dee said, as tears welled up in her eyes. "You aren't gonna be one of those stuck up movie stars now that you have a pretty fur vest, are you?"

"No, no, Miss Dee Dee. I'm nice movie star," she said.

With that, she hugged and kissed Dee Dee again, and then it was everyone else's turn for a hug.

When she made it over to Mama Tee, the old woman held her in her arms for a long time.

"Yes, ma'am, Jerri Faye. You'ze a beautiful movie star, just as beautiful and special as you can be," Mama Tee told her.

Destini saw the tears running down Mama Tee's wrinkled yellow skin, and she brought her a couple of tissues.

"Shoo, now girls, get on away from here," Mama Tee told Destini and Jerri Faye. "Bring me another cup of that coffee."

Mama Tee, as always, never wanted anyone to make over her when she got emotional. It was just her way.

After dinner, Destini's Uncle Duke insisted Nadine play her guitar, and that she, Wanda Faye and the children sing. That was all the prompting Nadine needed, and she quickly gathered everyone around to sing Christmas carols, since, according to her, Thanksgiving officially began the Christmas season. Even Mr. Hamp appeared a few minutes later with a Santa Claus hat, which he placed on Mama Tee's head. She smiled wide and joined in the fun and the singing.

A short time later, Mrs. Fernandez, an

accomplished pianist, sat down at the old Steinway Baby Grand and played a beautiful Christmas carol, Spanish style. She and her entire family sang to the delight of everyone.

"O Santissimo,
O Felissimo,
Grato tiempo de Navidad.
Al mundo perdido,
Cristo le ha nacido,
Alegria, Alegria, Cristiandad!"

When they finished, Mr. Fernandez asked everyone to stand and sing with them, "God Bless America".

"After all, this is an American holiday," he said.

As everyone sang the words, Wanda Faye looked out across the group in the lodge and she felt blessed. There were African Americans, Cuban-Americans, Pentecostals, Methodists, Catholics, gay, straight, a Down's syndrome child, and even a standard poodle named Chanel.

She thought to herself, "This is America."

She couldn't help but think about Miss Margot, too, and one of her recent shows. Miss Margot said something about America being like a big patchwork quilt. Each piece, she said, was a little different and unique, but each piece added something to the quilt.

"She was so right," Wanda Faye thought. "The quilt spread over Camp EZ today has been a warm and loving one. Happy Thanksgiving, Wanda Faye."

Chapter 4

Chester gives thanks, so does Daddy

Not too far above the Florida-Georgia state line, the congregation at the Ludowici House of Prayer was celebrating their own special Thanksgiving. Brother Chester Easley was playing bass guitar better than he ever did and he was leading the other members of the musical ensemble in an old hymn called "Heaven's Jubilee".

Some glad morning we shall see Jesus in the air,
Coming after you and me, joy is ours to share.

Shouts of "Glory to God" and the tinkling sounds of the shaking tambourines resounded throughout the little sanctuary and then spilled out the open windows, as a cool breeze flowed throughout the church, energizing the entire congregation.

Up and down the aisles, people of all ages raised their hands toward heaven. A few of the congregants even danced up and down the center aisle of the church, as they were filled with the Holy Ghost.

The singing reached a fevered pitch when the final words of the chorus were sung.

Oh, what singing, Oh, what shouting,
On that happy morning when we all shall rise.
Oh what glory, Hallelujah!
When we meet our blessed Savior in the skies.

"Oh, glory, yes, thank you, Lord Jesus! Glory, glory to God!" Chester shouted, as the song came to a close.

Once everyone was seated again and the band members returned to their loved ones in the pews, Chester took to the podium.

"Oh, beloved, what a Thanksgiving we are having today, but it is nothing compared to the one we're going to have when we cross over Jordan and get home," Chester said to the congregation. "I don't know about you, but when He calls my name, I'm ready to go home."

Many hearty "Amen's" were shouted and then Chester continued.

"As long as the Lord lets me live, dear brothers and sisters in Christ – and I don't know how long that will be – I will be doing His work. I spent so many years wandering in the wilderness of sin, and I came up with nothing. I was empty, dry, and felt bone dead. All of that changed, though, and not because of anything I did, but because of the one who loves me unconditionally, and the one who loves you. He is the one who came to earth, willingly gave his life and died for you, and who came up out of that grave. Today, He lives for you."

More hearty shouts of "Amen" and "Glory to God" rang out through the sanctuary.

"That is the reason today and every day is Thanksgiving for me, and that's the reason I know, as the banner says behind me, Jesus is the answer," Chester continued. "Not too many weeks ago, I went to sleep after praying, and in a vision I saw this banner. I saw a place where this church would attend to the physical and spiritual needs of our community. Today, we are breaking ground on our Jesus is the Answer Center, and with the tickets we've sold from our Thanksgiving dinner today, and the love offerings we've taken up, we have enough to step out on faith and start the construction on our multi-purpose building that will serve as a lighthouse of hope for everyone."

Chester had been quite busy since his revelation dream a couple months ago when he realized his goal in life was to honor and serve the Lord and help wayward souls along the way. He had managed to reel in quite a few radio stations throughout the state of Georgia to broadcast his sermons.

Each Sunday morning and Sunday evening service, as well as many special holiday church services at the Ludowici House of Prayer were broadcast live.

Chester's new mission in life doing work for the Lord kept his mind off the atrocities and the sexual abuse he had suffered at the hands of Daddy while he was in the state prison.

"I finally feel good about myself," he said each night before going to sleep. "Thank you, God, for watching over me."

❧ ❧ ❧ ❧ ❧ ❧ ❧ ❧ ❧ ❧ ❧

Meanwhile, sitting in the prison library at Georgia State Penitentiary, was an inmate by the name of Dexter, known by his cellmates as Daddy, who was pretending to read the Bible. He was pretending because he couldn't read, but every once in a while he liked spending time in the library because it was quiet.

Today, he smuggled in two pieces of pecan pie and gave one to the officer who was sitting at the desk. In return for pie, the officer reached into his desk drawer and handed Daddy a small, battery operated CD player and radio.

Daddy normally just listened to the CD with earplugs, but today, for some reason, he switched the control the wrong way and he heard a familiar voice on the radio.

"I love you, and more importantly, Jesus loves you," Chester said across the airwaves. "Remember, I love you and Jesus loves you, and once Jesus puts His arms around you, He will never let you go. You're His child then, and He'll never let you go."

A huge smile came across Daddy's face and he quietly whispered, "I found my little man. Daddy's found his little man. Daddy ain't never goin' let go of his little man. Oh, Happy Thanksgiving, Daddy's found his little man."

"Shhh," the officer warned him. "Not so loud. What's the matter with you? Do you need help?"

"Lord, no sir, you done helped me more than you know. I found something I lost. Oh, lordie, yes, I found it. It sho' is a happy Thanksgiving."

"This is WDSQ, the voice of South Georgia radio. We have brought you, live today, a broadcast from the Ludowici House of Prayer," the radio announcer said. "You have just heard singing by the House of Prayer Ensemble, Reverend Chester Easley, director. Tune in on Sunday when we'll bring you worship live from the Ludowici House of Prayer."

The broadcast ended with the Ludowici Prayer Ensemble singing "Amazing Grace".

"Oh, how sweet the sound that saved a wretch like me," Daddy said quietly to himself, as he listened to the words.

Later, as he walked down the corridor toward his cell, he was smiling so big that his teeth were glowing. He kept singing over and over, "I once was lost, but now am found."

Chapter 5

Destini's sleeping dog

The day after the Thanksgiving feast, Destini Wilson stood on the back lawn of the Camp EZ lodge and looked down at the slowly moving black waters of the Suwannee River, she breathed in the cool, crisp autumn air. Fall along the upper Suwannee was her favorite time of year. The leaves turned from green to golden, then from russet to deep red. Almost overnight, with the first frost of the season, the Sweet Gums, hickory trees and even the old cypress trees seemed to vie for attention to see which one could wear the brightest fall garment.

Destini knew all about the history of Campbell County and the small river town of Seraph Springs where she was born and raised, however, the land in and around this part of the county could write its own book and tell its own story. This was not the rich, fertile cotton land of the Mississippi Delta or Alabama's Black Belt. This was timber land, and it grew some of the best pine trees in the world.

Hamp Brayerford, the owner of Camp EZ, had related many stories to Destini over the years about his lineage. As she sat underneath a shade tree taking in the beauty of the river and all the fall colors, her mind wandered back to all those stories Hamp had told her.

His father, Hamp Brayerford Sr., worked as an overseer on the different farms belonging to his wife's family, the Allison's. The Allison's were the closest thing this part of the world had to antebellum aristocracy, as they had, at one time grown a lot of Sea Island Cotton, and later, flue cured tobacco on a number of farms in and around Seraph Springs.

The late Captain Watson Belmont Allison had been a hero in the Confederate Army. After the war, when all the radical reconstruction was over and done with, he was made postmaster of Seraph Springs. He also opened a general store that sold everything from soup to nuts.

Captain Allison's unwillingness to give up the sharecropping system and utilize diversified farming methods, however, forced the family to sell off more and more of their acreage through the years to maintain their lifestyle. Meanwhile, their farming business continued to lose money.

Right before the First World War, there was a major economic panic, in which Captain Allison over-extended himself. Seemingly overnight, the Allisons lost the big house overlooking the Suwannee River in Seraph Springs, as well as the cotton warehouses that had once been so profitable. The family moved to a smaller Victorian bungalow on one of the large farms north of town. Even though they kept most of their furniture, and the farm was a beautiful place, the Captain's wife hated it and became extremely depressed.

The local doctor prescribed a nerve tonic for her that was mostly laudanum, and soon she was taking it more and more, and lying in her darkened bedroom day in and day out. One morning, their maid, Miss Sukie, went in to check on her and found her dead.

On her tombstone was written, "A rose here on earth, a rose up in heaven."

The Allison's teenage daughter, Lillian Sophia, felt that statement on her tombstone was true. Her mama was too fine and delicate for this world. Since she lived mostly in the past and couldn't adjust to changes in the world, it was, for her, a blessing to move on to another world.

Hamp Brayerford Sr. began seeing Lillian right after she graduated from high school. At first, it was just randomly, when he would catch up to her when she was out riding the acres of her father's farms. He was definitely interested, though, and later, he asked Captain Allison for permission to formally call on her.

Captain Allison, having undergone some of the horrors of a Yankee prisoner of war camp, and having lost his arm to gangrene, was more of a pragmatist than his delicate departed wife. He knew if the Allison family was to have any chance of propelling itself to prominence in the twentieth century, then it would have to be through the sons and daughters of Hamp Brayerford Sr. and his daughter Lillian Sophia Allison.

Captain Allison watched and learned as young Hamp taught him about the naval store industry. Hamp was a hard worker, wholesome looking and good natured, as well. Captain Allison had nothing against him, other than his lack of a pedigree, which, he felt in most cases wasn't that much of a drawback. After all, what did it matter how many illustrious ancestors one had when, in today's world, most of them couldn't buy a cup of coffee?

The marriage of Lillian Sophia Allison to Hamp Brayerford Sr. in the sanctuary of Seraph Springs Methodist Church in the fall of 1919 brought much love to the young couple. Within six years, two children were conceived; a daughter, Elizabeth "Bessie" Brayerford, born in the spring of 1922, and Hamp Brayerford Jr., who was born November 7, 1927.

Lillian loved her husband dearly, but found that a man building an empire had little time at home. When he was home, though, he doted on the children and made a point of spending quality time with them, taking them on long jaunts through the flat woods and out to the farms.

He made his money in naval stores, a major industry that was prevalent throughout much of the South through the Second World War. Naval Stores carried products derived from pine sap, which included items such as soap, paint, varnish, linoleum, lubricants and even shoe polish.

Pine resin was extracted from thousands of pine trees and was distilled into mineral spirits. In this area of north Florida, when a person referred to someone living at the One Mile Still or the Five Mile Still, they were referring to the site of an old turpentine distillery.

During the years that followed, even during the Depression, when so many lost so much, the Brayerford fortune grew, due in no small part to Hamp Sr.'s business acumen, and the fact that he believed in keeping cash stashed in a number of safes and vaults he had hidden at various locations all over his vast timber empire.

Like his father before him, Hamp Sr. had a distrust of most banking institutions. He decided early on that his money would only go in a bank if he owned it. That dream became a reality in the fall of 1934, when he purchased controlling interest in three of the major banks in the area.

In the early 1960s, huge deposits of phosphate were found in the county, and an international company came in to become Campbell County's largest employer.

By the time Hamp Jr. reached the age of twenty-one, the Brayerford timber empire covered nearly 50,000 acres in four north Florida counties. The phosphate mining operation that came to the county paid the family millions of dollars for their interests in several sections of land on which the plant would be operating.

Timber, agriculture, phosphate and banking kept Hamp Jr. busy, but he loved it. His favorite pursuit in his limited free time was enjoying the recreational activities his land afforded him.

He had always been an avid hunter and fisherman.

He never dreamed that one day people from the urban areas of the state and the nation, not to mention all the foreigners from other countries around the world, would actually pay money to hunt and fish.

When he realized the money to be made from something he had always loved, he decided, after some deliberation, to build Camp EZ. It was situated on the site of an old pine slab shack where he and his daddy spent many wonderful hours together just watching the Suwannee River flow south on its way to the Gulf of Mexico. Of all the seasons of the year, his favorite had always been autumn.

Autumn meant wood fires; big bonfires built down near the river by Hamp Jr. and all the others who worked at Camp EZ. The smell of pine lightwood or "lightard" fires sent out a perfume that mixed with the tangy scent of the millions of slash pines covering the flat woods. Even the old palmettos seemed to rejoice and have new life.

"Well, enough reminiscing," Destini said with a sigh. "I better get back to work."

She went back into the lodge to check on the sweet potato pies that were baking in the oven. Even though she was purchasing cakes from Salvation Sweets, operated by Miss Jewell and Sister Velma, the folks at the camp still requested she make her famous sweet potato, pecan, and chess pies.

When guests requested she make the desserts, she pretended it was a bother, but secretly, she was overjoyed. She loved her time at the lodge, especially when it was quiet like it was today.

After she checked on the pies, which weren't quite done yet, she stepped out onto the back porch for one more glimpse of the beauty of autumn.

Coming from the open window of the upstairs master bedroom suite, she could hear the television and knew her young daughter, Bunnye, was safe inside watching cartoons. A few minutes later, when she went upstairs, she was, to say the least, a little surprised. There, lying on top of the quilted bedspread watching television with Bunnye was Mr. Hamp.

"Well, well," Destini said. "They say we are a child twice."

"That doesn't apply to me. I hope I never grow up," Mr. Hamp said, and he handed Bunnye another animal cracker.

"Y'all are gonna get them cracker crumbs everywhere," Destini told them. "Be careful."

"Will you go on, please, ma'am," Mr. Hamp said. "We want to see what happens with the fox and the hound."

"Just ask Bunnye," Destini said. "She can quote it for you she's watched it so many times."

"She is a mighty smart young lady, and we love watching TV together," the old man said.

"You goin' spoil her, and she won't be fit for nothing," Destini warned him.

"Oh, yes, she will," he said. "She's going to be a brilliant lady, and she can become anything she wants to become. I'll see to that. Bunnye will never have to depend on a man, unless she *wants* to depend on one. She's my girl, and my girl is going to have the best in this world."

Bunnye looked up at him, and after putting an animal cracker in his mouth, she said, "No, Mr. Hamp. I'm Mama's girl."

"Well, can't you be my girl, too?" he asked, pasting a big frown on his face. "I don't have a little girl. Will you be my little girl, too, Bunnye? Please?"

Bunnye looked at her mama with huge question marks in her eyes.

"Mama, can I be Mr. Hamp's girl *and* your girl?"

For just a second, Destini had to turn away, but when she turned back to her daughter she was smiling.

"Of course, you can, Miss Easter Bunnye Wilson. You can be our girl. You *are* our girl," Destini assured her.

"See?" the old man exclaimed, as he chewed on his cookie. "You are our girl, and you'll always be our girl."

Destini suddenly turned on her heels and hurried downstairs to check on her pies in the oven. After she set them on the counter to cool down, she went back upstairs.

Before she made it to the bedroom, she could hear the familiar snoring of Mr. Hamp. Bunnye was still watching the movie, but Mr. Hamp, long time bachelor and the wealthiest man in three counties, was sleeping with an elephant-shaped animal cracker on his forehead. Destini recalled something Mama Tee said once long ago.

"Honey, it's best to let sleeping dogs lie."

Chapter 6

There's a storm out over the ocean

The Vo-Tech school gave all their students two weeks off for Christmas and Wanda Faye was counting down the days. She, Nadine and Destini were busier than a peg-legged man at a behind kicking getting everything ready for the holidays.

One day, Wanda Faye suggested they take a couple of days for themselves and head over to Jacksonville to get their Christmas shopping completed, since there weren't many department stores to choose from in the area, unless one wanted to do all their shopping at Wal-Mart.

When Destini mentioned their plans to Mr. Hamp, he immediately picked up the phone and called Dee Dee, who said she'd be more than happy to have them come over and stay at her condo. She had, for a short time, rented an apartment in Jacksonville, but now she had a huge three bedroom condominium right on the St. Johns River. She told her uncle to send the girls over and that her place was theirs.

Dee Dee worked as a buyer for the women's department of one of Jacksonville's most exclusive department stores and she was gone or working late most of the time. With it being so close to Christmas, though, she said she'd be in town and was determined to be a good hostess for the girls, as they had been so good to her.

"Thank you, Dee Dee," Mr. Hamp said. "I'll let the girls know and...."

Destini grabbed the phone from Mr. Hamp.

"Now, Dee Dee, we just country girls, you know. We don't expect no big fuss and nothin' fancy, either."

"Oh, really? And what do you think I am?" Dee Dee asked her. "Hell, I'm still country as cornbread. By the way, Destini, will you cook us some greens and cornbread one night while you're here?"

"Girl, you is crazy. Living over there in that fancy condo all dolled up by one of them big interior designers, and you wantin' me to cook collards and cornbread? Jesus, help us."

"Honey, you can take the girl out of the country, but you can't take the country out of the girl," Dee Dee told her, laughing. "Every night's gonna be a slumber party while y'all are here. If you want to go out, we'll go out, but if you don't want to go out, we'll just have a good ol' time right here."

"Sounds good to me," Destini said. "We ain't gonna be with you for a long time, honey, but we aim to have a good time."

Two days later, the girls departed for Jacksonville, which was about a two-and-a-half hour trip from

Seraph Springs. Their first stop was to a jeans outlet store on the outskirts of the downtown area and each one of them bought a pair of brand new Levi's.

They arrived at Dee Dee's condominium just after five o'clock in the afternoon and ventured into the spacious lobby. Behind a desk off to the corner was a nice looking young man wearing a royal blue, gold and white uniform.

"Well, ain't he dressed up slick? He looks like he ought to be marching in a band or something," Destini said, eyeballing the guy up and down.

"I think he's what you call a doorman," Nadine told her. "You know, like Carlton on that old TV show *Rhoda*."

"How's that?" Destini asked.

"You remember that old show, the re-runs of *Rhoda*, and that man would call over her intercom and say, "This is Carlton, your doorman." Well, I think that's Dee Dee's doorman. He's probably got her keys or a message for us, or can fix it where we can get upstairs."

"Should we tip him?" Wanda Faye asked.

"No, crazy girl," Nadine said. "This ain't no hotel. This is a condominium complex. We don't tip him, not unless he carries up our bags, and he ain't apt to do that."

Destini wasn't the least bit shy, and so she walked over to the guy.

"I'm Destini Wilson. We being expected by Miss Dee Dee Campbell," she said.

The young man smiled and said, "Ah, yes, she is

expecting you. If you'll just get in the elevator and press the button that says Penthouse, the elevator car will take you directly up into Miss Campbell's home."

"Sho' nuff?" Destini asked, opening her eyes wide in astonishment.

"Yes, ma'am," he said. "I turn a little key down here and it takes you right up. When the doors open, you'll be stepping out into her foyer."

"Well, I'll be…" Destini said.

"Welcome to the Belle Avanti," the guy continued. "We are so pleased to have you visit us, and if I don't see you ladies again, happy holidays."

"Happy holidays to you, too, Bill," Destini said. "I hope you don't mind me callin' you by your first name. I see it on your name tag."

"Oh, no," the young man said. "That's what I am called by everyone here. Only my mother calls me William, and only when she's mad at me."

His joke was lost on Destini, who was still shaking her head at the fact the elevator would take them right into Dee Dee's condo.

"Well, Merry Christmas and Happy New Year to you, Bill," Destini said, and the girls entered the elevator.

Just a brief time later, they stepped out of the elevator car and into a large foyer.

"Wow, this is awesome!" Nadine said.

"Yeah, and look at that skyline!" Wanda Faye chimed in, as she went over to sliding glass doors and stepped out onto the terrace that overlooked the river.

"Look at all them twinkling lights," Destini said, as

she stopped to admire Dee Dee's seven foot tall Christmas tree in the corner of the living room, which was lit up in black, white and red lights with matching colored ornaments. "It's pretty, but there ain't nothin' very personal or homey about it."

"It looks like it's been done up by a florist shop or Maybe she's got her own personal decorator," Nadine said.

"Well, here's your answer," Wanda Faye said, and she picked up a brochure that was sitting on the coffee table. "Richard Blair Designs, Jacksonville's finest flower shop," she read on the front of the brochure. "If you ask me, it suits Dee Dee to a T."

"Girls, come look at this!" Nadine squealed from the kitchen.

In the corner beyond a row of floor to ceiling cabinets was a small artificial green spruce tree. It was decorated with dozens of dog biscuits, a black and red, jeweled dog collar, and a variety of squeaky toys.

"Oh, my goodness," Wanda Faye said. "Leave it to Dee Dee to pamper that little mutt."

"Hey, she left us a note," Nadine said, as she wandered into the dining room.

On the glass-topped table was a note written in Dee Dee's unmistakable scrawl.

Girls, make yourselves at home. I'll be home around seven. There are soft drinks, orange juice, bottled water and beer in the fridge. I made y'all a cheese and fruit tray, and there's some crackers on top of my breadbox by the stove.

Go ahead and open the boxes I have for you under the tree.

I've bought all of you some sparkly things to wear out tonight. I have something special and important you all need to see, especially you, Destini. What I have to show you tonight, I believe, will help you a great deal in the future.

Go ahead and refresh yourselves and welcome to my little home. I am running late, since I have to pick Chanel up from the groomers. All our love, Dee Dee and Chanel.

It didn't take the girls long to start tearing into the presents Dee Dee had left for them. Inside the boxes were exquisite Christmas themed sweaters and each one was unique.

"Wow, these are really nice," Wanda Faye said.

"They'll look perfect with the new jeans we just bought," Nadine added.

"Well, since it looks like we're goin' out tonight, we'd best be getting' ready," Destini said.

Dee Dee's master bathroom was so huge that there was more than enough room for all three girls to apply their makeup in front of the gigantic mirror above the double sinks. They took turns working on each other's hair and then it was time to get dressed for an evening out on the town. When Dee Dee and Chanel arrived just after seven o'clock, they were ready for a holiday adventure.

After Dee Dee freshened up and fed Chanel it was almost eight o'clock.

"Y'all are probably starving by now, so how about we go get a bite to eat first?" Dee Dee suggested. "I know just the place, too."

By eight-thirty, the girls were seated around a table

at Martino's Italian Restaurant sipping on the house special red wine, Valpolicella.

"This is one of the best hidden secrets in Jacksonville," Dee Dee said. "Wait until you taste their lasagna. It is to die for."

After the girls finished their main course, they all agreed that Dee Dee was right about the quality of the food. In her usual southern belle flair, Dee Dee didn't disappoint the girls as she wooed the owner, Alfredo Martino, who had come by their table to ask how they liked their meal. She had him so taken by her charm that he offered the girls coffee and dessert on the house.

"This is delicious," Wanda Faye said, after taking a bite of her dessert. "What is it?"

"It's a Cannoli," Dee Dee said. "Isn't it heavenly?"

"It sure is," Wanda Faye said.

As they prepared to leave, Wanda Faye, Nadine and Destini thanked Dee Dee over and over for treating them to such a fabulous dinner.

"Think nothing of it, ladies," she said. "As many wonderful meals as I've eaten that you gals have prepared, this was the least I could do. By the way…"

"Stop right there, Dee Dee," Nadine said. "I know what you're gonna ask, and yes, Mama sent you one of her chocolate swirl cakes."

"Oh, that's wonderful," she said. "Tell her I said thank you. You know it's my favorite in the whole world. That and…"

"My sweet potato pie," Destini said, completing the sentence for her. "Yes, girl, I brought you one of them, too, and tomorrow, if you'll take me around to the Winn Dixie to buy some seasoning meat, I got some collards I'm gonna fix for you."

"Y'all are angels," Dee Dee said. "Angels sent from heaven. I love you, love you to death. I've always believed in friends helping each other out. One thing Aunt Hattie always told me was that knowledge is power, and that's what my little outing with y'all is about tonight. Knowledge and power."

"What are you talking about?" Destini asked.

"Just follow me, girls," Dee Dee said, with a sly grin. "Just follow me."

Minutes later, Dee Dee pulled her Range Rover up to the curb of a building about four blocks away. Outside above the sidewalk was a neon sign with the words "Pink Flamingo" flashing on and off every few seconds. The sign had a huge pink flamingo flanked by a chartreuse green palm tree that could be seen for blocks.

Standing in front of the establishment were a lot of young men, many of whom were dressed in extremely fashionable clothes.

"What kind of place is this?" Nadine asked. "Is it a bar or what?"

"You'll find out soon enough," Dee Dee said. "Let's just go in and sit down and order some drinks, okay? The show is about to begin and we sure don't want to miss it."

Dee Dee, it seemed, had already reserved a table for them that was a little left of center stage and sort of in the shadows. Even though they were sitting in a darkened corner, they still had a decent view of the stage.

While they were ordering a round of drinks, Wanda Faye was checking out the rest of the patrons in the club. With the exception of one or two women, they seemed to be surrounded by all men. Some of them were even holding hands.

Destini was busy checking the place out, as well.

"Sugar, sugar in the blood," she whispered to Wanda Faye. "Sweet... this is one of them sweet bars."

"Oh, my goodness," Wanda Faye whispered back. "I was just reading about these places in some of those old issues of Cosmopolitan at Camp EZ the other day. Destini, this is a gay bar."

"Sho' nuff is," Destini said. "Pretty soon you'll see 'em up there dancin' with each other."

"This is a great floor show, girls," Dee Dee said. "One of the best in town."

Wanda Faye was too shocked to say anything. Meanwhile Destini was whispering in Nadine's ear. The three girls were noticeably stunned with their eyes as big as saucers, as they glanced from one table to the next.

"Here we go, girls," Dee Dee said, with a huge grin on her face. "Hold onto your seats."

The emcee came onstage dressed in a tuxedo and he announced the first act. When the curtains were pulled back, there stood what appeared to be Sophie Martin. Immediately, the girls began clapping. Upon closer inspection, though, it wasn't Sophie. It was a man dressed up like Sophie, and he was singing

Sophie's hit tune "Marlene".

"He looks authentic, doesn't he?" Dee Dee asked the girls, seeming truly caught up in the act. When she saw the stunned looks on the girls' faces she laughed. "Oh, come on. He's a female impersonator."

"You mean a drag queen, don't you?" Destini replied, but Dee Dee didn't hear her.

After forty-five minutes of watching Sophie Martin, Barbara Streisand and Cher, who were all decked out in extravagantly beautiful gowns, and downing two more drinks a piece, it was time for the last act of the first set. Dee Dee said it was the one everyone had come to see. Then, she snatched a camera from her purse.

"We'll want photos of the headliner," she explained to the girls. "You'll want to keep them in your scrapbooks. Later, you can look back and remember the wonderful time we all had tonight, and how enlightening and entertaining it was."

"Well, this oughta be good," Destini whispered to Wanda Faye.

Just then, the emcee walked up to the microphone in the center of the stage with the spotlight aimed at his face and the entire crowd quieted down.

"And now, ladies and gentleman, we have a rare treat for you," the emcee said. "This Southern Belle direct from Memphis, Tennessee can sing the birds out of the trees. Tonight, in a limited engagement, she is here to do a few holiday selections for us. Please give her a warm welcome, the beautiful and talented Miss Carla Eileen."

When the lights came up, there was a collective

gasp among the girls. Standing onstage, in a long, cranberry velvet gown, was one of the most beautiful women Wanda Faye had ever seen. She began singing, "Have Yourself a Merry Little Christmas", milking each line for all it was worth.

"She's not lip synching, either," Dee Dee said. "What a voice, huh?" and then she turned back around and aimed her camera at Carla Eileen.

Meanwhile, Destini was scrutinizing the female impersonator carefully.

"There's something about those eyes," she said to Wanda Faye. "And that nose... and oh, dear Lord in Heaven, that tattoo!" she gasped.

"What tattoo?" Wanda Faye asked.

"On his left pinkie," Destini said. Then she drew in her breath, and said to Dee Dee, "I think you better take that photo now, 'cause I'm goin' be ready to leave from here in just a second."

Right on cue, Dee Dee snapped a picture and then another and another.

"Are you sick?" Nadine asked Destini.

"Let's just say, I've felt better," Destini said.

Dee Dee put her camera back in her purse and turned to face the three girls. Her eyes were gleaming and a sly grin spread across her face.

"By the way, those are blue contact lenses Miss Carla Eileen is wearing," Dee Dee said. "You girls remember this night. Also remember that knowledge is power. As much as this hurts you, Destini, and as much as it hurt me, don't let go of these pictures once I make copies for y'all. I'm thinking the time might come when you might need them. This is my Merry Christmas to all of you."

"What the hell are you two talking about?" Nadine asked.

Destini reached in her purse, took out a pen, and scribbled something on the back of a cocktail napkin. Then, she showed it to both Nadine and Wanda Faye. On the napkin she had written, Carl Alvin.

"Noooo…" Nadine said, covering her mouth and staring more closely at the singer.

As the girls were leaving, Dee Dee grabbed a few copies of the leaflet advertising Carla Elaine's appearance, and they were out the door.

On the drive back to Dee Dee's condo, no one spoke for the longest time.

Finally, Dee Dee said, "I love you all, but remember when we watched that *Godfather* movie and the man said to keep your friends close and your enemies closer?"

"I believe you're onto something," Destini said, shaking her head.

"I know y'all know what I'm talking about," Dee Dee said, as she pulled into the parking garage of the condo. "Just know I am on your side in this one."

The three girls didn't say anything. They just kept looking at each other, shaking their heads in disbelief.

"Now, let's not think anymore about this," Dee Dee said. "I want to talk about the reception we're going to give Wanda Faye and Dink next week at Aunt Hattie's house."

After the initial shock wore off and the girls all

changed into their pajamas, they ended up staying up half the night, sipping on coffee and Irish cream, and laughing together, as Dee Dee played Elvis Christmas songs, one after the next on the CD player. Chanel seemed to be in the holiday spirit, as well, running around the condo with a bright red Christmas bow tied in her hair.

Wanda Faye thought about Margot Smith and remembered something she once said.

"Real friends are like the roots of a mighty oak. They'll stick with you, no matter what kind of storm blows."

As the night wound down, Destini was the first to go to bed. As she walked down the hall to the spare bedroom, she was singing an old song. Wanda Faye smiled, as she pictured her getting out of her fuzzy pink bedroom slippers, while she continued singing the words to the song.

An uneasy feeling came over Wanda Faye just then and she didn't know why. She was having such a good time, but in the pit of her stomach she had a feeling something was brewing, especially with the song Destini was singing.

"There's a storm out over the ocean, and it's moving this a way,

If your soul's not anchored in Jesus, you will surely drift away."

Chapter 7

Carl Alvin's secret

That night, a storm did blow in from the Atlantic. It wasn't severe, but it left about three inches of rain across the entire county, as well as much of northeast and north central Florida. It was definitely a signal that the weather was changing. By three in the morning, the mercury had dropped twenty degrees.

At Fernandina Beach, just northeast of Jacksonville, Carl Alvin Campbell turned the key on his beachfront condominium. It had taken him longer than usual to remove all the heavy makeup he wore as part of the show at the Pink Flamingo.

He enjoyed the club, but because of his high profile in the legal community, he always went in drag, even when he wasn't performing. He knew he was playing a dangerous game, but he had hired one of the best theatrical makeup artists in the area to do his makeup. He paid him handsomely for his talents, as well as his promise of confidentiality.

It was only during the yuletide season that he dared

come out as Carla Elaine and take center stage at the club. Tonight was different than all the other times, though. He had an uneasy, queasy feeling nagging at him. He could never see the audience that well from the stage because of the dim lighting, and especially with the contact lenses he wore that disguised his true eye color.

He did, however, see flashes of light and knew someone was taking photos of him from off to the side of the stage. It wasn't that unusual for people to take pictures of him at the club, and most times he was actually flattered, but this time was different.

His curiosity had gotten the better of him, and before he left the club, he asked the manager about it. He told him it was a group of young women who absolutely loved the performances.

The manager wasn't being entirely truthful, though. He didn't tell Carl Alvin that the person taking the photos was Dee Dee, who had given the manager and the waiter a generous tip, telling them both to be as vague as possible if Carl Alvin started asking questions.

Of course, her tip was large enough that the manager and waiter suddenly developed selective amnesia.

As Carl Alvin poured himself a nightcap, he noticed his bedroom light was dimly lit and a smile crossed his lips. When he went inside, he could see through the semi-darkness the beautiful and muscular body of his current play thing, Grant, lying on his bed. On a chair in the corner, was a football jersey. It was grass stained and dirty as it had been worn the night before at a major college game. Grant was the star quarterback for a well known university team and his home was in a town not far from Turpricone.

His mother was a waitress at one of the local restaurants Carl Alvin frequented when he had business in the neighboring town. Grant's father, a mechanic for one of the local watermelon packing companies, had long since vanished, leaving his mother with a pretty, but worn face to raise her boy as best she could.

When Carl Alvin first spotted the young Adonis, he saw opportunity knocking for him in a huge way. It wasn't often an opportunity came along to have all his physical desires fulfilled and in such a pretty package.

The young twenty-year-old found Carl Alvin to be extremely generous. After the first couple encounters, he told Carl Alvin that he really enjoyed their times together.

As desire welled up inside him, Carl Alvin quietly shut the bedroom door and then sat down on the bed beside Grant. He ran his hands down the young man's neck and back, and then leaned down and whispered in his ear.

"Kickoff time, Bud," Carl Alvin said, and then he kissed him long and hard on the mouth.

Outside, the wind continued to blow, while bright streaks of lightning lit up the sky, followed by rolling claps of thunder.

Chapter 8

The fragrance of pine and cedar permeated throughout the screened back porch of the lodge at Camp EZ. It was a tradition each year around the Christmas holidays to fill various decorative containers with pine, cedar, holly, ivy and magnolia and place them in all the rooms at the lodge.

Each year, Mr. Hamp insisted that the lodge be decked out with fresh holiday greenery from stem to stern. Wanda Faye, Nadine, Destini and all their children had volunteered for the job this year and they were having a blast.

Along with the holiday greenery, huge wooden bowls in the kitchen and dining area would hold fresh citrus fruits, such as navel oranges, tangerines, tangelos and grapefruit, which were shipped to the lodge by the Fernandez Trucking Company.

Several rough, pine bark bowls held an assortment of nuts, along with nutcrackers and picks for anyone who was so inclined to crack them open.

Christmastime at the lodge kept the children busy after school each day, beginning right after

Thanksgiving on up until Christmas day. The Saturday after school let out for Christmas vacation, Destini was placed in charge of decorating a twelve-foot tall, live cedar tree in the main social area of the lodge, which Mr. Hamp and his boys made certain was in no danger of toppling over. Meanwhile, the children were busy stringing popcorn and cranberries for the garland that would drape the tree.

Mr. Hamp had an affinity for the large, old-fashioned, colored Christmas bulbs, but as the old bulbs gradually burned out over the years, he was finding it harder and harder to find replacement bulbs. He also insisted on using lots and lots of silver icicles. Destini made sure the children strung them one strand at a time on the tree, just the way Mr. Hamp liked it.

About a third of the way through the tree decorating process, Destini suggested everyone take a break.

"Anybody for some hot chocolate and freshly baked chocolate chip cookies?" she asked.

In less than a second, all the kids dropped what they were doing and followed her into the kitchen.

"Look at her, Wanda Faye said, laughing. "She's the pied piper."

"No, I'd say she's more like Mrs. Claus with the cookies," Nadine chimed in. "Hey, Mrs. Claus!" she shouted toward the kitchen. "Don't forget about your adult workers out here! We ain't elves, but we'd still like some refreshments!"

"Mrs. Claus is getting' your things for you now, Miss Nadine!" Destini shouted back. "Is there anything else I can get for you? A mint julep, perhaps, or a hot toddy?"

"Not right now, Prissy!" Nadine shot back. "Just the hot chocolate and one of those cookies! Miss Scarlett and Miss Melanie out here are developing a mild case of the vapors, even though it's December. We don't need a nap, so no need to bring the feather fan out here. Just shuffle on out when you have a minute and we'll be delighted."

The three girls had played this game a thousand times, ever since they were children. *Gone with the Wind* was their favorite movie of all time. There was never any ill intent and Destini never took it as derogatory. All three of them were intelligent enough to see the humorous side to the ways of old.

About ten minutes later, the three dear friends were seated on the sofas sipping their hot chocolate, while the kids were clamored around the kitchen table enjoying their snack.

"Hey, here comes Mr. Hamp," Nadine said, pointing toward the front bay window.

"That's odd," Destini said. "He hardly ever comes over here before dark during huntin' season."

She went over and opened the front door and watched him get out of his truck. He was dressed in his khakis, a flannel shirt, his University of Florida Gators cap, and, of course, his Brougham shoes with no socks. He also had a strange look on his face.

"Younguns!" he called out to the children, as soon as he stepped inside.

Within seconds, all the kids were standing in front

of him.

"I want y'all to go get my hunting dogs out of the box and put them in the dog pen for me down there behind the house," he told them. "Little Chet, Victor, Dale and the twins know how to catch 'em by the collar. Jewell Lee, since you and Bunnye are the youngest, I want the two of you to hold the door to the dog pen and don't let them dogs out once they're inside."

"We won't, Mr. Hamp," Bunnye said.

"Little Chet, you make sure they have plenty of fresh water in their troughs. These ladies and gents had a tough day running all over them woods up north of here. I'm sure they're all thirsty now."

As soon as the kids took off, Mr. Hamp sat down on the couch, still with a concerned look on his face. He wasted no time getting straight to the point.

"Girls, you gotta finish up here now," he started. Nadine, I want you to get all these children over to your house. I talked to Louie already and he'll be there to look after them."

"My God, Mr. Hamp, what's wrong?" Nadine asked.

"Y'all need to go on to the hospital as soon as you can," he said. "Miss Jewell called my cell phone a little while ago. She's never called me in all the years she's had my number, so I knew it was important and I knew I had to answer it.

"Oh, my God!" Wanda Faye shrieked. "Has something happened to Mama? Is she okay?"

"Your mama's fine," he assured her. "She didn't

want to call y'all here because she knew it would upset you. It's Brother and Sister…"

Before he could finish his sentence, Wanda Faye started crying.

"It's Jerri Faye, isn't it?" she asked.

"I'm afraid so," Mr. Hamp said. "She's bad off. Wanda Faye, you got to buck up now, gal. You can't let these children see you like this. You need to get a hold of yourself. All you girls are going to need all your strength over the next couple of days. The doctors don't seem to think it's going to be long."

"Lord, Jesus, please be with her, sweet, sweet baby," Destini said, crying. "She always did love Christmas so."

"Well, hell!" Mr. Hamp shouted. "Take it to her, Destini! I mean it. Take Christmas to Jerri Faye. Here's a thousand dollars. If you need more, I'll get it to you. Get her a little tree, some decorations, and make that baby's room into a Christmas scene she'll never forget."

Wanda Faye had never seen the emotionally demonstrative side of Destini toward Mr. Hamp before. After she took the money from his hand, she kissed him on the cheek.

"The Lord bless you, Mr. Hamp," Destini said, and then the two of them shared an embrace.

"Yes, he has, Destini," he told her. "He's been good to me all my life."

While Nadine and Wanda Faye rounded up all the kids, Destini stayed and talked with Mr. Hamp a while.

"I wonder if Dee Dee is at Miss Hattie's," she said

to him. "If she is, she'd wanna go with us. You know she's always loved Jerri Faye."

"She's meeting y'all at Nadine's," Mr. Hamp said.

"Say what?" Destini exclaimed.

"She's meeting y'all at Nadine's," he repeated. "I called her already and she's on her way. Y'all are going to ride with her down to Gainesville."

"Good, that was mighty nice of you," she said.

"I reserved a room for y'all at the hotel across from the hospital," he went on. "I got a room there for your mama and the preacher and his wife, too. You have my phone number, Destini. You call me, you hear? I ain't much for being around the sick bed, but I love that little girl. God bless her. Sweet and kind is all she's ever been. Just keep me posted."

"I will, Mr. Hamp and, again, thank you."

Just then, Wanda Faye walked in and told Destini they were ready to go.

"Go on, now," Mr. Hamp said. "When y'all get down there, put on happy faces and be smiling with them pretty Christmas sweaters on. If that baby goes out to meet her maker tonight, I don't want her last visions of y'all to be sad. Show her what you're made of. Rise and shine."

"Rise and shine," Wanda Faye thought.

It was always a favorite song of Jerri Faye's.

Rise and shine and give God your glory, glory, children of the Lord."

On the way to Nadine's house, it wasn't "Rise and

Shine" reverberating through Wanda Faye's mind. It was that old spiritual. She could hear the words clear as day.

"There's a storm out over the ocean, and it's headed this-a way.

If your soul's not anchored in Jesus, you will surely drift away."

Chapter 9

It had been about two-and-a-half hours since Mr. Hamp broke the news about Jerri Faye. When Dee Dee, Nadine, Wanda Faye and Destini walked into Jerri Faye's hospital room they weren't prepared for what they were about to witness.

"Oh, dear, look how weak and frail she is," Wanda Faye softly said, when she saw her lying in the bed.

Her hair, which was always combed and fixed perfectly, now lay straight and stringy across her pillow. Her complexion wasn't rosy and happy anymore, either. It was pale as a sack of flour. Her normally bright, blue eyes now had a glaze over them.

Sister Velma and Miss Jewell were sitting side by side right next to the bed and neither one of them spoke when the girls arrived.

Wanda Faye could see her mama's lips moving in silent prayer, and she knew in her heart that she was sincerely concerned. When she finally looked up and acknowledged the girls' presence, she shook her head and Wanda Faye knew exactly what it meant.

Jerri Faye began to rouse a bit and Dee Dee rushed

to her side.

"Well, look here, our Christmas angel came to Gainesville to have a big Christmas party, and we found her," Dee Dee said, as she clasped her hands around Jerry Faye's. "She thought she was going to play hide and seek and leave Wanda Faye, Nadine, Destini and me at home, but we found our angel."

"Oh, thank you, Jesus," Sister Velma said, as tears streamed down her face.

Wanda Faye knew she could always count on Dee Dee during the darkest of times. Mr. Hamp once told her that Dee Dee could cry a bucket of tears, but she was just like her daddy, Carter Wilson, who was his best friend.

"She's got more grit than a damned Bengal tiger when she has to," Wanda Faye recalled him saying.

He told her he watched her daddy get peppered across his back with bird shot out at the farm one day by a young boy from Miami. Mr. Hamp said he wanted to take him to the doctor, but Carter wouldn't have any of that. He just ripped off his shirt, took a few swallows of homemade moonshine and told Mr. Hamp to dig them out with his pocket knife. He never hollered or flinched the entire time. After all the birdshot was removed, Carter told Mr. Hamp to pour some moonshine on the cuts, put band aids on them and he was ready to go out and do some more bird hunting.

"That's the kind of stock Dee Dee comes from," Mr. Hamp told Wanda Faye.

Jerri Faye began to giggle at the sound of Dee Dee's voice. When she spotted the other girls, her face brightened.

"Nay Nay, Wannie and Desti," she called out.

Each one of them took turns hugging Jerri Faye, and as they promised Mr. Hamp, no tears were shed.

All of a sudden, Dee Dee started singing "Jingles Bells" and she was terribly off key.

Jerri Faye looked at her and said, "Dee Dee, you pretty, but you ain't singing that song good."

Everyone in the room burst out laughing. Dee Dee had one of the most trained singing voices in the South and had studied with some of the world's best vocal coaches.

"You know, honey, that's one song that's always been hard for me, but I'll bet you and the girls could sing it," Dee Dee told her.

That's when everyone in the room sang the song with gusto, even Jerri Faye. One of the floor nurses happened to walk past the room and she had to stop and listen for a while, smiling and even joining in for the last chorus.

Before the girls left Jerri Faye's room that night, Wanda Faye noticed Dee Dee was out in the hallway talking to someone on her cell phone. She never volunteered any information about the call, not even who she was speaking with.

The next morning when they arrived back at the hospital, the nurses and everyone else in the ward were talking about Jerri Faye's Christmas miracle.

Her entire room was Christmas from stem to stern, just as Mr. Hamp had ordered and it wasn't a florist shop kind of chic. It was the work of folks who knew

Jerri Faye. Dee Dee had a grin on her face a mile wide.

"What did you do, Dee Dee?" Wanda Faye asked.

"Oh, come on, now," she said. "Don't y'all believe in Santa Claus? I do. How about you, Jerri Faye?"

"It's so pretty," Jerri Faye said. "All the lights and the tree. It's just like at church and at home."

"Yes, honey, it is, isn't it? Just like the House of Prayer at Christmas," Dee Dee said.

Just then, Jerri Faye's doctor came in and asked everyone to step out into the corridor. That's when Dee Dee told the girls that she had called Miss Jewell's Bible Drill team captain, and told him if he wanted a thousand dollars for their Christmas party, he had to bring the team and work through the night to have the room ready by the time Jerri Faye woke up in the morning.

"Lord," Miss Jewell said, shaking her head. "They must have stripped the closets clean at the church, but I don't care. If it makes this angel smile, I don't care. I do thank you, Dee Dee. You are an angel."

"You is something else, girl," Destini said. "You got more tricks up your sleeve than David Copperfield."

When the girls were allowed back into the room they were able to take in the full effect of what had been accomplished. The small Christmas tree on Jerri Faye's nightstand was covered with the hand crocheted stars and angels that had always decorated the tree at the House of Prayer. Dozens of tiny white lights twinkled on the tree that was filled with colorful ornaments.

On her windowsill was the ceramic nativity set that was made many years before by the youth of the church out at Miss Vera Chambers' Ceramic Studio. Miss Vera was a longtime member of the church and she was always inviting the youth out to her studio to make holiday figurines as presents for parents and grandparents.

The nativity set was done up in a white pearl, iridescent finish with light blue highlights and it was beautiful.

The Bible Drill group had even taken the brass cross that stood behind the pulpit where Brother Linton preached each Sunday and placed it on the wall in front of Jerri Faye's bed. Around it, they had strung white lights so the cross would be visible day and night.

The only thing Dee Dee purchased was a moveable, lighted Santa Claus. Beside it was a golden sleigh filled with brightly wrapped packages and surrounded by gorgeous red poinsettias.

Throughout the day, the girls kept Jerri Faye entertained, coloring pictures with her and singing Christmas carols. Everyone in the room had their own personal Santa Claus hat, too.

For lunch, Dee Dee brought in banana splits and Sundaes for everyone, including all the personnel of the hospital who worked on Jerri Faye's wing.

Shortly after noon, Jerri Faye grew weary and drifted off to sleep. Sister Velma sat near her bed on one side and Destini sat on the other, humming Christmas carols, while stroking Jerri Faye's hair.

Just as the sun was beginning to set, Wanda Faye

looked out the window and saw what looked like a seagull fly across the manmade lake in front of the hospital. She thought about Destini's song, "There's a Storm Out on the Ocean", but she all she could hear was Destini's soft voice singing, "Sleep in heavenly peace, sleep in heavenly peace."

Then, as if the Westminster Abbey clock had just struck midnight, Wanda Faye heard the dreaded steady bleep, bleep, bleep of the heart monitor machine. It was then she knew their beloved Jerri Faye was gone.

"She was one of God's special angels and now she'll live with Him all the time," Destini softly said, as she lightly stroked her face.

Dee Dee cradled Sister Velma in her arms as she wept, and the girls had their arms around their mama, who was silently weeping. Just as Destini was about to go around the side of the bed to console Brother Linton, Mr. Hamp came into the room with Dink right behind him.

Mr. Hamp never said a word. He simply held out his arms and Brother Linton fell into them.

Wanda Faye went over to the window again and she spotted the white bird flying toward the east. Destini came up beside her and held her hand.

"Will you do something for me, Destini?" Wanda Faye asked.

"Anything, baby."

"Will you sing that song for me? The one you were singing that night in Jacksonville?"

Without another word, and as clear and beautiful as any angel, Destini began to sing.

"There's a storm out over the ocean, and it's headed this-a-way.

If your soul's not anchored in Jesus, it will surely drift away.

Somewhere in the shadows of the evening, Wanda Faye could feel Jerri Faye Linton's sweet spirit breaking through the bands of earth and drifting away to her heavenly home.

Chapter 10

News of Jerri Faye Linton's passing spread quickly throughout the town of Seraph Springs. Within hours, there were pale pink satin bows with streamers attached to all the utility poles along the main drag through town. Even more pink bows were attached to the fences and front doors of nearly every resident in town, as well as along the school fence, and on the storefronts of all the businesses in town.

Seraph Springs, with its multi-cultural population of Caucasians, African Americans and Hispanics, all demonstrated their respect and love for Jerri Faye, a Down's syndrome child, who never failed to smile and show love for all those around her.

Her wake a few days later drew hundreds of people who wanted to pay their respects. There wasn't a dry eye in the sanctuary at Seraph Springs House of Prayer, especially when Brother Linton and Sister Velma placed inside the coffin Jerri Faye's pink and white crocheted afghan, her favorite Barbie doll, her Lifetime Achievement Award for Superlative Performance from the House of Prayer Bible Drill team, and a small white

Bible.

The following day at the funeral service, there wasn't a vacant seat in the sanctuary or in the fellowship hall, where television screens were set up to simulcast the services. The parking lot was full, and all up and down the side streets there wasn't a parking space to be had.

Never had the House of Prayer been as full as it was on this cool December night. It was more than evident that Jerri Faye had touched the lives of many in the small town of Seraph Springs, as well as surrounding communities.

Hundreds of floral tributes surrounded Jerri Faye's ornate white casket with its pale pink lining, as she lay in repose. Dee Dee had offered to help the Linton's with the family floral piece, which could only be described as breathtaking.

Pale pink spray roses, tiny white orchids, lilies, maiden hair fern, and lilies of the valley covered the top of the casket. Inside, pinned to the lining, Wanda Faye, Nadine, Destini and Dee Dee had pinned a small corsage floral tribute with a special message.

The next morning during the funeral service, even more people turned out to pay their last respects.

"Precious memories, unseen angels, sent from somewhere to my soul.
How they linger, ever near me, and the sacred past unfolds.

The plaintive words of the old gospel song drifted through the House of Prayer and out onto the streets.

Wanda Faye, Nadine, Destini and Dee Dee were all crying, as they stood side by side next to the piano singing the song in honor of their beloved friend, Jerri Faye Linton.

The four girls were dressed in suits and dresses in various shades of pink, Jerri Faye's favorite color. Miss Jewell was sitting nearby with a box of tissues and kept passing them out to the girls, as well as others sitting near her.

As the girl's launched into the second verse of the hymn, the children and young people who were members of the Bible Drill team, came up to sit on the two pews behind the Linton's. All of the children were dressed in spring colors of light pink and white, despite the winter season.

Wanda Faye nearly lost control when she saw the children. She knew the effort it had taken for some of the mothers and grandmothers to outfit the kids. Indeed, sewing machines throughout the south end of the county ran for many straight hours, lovingly making dresses, skirts, shirts and blouses.

Each of the children carried a pale pink rose and came forward to lovingly place their floral tributes on Jerri Faye's casket.

The last two children brought with them a large standing heart-shaped spray, covered with pink and white silk flowers, and on it was a white, plastic telephone. The receiver was off the hook and across the front of the heart, written on a pale pink ribbon in silver glitter, was the caption "Jesus Called". The children and everyone in the church knew how much

Jerri Faye loved talking on the telephone.

Meanwhile, the singing continued.

"Precious father, loving mother, fly beyond the lonely years and old home scenes of my childhood.

In fond memory appears precious mem'ries. How they linger, how they ever flood my soul.

In the stillness of the midnight, precious, sacred scenes unfold."

Perhaps it was the appearance of the children or the song, nobody was certain, but Sister Velma abruptly stood up and held up her hand for everyone to stop singing. In all the years folks had known her, they had never witnessed her be so forward. The entire congregation went silent.

"Brothers and Sisters, today I want to give a word of testimony, and this comes to me as a gift from the Holy Ghost," she said. "These words are not my own. They belong to Jesus."

From across the sanctuary came the "Amen's" of support and then others in chorus who shouted, "Help her, dear Jesus, help her, Lord."

Sister Velma seemed oblivious and merely continued speaking.

"Sister Mary Lee, as I speak, please continue playing "Precious Memories". When I'm finished, I want these children, these precious Lambs of God, who were so much a part of Jerri Faye's life, to come and sing her favorite, "Jesus Loves Me".

Sister Velma took a deep breath and wiped away

the tears that had fallen down her cheeks.

"Wanda Faye, Nadine, Destini and Dee Dee, you girls are grown, and three of you have children of your own, but you're my children," she continued. "You always have been. I want you to come join these little children and sing. Sing it like you mean it, just like Jerri Faye would have wanted you to."

The four girls came up and stood behind the children who were gathered near the casket.

"When you sing the second and third verses, I want all of you here to sing it to the Glory of God, just the way my beloved always sang it," Sister Velma said to the crowd. "My Jerri Faye was seeing someone, and she felt something that is so special and precious, for Jesus was with her all the time. Not just part of the time, but all the time. As a mother, I am indebted to the Lord Jesus Christ for entrusting me with Jerri Faye for twenty-five years. I was over forty years old when I had her and I knew she was going to be a special angel before she arrived. The doctors told me I had an option, but I shook my head to that doctor and said, "No option." The Lord sent this gift to me and I am going to lovingly tend to her."

Across the sanctuary there was quiet sobbing and, in a few cases, outright weeping.

"Today, beloved, if I could say one thing to you, don't cry for this baby," Sister Velma went on. "Don't cry for me and the preacher. Rejoice and be happy, for we have been blessed all these years to be in the presence of one of God's special angels. Some people never have that chance. They never have that privilege."

Sister Mary Lee began to play and the children sang the first few verses. The four girls sang with them for the next few stanzas and then the entire congregation joined in.

"Jesus loves me, this I know,
For the Bible tells me so.
Little ones to Him be known,
They are weak, but He is strong."

As the piano struck the chords and played the song, Wanda Faye could see a change come over the faces in the congregation, and she could feel it as it surrounded and enveloped the House of Prayer.

Destini grabbed her hand, and with tears running down her face, she shouted, "She's happy now! Oh, Jesus, she's happy now! She's smiling and she's happy now."

Nobody said a word, but the smiles became larger and larger, and the weeping soon stopped. As the congregation continued singing, Destini would intermittently shout, "She's happy now!"

Wanda Faye looked at all the faces, many loving and familiar faces, and she thought, "Yes, Jesus loved her."

Brother Elvin Jackson, the elderly African American pastor of Destini's church, Mt. Nebo A.M.E., drove the school bus for special needs children at the Seraph Springs School. He was Jerri Faye's bus driver for most of her time in the public schools of the county. Once the song finished, he came up to the pulpit.

"Brothuhs and sistuhs," he began. "They's a lot I could say to y'all, but I'm not gonna do it. Sister Velma and these children have said and done it all. This baby, Jerri Faye, is now happy in her heavenly home, as Sister Destini testified under the power of the Holy Ghost. Since the family has requested no interment, we are going to join hands and say the Lord's prayer, and I will simply say before we do, "Father into your hands, I commit the beautiful spirit of this baby, Jerri Faye Linton. May she rest in peace. I know she's already a joy to you in your kingdom."

The old man glanced over at the casket and brushed a tear from his eye.

"Jerri Faye, baby, we are not saying goodbye precious," he said. "Just like you used to say when you got off my bus each afternoon, we'll say, I'll see you in the mawnin."

As the undertakers rolled the casket out of the sanctuary, the congregation again, sang, "Jesus Loves Me."

Wanda Faye thought about Miss Margot Smith as the casket was being rolled out, and how she said on her program not long ago about tears being turned into joy. This was one of those times.

Chapter 11

For the first time in the town's history, the elementary school closed down for the day in honor of Jerri Faye Linton's funeral. Some folks insisted it was at Mr. Hamp's request and others speculated that Dee Dee was the one who called the superintendent and told him he would surely regret it if the school in Seraph Springs wasn't shut down for the day, so that all the kids could attend the funeral services.

Whoever was responsible, though, succeeded, and the school was closed for the day, except for the cafeteria, which stayed open for four hours, so that the hundreds of mourners in town could gather for a meal after the funeral.

Pan after pan of fried chicken, sliced hams, potato salad, fresh string beans, acre peas, collard greens, sweet potato soufflé, deviled eggs, and desserts of all kinds, including banana pudding, pound cake, old fashioned coconut cake, red velvet cake, pecan pies, sweet potato pies and coconut pies. In one corner of the dessert area, the Bible Drill children had placed a pan of Jerri Faye's favorite Rice Krispy treats decorated with M and M's. It was Jerri Faye's favorite.

Close to five-hundred people were fed and nobody went away hungry.

"Would you look at all these people?" Dee Dee said to Wanda Faye and Nadine. "All of them are here because of the positive impact Jerri Faye had on their lives. All she knew was love. All she knew how to show was love. It makes you wish those powerful folks in Washington would get a clue, doesn't it?"

"Yep, sure does," Nadine said.

Just then, Wanda Faye caught a glimpse of someone in the crowd and it sent chills up and down her spine. He had just given Sister Velma a hug and then went out the door. She rushed over to the door and looked outside.

A storm was brewing to the west and dark clouds were quickly settling over the town. In the distance, bolts of lightning were striking every few seconds illuminating the sky. When she looked down the driveway, she saw a dark blue van pulling away. On the side written in gold letters was "Ludowici House of Prayer".

She turned hot, then cold, then hot again, but, somewhere deep inside of her, she decided not to say a word to anyone. She'd heard through the grapevine that Chester Easley had started a ministry in Ludowici to help those who were down on their luck. On a recent Sunday evening, Wanda Faye was surfing through radio channels at home and could have sworn she heard his voice. The station was filled with so much static, however, that it was difficult to say with certainty it was him.

As she stood in the doorway, her head was reeling from the events of the past two days, and now, to add Chester to the mix was the last straw.

"Wanda Faye, is that you?" a familiar voice rang out behind her. "Are you out here nabbing a cigarette, girl?"

It was her friend, Lollie, from the Vo-Tech school.

"Oh, my goodness!" Wanda Faye squealed. "Come here and give me a hug. How are you doing?"

"I'm doing fine... well, not great, but I won't burden you with my troubles after all you've been through today."

"What are you talking about? I've always got time for you."

Lollie didn't say a word. She just lowered the shawl she had around her shoulders. When Wanda Faye saw the dark bruise marks up and down both her arms, she had a sudden flashback of those horrible days living with Chester. Lollie fell into her arms and began to cry.

"What am I gonna do, Wanda Faye? I don't know what to do."

Wanda Faye gently rocked her in her arms, and said, "We'll talk it about it, honey. Did you come here by yourself or with Miss Sissy?"

"I'm here with Aunt Sissy," Lollie said.

"Well, hold on just a second, baby," Wanda Faye said.

Wanda Faye motioned for Nadine to come over and the two girls met in the middle of the cafeteria.

Wanda Faye whispered something to her and Nadine nodded and walked away, while Wanda Faye hurried back to where Lollie was standing by the doorway.

"It's all taken care of," Wanda Faye assured her. "We're going to celebrate the life of our friend, Jerri Faye, tonight and you're coming with us. Destini has arranged for us to have a slumber party out at Camp EZ. She said Mr. Hamp shut down the camp today, but he told us we were welcome to go out there after all this is over. Don't you worry, Lollie. Between all of us, we are going to help you."

"Thank you so much," Lollie said, as a fresh stream of tears rolled down her cheeks.

"The first step to bringing your troubles to an end starts today," Wanda Faye told her. "Go on and fix yourself up in the bathroom. Then we'll have some cake and coffee. After that, we'll be ready to go out to the camp where we're gonna light some candles down by the river, sing a few songs, and maybe have a glass of wine or two. We're gonna celebrate Jerri Faye in our own way, and then we're gonna celebrate a new beginning for you."

As Lollie walked away, Wanda Faye again reflected on so many things; Destini's shouting outbursts inside the church, the sight of Chester just a few minutes ago, and now Lollie coming to her pleading for help. It was all too much.

As she was about to put her apron on and resume her duties in the food line, Dink snuck up behind her and put his arms around her waist.

"Guess who?" he asked.

"Okay… tall, dark and handsome… I'm thinking maybe that young Tim Tebow from the University of Florida. Go Gators!" she said, laughing.

"All right, now," Dink said. "That'll be enough of that."

Wanda Faye turned around and gave Dink a big hug and then she kissed him.

"Thank you, honey," she said.

"What for?" he asked.

"Just for being here and being you," she said. "Being here in your arms is the safest place in the whole wide world."

Chapter 12

It was close to seven o'clock by the time the girls got on the road to head over to Camp EZ that night. On the ride over in Nadine's van, Dee Dee surprised everyone with a thermos full of coffee that was laced with Bailey's Irish Cream. As they drove along, they sang Christmas carols and drank the Christmas coffee, as Destini had dubbed it.

"We better not drink much more of this or we won't ever get our candles lit tonight," Wanda Faye said, after she finished her first cupful.

"I know one thing," Nadine said, grabbing onto her stomach.

"Got you covered, girl," Destini said.

"What are you two talking about?" Wanda Faye asked.

"We spent so much time serving everyone else, well, I don't know about y'all, but I ain't had a bite to eat since that little sliver of toast with blackberry jelly this morning, and it done left me a good while ago," Destini said.

"Oh, thank the Lord," Wanda Faye said. "What did

you bring for us?"

"You know I know how to make a feast, honey. I'm the one does it for all them rich, white folks. I got us some sliced ham, smoked turkey, fried chicken, potato salad, a jar of my melt-in-your-mouth, bread and butter pickles, some of them yeast rolls the lunchroom ladies made, and a whole pecan and sweet potato pie. Now, white girls, who's your mama? Come on. Say it, say it."

All the girls started laughing hysterically, and they laughed even harder when Dee Dee reached in her gazillion dollar Prada bag and pulled out a paper plate covered in tin foil. Inside were a dozen deviled eggs.

"Hell, girls," Dee Dee said, laughing. "This ain't my first damned trip to the rodeo. I saw Destini nabbing those snacks bit by bit, and stashing them down in that damn grocery bag. I knew what the deal was. After all, what's a picnic without deviled eggs?"

"Girl, you is crazy!" Destini said, laughing some more. "I mean crazy!"

"One more thing," Dee Dee said. "Don't y'all let this make you sad now. I want us to have one of these with this coffee."

"Oh! I know what it is!" Nadine shouted.

Out of Dee Dee's bag came another tin foil wrapped object. Inside were five of the M&M covered Rice Krispy treats made by the Bible Drill team.

"These were her favorites, you know," Dee Dee said, and then she handed one to each of the girls. "To Jerri Faye, Merry Christmas and happiness always. We love you, baby."

"Yes, yes," Destini said. "Baby girl is happy now. Yes, she's happy now."

Once they arrived at the lodge, Destini unpacked the grocery bag full of food, along with Dee Dee's goodies, while Nadine spread two old blankets on the hardwood floor. Dee Dee had gone into the kitchen to grab plates, silver wear, napkins and wine glasses for everyone.

Reality struck as soon as Lollie removed her shawl and revealed her bruised arms. There was a collective gasp from everyone, even Wanda Faye. She had only seen a few of the bruises earlier, but now she could see all of them, even the ones around her neck. It was beyond unimaginable that someone would abuse her friend like that. By the same token, it was easy for her to sympathize after what she went through with Chester.

"My Lord, girl!" Destini gasped, as she rushed to her side. "What in the world, or *who* in the world did this to you?"

Lollie tearfully related to the girls how her boyfriend, Jimmy, a pharmacist from up near Valdosta, had lately begun grabbing her much too roughly and shoving her around. She explained there were extended periods of time, however, when everything seemed to be all right, times when there would be no arguments or fighting, and life with Jimmy seemed perfect.

"I'd be thinking, okay, he must have just been having a bad day and everything is going to be fine from now on. Then, all of a sudden, he would change in an instant, like Jekyll and Hyde."

"You said Jimmy is a pharmacist and he owns his own drugstore?" Dee Dee asked, rising her eyebrows.

"Yes, ma'am," Lollie said. "He's owned it since his Uncle Bascom died about five years ago and left the store to him."

"Honey, please don't call me ma'am," Dee Dee said. "It makes me feel like an old woman. Dee Dee will work just fine."

"I'm sorry… Dee Dee… Anyway, his uncle and his aunt, Polly, didn't have any children. Jimmy's aunt died from pancreatic cancer about ten years before his uncle died. The two of them put Jimmy through college and pharmacy school."

"I see," Dee Dee said, stroking her chin. "Where were his parents?"

"Well, Jimmy's daddy was a high school football coach and he was killed in a car wreck coming home from a coaching clinic in Atlanta when Jimmy was about three years old," Lollie explained. "His mama loved him so much that she never remarried. She could never find anyone who was as wonderful as he was."

"Did his mama work?" Dee Dee asked.

"Oh, yeah, she was an elementary school teacher, but, of course, she didn't make enough money to put Jimmy through college. Teachers don't earn that much, you know. All she could do was provide a roof over their heads and enough food to eat so they didn't starve. She did all she could and it kept them off welfare, but it was the bare minimum."

"Wow, that's so sad," Nadine said.

"Yes, it is," Lollie said. "Thank God, Jimmy's uncle

stepped up to the plate and took care of his sister. He and Polly did so much for the two of them. They're really sweet, gentle people, too."

"Yeah, I'm sure they are," Dee Dee said.

"That's what attracted me to Jimmy," Lollie continued. "He's not real macho or muscular, like some other men I've gone out with, but he's a sweet man with a wonderful sense of humor, and he's a gentleman. He made me feel so special."

"You mean he *was* a gentleman," Dee Dee interjected.

"When did things begin to change?" Wanda Faye asked.

"About three months ago," Lollie said. "I noticed he seemed to be hyped up at night. He started complaining he was itching all over when we'd go to bed at night. I put salve and ointment on him, and I even made him take Benadryl, but it didn't seem to help at all. Sometimes, he'd be up all hours of the night just scratching and scratching."

"Wow, that's weird," Nadine said.

"Yeah, and then there were the mood swings," Lollie went on. "He'd be mean as a junkyard dog one minute, and then sweet as a lamb the next, apologizing for what he did and what he said to me."

"Well, darlin', I can tell you what I think our little Jimmy's problem is," Dee Dee cut in. "I believe he's got the same problem Judge and Mrs. Wesson's son, Bill, had a few years ago. Have you ever found anything in his medicine chest or noticed prescription bottles lying around the house?"

"Oh, yes, lots of them," Lollie said, shaking her head. "Not too long ago, I told him he sure had a lot of prescriptions for pain medications. He said his doctor prescribed them for an ankle injury. You see, he broke it years ago when he was running track in college. Then, last year, he was out jogging, and damned if that same ankle didn't break again. You know, Dee Dee, I never noticed his mood swings being so intense until after he broke his ankle. Come to think of it, shortly after that was when I started noticing the major mood swings."

"Uh-huh," Destini mumbled.

"What do you mean, uh-huh?" Lollie asked.

"Honey, I believe your man, Mr. Jimmy, has become a pain pill popper," Destini said. "That's the reason he's actin' so crazy. Popping them things like Chiclets and can't get enough of 'em. I'll bet if you took a good look in that medicine cabinet, you'd see all kinds of goodies he's been giving himself. Stuff like Loritab, Vicodin, Oxycodone… yep, your baby doll is flyin' high on pain medicine and he's gonna crash and burn if he don't' get some help… and fast."

"I don't know what to do for him," Lollie said, as tears filled her eyes. "I want to help him. He's really a good person, I swear, but I don't know what to do."

"I know what to do," Dee Dee piped up. "Any of you girls watch *Intervention* on television?"

"Yeah, I think we've all watched it a few times," Wanda Faye said.

"Well, we're gonna have us an intervention with Mr. Jimmy McRae," Dee Dee said.

With that, she grabbed her cell phone and asked Lollie for Jimmy's phone number.

"No time like the present," Dee Dee said to her. "Let's call him and get him out here. We can make something up, and he'll come down here. Who could resist all of us, right?"

"Hold on just a minute there, Madame Hero," Destini interjected. "Before you start runnin' up that Ma Bell stock, let's think about this for a minute and do some plannin'. A little plannin' never hurt nobody, you know. I think we should go up to Lollie's place for supper one night."

"Is food all you ever think about?" Nadine asked, trying not to laugh.

"Girl, I ain't the only one in this quintet that loves food," Destini protested. "Take a look at all them chicken bones on your plate, missy. Looks like a fox cleaned out the hen house."

All the girls had a much needed laugh at Destini's humor.

"I think I know what you mean, Destini," Wanda Faye said when things calmed down. "Lollie, you could make a big pot of your killer spaghetti, and we could bring a big salad and some of Mama's desserts. Then we could have a slumber party at your place, Mark included. That way, you and Mark could do our hair for us."

"I see you know Mark quite well," Lollie said with a grin. "He loves that sort of thing as much as we do. He'll be in his glory helping us tease and twist our hair."

"No doubt," Nadine said, rolling her eyes.

"What do you think about asking the Vietnamese girls, Tang and Lee, to come over?" Wanda Faye added. "They don't know many people, and they're just as sweet and nice as they can be. Maybe they'll do manicures for us."

"That would be wonderful!" Dee Dee exclaimed. "I've wanted to meet them for a while now. I've heard so much about their new salon from Aunt Hattie. She said she loves them."

"I'll love havin' me a manicure and pedicure done, too, but I don't want them gals bringing no covered dish with 'em," Destini said. "No, ma'am. I ain't wantin' no noodles and poodles. No, ma'am."

"You are one crazy girl, Destini," Lollie said, and all the girls had another good laugh.

"You gotta be crazy to stay in this crowd," Destini said. "Sane just don't cut it. We all crazy, honey. I think you might qualify, but before we get too far off track, let's get back to pill poppin' Jimmy and him wanting to whip your ass ever' time he gets high on them pills."

Wanda Faye took Lollie by the hand and looked her straight in the eyes.

"You have Jimmy come over the night we get together and we'll confront this thing head on," she said. "He needs help, and he needed it yesterday."

"Yes, he does, and he's gonna either get it on his own or we're gonna scare him into it," Dee Dee added. "Carl Alvin's cousin, Hugh Jr., handled a case like this about two years ago over in Pittstown. I was working part-time in his office then. I'll tell you, that man came close to losing his pharmacy license. The only thing that saved him was an agreement he signed between him and his doctor, which was filed in the local judge's office that he attend a twelve-week rehab program up at Talbot near Atlanta."

"I remember when that happened," Destini said.

"It set him back a pretty penny, but it beat him losing his license," Dee Dee continued. "If Jimmy doesn't come around, I'm gonna let him know that I know what's going on, and that my cousin is licensed to practice law in Florida and Georgia, and he has lots of contacts. In the mean time, you need to move out of his apartment, Lollie, and go back to your mobile home out there on your Aunt Sissy's farm. Use any excuse you have to. Lie like hell, but get out of there and don't let him beat on you anymore."

"God, my place out at the farm is such a mess," Lollie said.

"Well, honey, they don't call us the Pentecostal cleaning queens for nothing," Wanda Faye said. "By day after tomorrow, when Nadine and I talk to Mama, she'll have her Bible Drill group out there with us and you'll be able to do surgery off the floor, but there's a trade off. You'll have to start showing up to church down here at the House of Prayer, and when Mama starts her cake selling for the group in earnest again around Easter time, you and Sissy are gonna have to really push her cakes. Mama won't come out and say it, but she expects it."

"Oh, I don't mind that a bit," Lollie said. "I love Brother Linton and Sister Velma, and I was raised

Pentecostal. I love y'all's church. As far as Miss Jewell and Sister Velma's cakes are concerned, Aunt Sissy bought several of them for Christmas gifts. Plus, she bought three of them for us to have at the house for Christmas."

"Well, it's a done deal then," Wanda Faye said. "Who says all those ghosts have to come to you like Scrooge to get you to make up your mind to do the right thing?"

"Hell, if Scrooge had all of us on his tail in that Christmas carol, we'd a made them ghosts look like kindergarten children," Destini chimed in.

As the girls enjoyed more lighthearted laughter, Dee Dee zipped into the kitchen. Seconds later, she was back with a bottle of Mr. Hamp's good champagne. It was even chilled.

"Mr. Hamp doesn't go all out on super expensive Cristal or Dom Perignon, but he always loves a bottle of Moet White Star on special occasions," Dee Dee explained, as she held up the bottle. "I promise you, he won't mind. I think tonight is about as special as special can be, don't you think?"

"Hand it over," Destini said. "I'll pop the cork. I'm gettin' pretty good at it."

After a bit of a struggle, Destini finally popped the cork and it went flying though the air, making a final landing in the fireplace.

"Hey, I only said I was *pretty* good," Destini said, as her face flushed red.

Destini filled everyone's glass and then the five of them stood in a circle.

"Girls, we're saying farewell to our old friend, who I know is soaring around up there and supporting us right now as we help this new friend," Dee Dee began. "Jerri Faye, God rest her sweet soul, never hurt anyone and she wouldn't want anyone to be hurt. You, Lollie, are a good girl and you don't deserve abuse from anyone, especially someone hopped up on pain pills. So, raise your glasses, ladies. Here's to Jerri Faye Linton and here's to Lollie Sears. Here's to friendship and love, and here's to hope."

"And in the words of that poor little crippled boy, Tiny Tim, God bless us everyone," Destini added.

❧ ❧ ❧ ❧ ❧ ❧ ❧ ❧ ❧ ❧ ❧

Later that night, along the banks of the Suwannee River just beyond the lodge at Camp EZ, the girls knelt down around an altar Dee Dee had made from palmetto fans, which she stuck into the ground. Inside the shrine, she placed a photo of Jerri Faye, along with one of her pink hair ribbons. As the girls lit their candles, they each said a brief something special about their childhood friend.

"She was sweet and kind," Nadine said.

"She always said I love you," Destini added.

"She was well loved," Lollie said.

"She was not made for this world," Wanda Faye said next.

"Now, she's in a world where she's at home," Destini said in conclusion. "Y'all see those old stars twinklin' up there above the river? If you'll listen real close, they're saying somethin'. They're sayin',

"Welcome home, Jerri Faye, but I got somethin' I wanna say to our new friend here tonight."

Destini held out her arms to Lollie and the two embraced.

"Welcome home, girl," Destini said, and she kissed Lollie's cheek. "We're your friends and friends help each other, and this is your home."

Lollie started crying, as did the other girls who, in turn, hugged her and said, "Welcome home."

Before leaving the river bank that night, each of the girls threw pink rose petals into the dark river and said Jerri Faye's name loud and clear. Then, they held hands and softly sang, "Jesus Loves Me".

As they were singing the last verse, a curious baby doe wandered down to the river's edge just across from them and drank from the dark waters of the Suwannee. All the girls saw it, but no one said a word, at first. They just watched in silence.

Seconds later, Destini stepped closer to the water and whispered ever so softly, "She's happy. She's happy now."

Chapter 13

Daddy comes a callin'

Chester Easley sat in his dining room that same night in Ludowici, Georgia. As he read his Bible, he thought a great deal about the events of the day. He knew he had taken a risk by going down to Florida for Jerri Faye's funeral, but he also knew he had to go.

The entire time he was in prison, the Linton's had never forgotten to write to him on a weekly basis. They also sent care packages on his birthday, Easter, Christmas and other special holidays. Along with the care packages they included copies of their Sunday school quarterly, daily devotional books, as well as copies of Brother Linton's sermons.

On many occasions, they sent him entire church services that had been recorded on CD's. He loved listening to them in the prison library. The recorded sermons and the music from the House of Prayer in Seraph Springs helped him through many dark hours while he was imprisoned.

He knew Wanda Faye had seen him today at the

school cafeteria, and he wondered if she would say anything to Dink, her new husband, or to Nadine, or, God forbid, to that colored girl, Destini. He was fairly certain it was her who made the midnight visit to him shortly after he came home from prison, and he sure didn't want a repeat visit from her.

Just as he was about to close his Bible where he had been studying Psalm 121, his telephone rang.

When he picked up the receiver and said hello, nobody spoke on the other end. He could tell someone was there because he could hear breathing. Three times he asked, "Who's there?"

Finally, in a low whisper, there was a voice. It was barely audible, but he heard each word distinctly and it made him shudder.

"You know who dis is," the voice said. "Dis is yo daddy. Daddy's comin' after his lil man. Get ready. Daddy goin' have his Christmas cheer. Daddy loves you. Merry Christmas."

Then the phone went dead.

Chester tried every which way to determine where the call came from, but his caller ID wasn't cooperating. Daddy, or whoever it was, seemed to have been quite the sleuth, making certain the number couldn't be traced.

Chester fell to his knees and began reciting the words of the 121st Psalm over and over, as tears streamed down his cheeks.

"I will lift up mine eyes unto the hills, from whence cometh my help. My help cometh from the Lord, which made heaven and earth," he recited.

Four times he repeated all the verses of the psalm. When he got to the one that said, "The Lord shall preserve thee from all evil," he interjected his own pleading words.

"Oh, dear, Jesus, I am your servant, and I claim this promise. I know you will protect me from all evil, and I pray and plead with you, Lord."

Even as he spoke the words, he couldn't help but realize that it was followed by the verse that stated, "The Lord shall preserve thy going out and thy coming in from this day forth, and even for evermore."

A feeling of dread quickly swept over him as he read the psalm yet another time. He knew God was merciful and gracious, and he knew all about his love and grace, but he also knew the wrath of God, as well as the power of the devil in the world.

He recalled one of the sermons Brother Linton had sent to him. The gist of it was that if you're busy doing something for the Lord, for the advancement of the Kingdom of God, then Satan won't let up on you. Brother Linton had said if a person reached a point in life where Satan wasn't bothering them, then they'd better be cautious, because he had them right where he wanted them.

"As long as a person is striving to do the will of God, Satan will keep right on working and tempting, just as he did to Jesus in the wilderness," Chester said from memory. "That's what Brother Linton said, and I believe it."

He thought about his situation. Since his return from prison, he had worked each and every day to put his old life behind him. He had attended AA meetings, and he even led several meetings in Waycross and Brunswick. He hadn't messed with any drugs, he hadn't had any alcoholic beverages, and although he had many offers, some from extremely attractive women, he hadn't kept company with any of them.

The thought of intimacy of any kind with anyone was repugnant to him after what he'd been through in prison at the hands of Daddy. He often wondered if he'd ever be able to lead a normal life in that way again.

Closing his eyes, he tried again to recite the psalm, but all he could hear were Daddy's whispered words before the phone line went dead. He knew he had to clear his mind from all these dark thoughts, and he was determined not to allow it to overpower him.

Instead, he thought about sweet Jerri Faye Linton. For a few minutes, thoughts of her brought him comfort. Thoughts of her and her sweet daddy and mama slowly took Daddy's voice away from inside his head. It was a tactic he'd been taught by the prison psychiatrist. In order to make negative or toxic thoughts go away, think pleasant thoughts, is what he was told. He made it through many dark hours and days by utilizing this method.

He thought of the card and the box of Rice Krispy treats topped with chocolate M&M's that Jerri Faye had sent to him on his last birthday.

"If only everyone in the world could have such a kind and caring heart," he thought.

Feeling much calmer now, he stepped over to the window and looked out across the open field beside his house. He smiled when he saw how beautiful the sky was tonight, with the moon and the stars shining so brightly.

He lifted the window and the cool December air rushed in. The fragrance of wood smoke coming from the neighbors' chimneys, as well as a light scent of pine permeated the air. He drew in a breath from the pit of his soul and savored the aroma.

Out toward the edge of the field, he spotted a beautiful baby doe. She lifted her head high and made her way to the spring-fed pond behind the house to partake of a leisurely drink. She obviously wasn't aware Chester was watching her, as she seemed not to be the least bit frightened. All he could do was drink in the beauty of the scene and thank God for allowing him to witness such a creature of beauty.

As the doe slowly crept back into the woods, Chester's heart was not filled with fear or dread any longer, but with contentment and happiness. He considered it a blessing.

"Thank you, Lord," he said. "I'm happy now. I'm happy now."

Chapter 14

Carl Alvin's ultimatum

Hattie Wilson Campbell's Yuletide Open House had always been the event of the year on the social calendar of Campbell County, and this year was no different. Anybody who was anybody in the five adjoining counties would be in attendance.

The party was normally set for two weeks after Thanksgiving. Usually, it was the same people, their children and grandchildren who made up the guest list, but this year there was a special addition because of Dink and Wanda Faye's recent marriage. They were the guests of honor.

People began arriving just after six in the evening, dressed in their finest and most elegant evening wear. As they entered the foyer, they were greeted by Dee Dee, who was radiant in a beautiful ecru colored lace skirt with a cranberry velvet blouse. She introduced each guest to the honorees, Wanda Faye and Dink, who both seemed quite nervous about being doted over.

Dee Dee had done her groundwork with both of them in a way only she could do, and the young couple were dressed so stunningly that they could have graced the environs of any of the fine drawing rooms in the region.

Miss Hattie stood next to them and she was resplendent in a black and silver, sequined evening sweater and long black taffeta skirt.

Throughout the evening, the guests kept oohing and ahhing over Hattie's elegant furnishings and antiques throughout the home, many of which were museum quality. The cornice boards in the house were truly works of art, as they had been custom made.

The wood that was used in the home was among the rarest, as the Wilson family had been in the lumber business for generations as importers and exporters. Mahogany, birds-eye Maple and other rare woods were used in each of the intricately carved mantels, which sat above the numerous fireplaces throughout the house.

A gigantic twenty-foot Christmas tree in the formal drawing room glistened with red and gold ornaments. They were ornaments that had been carefully selected through the years, as Miss Hattie was a world traveler and loved bringing home collectibles for her tree.

Her antique dining table was centered with a sterling silver sleigh that she purchased when she went to England on her twenty-first birthday. She brought it back as a present for her mother, and each year she decorated it with white roses, holly, pine, and English ivy. The simple elegance of everything in the house had always been widely discussed and admired by all who entered her home.

Arriving fashionably late tonight was Carl Alvin. He waltzed through the receiving line as if he was royalty to congratulate Wanda Faye and Dink. Beside him was Jane, a big Midwestern lady accountant he took with him everywhere as a decoy. Right behind them was a young man accompanied by Amy Wesson, Dee Dee's goddaughter and granddaughter of Judge and Mrs. Wesson. Amy introduced the young man as Grant Martin.

"He went to Wilson High School, Aunt Dee Dee, and now he's the quarterback at the state university," Amy explained.

"Well, well," Dee Dee said, eyeballing him up and down and smiling wide. "It makes me wish I were younger. Welcome, Grant. So, how did you meet our sweet Amy?"

"Oh, Uncle Carl introduced us," Amy said. "Grant is doing intern work for him. He wants to be a C.P.A."

"Really, now?" Dee Dee cooed. "So, Grant, what area of accounting is of interest to you?"

"Well, um, I'm not quite sure just yet, Miss Wilson. I've just started and all."

"Well, now, don't you have nice manners, Grant, but it's Dee Dee. I am Carl Alvin's cousin and we have always been *very* close." Without missing a beat, she added, "Well, y'all are such a beautiful, young couple. I hope you have a wonderful evening, and Grant, Merry Christmas. I hope we see more of you."

"Thank you, Miss... I'm sorry... Dee Dee," he stuttered.

Once all the guests arrived, Dee Dee eased her way over to where Carl Alvin and Jane were standing. Jane was laughing much too loud, as she always did, and then she mentioned something about going out on the terrace for a smoke.

"Oh, honey, do feel free," Dee Dee told her, as she came up beside her. "There are plenty of ashtrays out there and even a big box filled with cigarettes if you run out. Can I get the bartender to freshen your drink for you before you go out?"

"No, I'm fine," Jane said. "I just got a fresh one. If the two of you will excuse me, I'll be back in a jif."

As soon as Jane scooted out onto the terrace, Dee Dee grabbed Carl Alvin by the elbow, steered him across the hall to the guest bedroom, shut the door and locked it.

"Carl Alvin," Dee Dee said as sternly as she could muster. "I don't care with whom you go and how much you like to dress up in women's clothes in your secret life, but I'm here to tell you, you don't poop where you eat. You bringing that boy in here to this party…"

"Dee Dee, I think I'm in love," Carl Alvin interrupted her.

"Then you're a bigger damned fool than I thought," Dee Dee said, shaking her head. "You're a good looking man Carl Alvin, but all that boy wants out of you is what you can give him. When he's through getting all he can, you'll be yesterday's news. He wants to go places, and, right now, you're his step up the ladder."

"Oh, come on, Dee Dee, give me a break."

"Look, don't make any more of this than what it is. What have I told you time and again? When Uncle Hamp dies, you can leave here and go to Miami or New York, or wherever you want to go. Hell, you won't have to be an accountant anymore if you don't want to. You won't have to get up in the morning if you don't want to, either, but you're playing a dangerous game… a very dangerous game."

"You're making way too much of this, Dee Dee," Carl Alvin said. "I know what I'm doing."

"Do you think because Wanda Faye, Nadine and Destini are not as educated as you, and don't have as much money as you that they don't know things? They're some of the smartest people I know, and they can pick up on even a hint of scandal. They know all about you, Carl Alvin, and you know they know, but they've never said a word, and never would because of honor. You keep on being reckless and crazy if you want. Just remember, though, if Uncle Hamp ever picks up on what's going on, you'll find out soon enough what it's like to get along on nothing but your miniscule accountant fees. Face it, Carl Alvin. It wouldn't pay for all those designer clothes and custom-made shirts and shoes you love so much."

Carl Alvin turned white around the mouth and began sweating.

"You wouldn't say anything to him, would you Dee Dee?"

"Not just yet, but you hear me, Carl Alvin. I don't care how sweet that little boy is. You'd better get rid of him before the holiday is over. Find a way and get rid of him. If you can't do it, give me a call, honey, and I'll get rid of him. Do you hear me?"

"Yes, I hear you, cousin."

"Before I go, one more thing, darling."

"What, Dee Dee?"

Dee Dee smiled a big Miss America smile and gave him a kiss on the cheek.

"Merry Christmas, Sugar Plum. I hope Santa is really good to you this year," Dee Dee said.

As they walked out of the bedroom, Carl Alvin stopped in the doorway and motioned for one of the waiters to come over.

"Would you bring me another glass of wine, please?" he asked the waiter, and then he handed him his empty glass.

After pulling a handkerchief from his pocket and wiping the sweat from his forehead, he stared at Dee Dee's backside as she gallivanted into the dining area.

"Happy holidays to you, Mrs. Grinch," he muttered. "You sure know how to steal a man's Christmas."

Chapter 15

"This spaghetti is so tasty, Lollie," Destini said, after swallowing her first mouthful. "You'll have to invite me over after the holidays and show me exactly how you make this, girl."

Destini was savoring each bite of the wonderful meal Lollie had prepared for their undercover slumber party, which had gained two more guests since they originally planned it. Aside from Lollie, Wanda Faye, Nadine, Destini, Dee Dee and Mark, Miss Sissy and Carl Alvin had also been invited. Lollie's boyfriend, Jimmy, hadn't arrived yet, but he had had phoned earlier and said he would be there by seven-thirty. He insisted the group go ahead and eat without waiting on him.

Dee Dee had persuaded Carl Alvin to join in, even though he told her he felt uneasy about joining in, but despite himself, he seemed to be having a good time.

"May I have another glass of that wine, honey?" Miss Sissy asked Lollie. "It's just so refreshing and it tastes divine."

"You don't find it too sweet?" Lollie asked, as she

poured her some more of the sparkling wine.

"Oh, no, honey. I like my wine to taste like Kool Aid, and I don't trust a wine that comes with a cork in it. I like the screw tops the best. They're so much more convenient."

Wanda Faye wasn't sure whether Miss Sissy was being complimentary about the wine or sarcastic. Sometimes it was hard to tell with her.

Miss Sissy raised her glass and announced to everyone at the table, "Here's to all of you. Merry Christmas."

"And Merry Christmas to you, Miss Sissy," Carl Alvin said. "You are a vision tonight. Simply a yuletide vision," he added, as he admired her sweater.

"Oh, this old thing? I've had it for years," Miss Sissy said.

She stood up to model her lighted Christmas sweater so everyone could see it.

"It's battery operated, you know," she went on. "I asked the girl at the store in Atlanta if it would shock me, but she assured me it wouldn't. Don't you just love all the twinkling lights on the Christmas tree and this little star at the top?"

"I love your earrings," Dee Dee said. "They're shaped like old fashioned Christmas light bulbs. You know that's the kind Uncle Hamp still uses on his tree out at the lodge. Those earrings just set the sweater off."

"Oh, they do, don't they? Thank you so much, Dee Dee," Miss Sissy said, blushing. "You know, honey, it's been a long time since I've seen you. You came in the shop last year with your Aunt Hattie when she was getting her hair done, didn't you?"

"Yes, it's been a while," Dee Dee said.

"If you ever need me to do anything for your hair, or if you want to get your nails done while you're in town, just give me a call, baby. You are a beautiful lady."

"Why, thank you, Miss Sissy. How kind you are. I know how everyone considers you the arbiter of beauty here in this part of the world. I can see I'm going to be president of your fan club soon."

"You sweet thing," Miss Sissy said. "Just for that, if you'll come in before Christmas, I'll give you one of my complimentary, signature tote bags. These girls all have one, and they love them, don't you, girls? Let me look at your hands. Uh-huh, you need to go see Tang and Lee before Christmas and get your manicure and pedicure touched up. I want you to come in early the morning of Christmas Eve. We'll all be working until noon."

"You mean you'd take me on Christmas Eve?" Dee Dee asked, raising her eyebrows.

"Oh, of course, honey," Miss Sissy said. "We'll even have us a Mimosa or something. I love Christmas. You know…"

Just then, the front door opened and in bounded Jimmy.

"Merry Christmas!" he yelled, as he made his way over to where the group was sitting.

He was carrying two red poinsettias and he gave one of them to Lollie. Then, he kissed her on the cheek and handed the other one to Miss Sissy.

"Well, ain't you the sweetest thing?" Miss Sissy said. "Go fix yourself a plate, Jimmy. We waited on you like one hog waits on another, sort of. We're about to have dessert, but you just sit right down and take your time, sugar."

Miss Sissy walked over to the card table that Lollie had set up with all the desserts. It was full of cakes, pies and puddings. The rest of the group was right behind jabbering about which dessert they wanted to try first.

Wanda Faye and Nadine had provided one of their mama's famous chocolate swirl cakes, as well as an old fashioned coconut cake. Destini brought a sweet potato pie and a pecan pie, and Miss Sissy brought her award-winning banana pudding.

"I know banana pudding isn't considered a Christmas dessert, but I love it any time of the year," Miss Sissy said, as she scooped some into a bowl.

"If you're a Southerner, banana pudding has no special timeline," Wanda Faye said, and she, too, spooned herself a heaping bowl.

"Is that coffee I smell perking?" Destini asked.

"It sure is," Lollie said. "It's some of that wonderful coffee you brought us from the camp."

"Oh, goodie, Camp EZ coffee," Dee Dee said. "It's the elixir of the gods."

Miss Sissy had already gone back to the table and sat down, diving right into the delicious sweets.

"Oh, this is good pudding," she said, licking her lips. "Umm, and this cake is absolutely delicious. I tell you, life is too short for people not to enjoy themselves. As I've always said, I'm not here for a long time, I'm here for a good time," she added with a hearty laugh.

Minutes later, the rest of the group joined her at the table with their plates and bowls bulging with a variety of different desserts, while Jimmy shoveled spaghetti in his mouth like a starved foxhound.

"Speaking of a good time, Jimmy, I'm glad you could join us here tonight, honey. I've been a little worried about you," Miss Sissy said, after she finished her dessert.

She was looking at herself in her compact mirror and touching up her hair. Then, she motioned for Lollie to pour her a cup of coffee.

"Oh, lordie," Lollie whispered to Destini.

"Testify, sister," Destini encouraged Miss Sissy, while Jimmy was looking at everyone out of the corner of his eye.

"Thank you, Destini, for that word of support," Miss Sissy continued, and then she wasted no time in moving over to the couch in the next room. "Now, Jimmy, since you've finished your spaghetti and your salad, I want you to come over here and sit by me!" she yelled into the dining room.

Jimmy just shrugged and did as he was told, and the rest of the group followed behind him.

"Mark, baby, go over there and get that cup of coffee I left on the table, would you, sugar? I do want to try some of that award winning coffee. You can add me a little shot of that Irish Cream, too."

"Is there something going on I should know about,

Lollie?" Jimmy asked, as he sat down beside Miss Sissy.

"I guess we'll find out in a moment," was all she said to him.

Jimmy was looking rather sheepish and nervous. Miss Sissy then took both his hands in hers and it was a stare down for a few moments.

"What do you mean you're worried about me?" Jimmy asked her.

"Why sugar, I'm worried about how you're going to live through the holidays."

"This is a joke, right?"

"No, I'm not joking, Jimmy," she said, and then she reached into her purse and pulled out a snub-nosed, thirty-eight caliber pistol. "I'm worried about how you're going to live after I take this gun, cock the trigger, and place it right here up against your temple. Now, I want you to bat your eyes, and what few brains you have in that skull of ours will go flying all over the place. Wouldn't that Christmas tree look might pretty with red snow all over it?"

Jimmy was so stunned he didn't know what to do. Mark and Carl Alvin looked as if they wanted to bolt and run.

"You're a crazy old woman!" Jimmy finally shouted, but he didn't move away from her. He sat still as a lizard about to pounce on its next meal "Have you lost your mind? Lollie! Somebody! Call the police!"

"Ain't nobody calling anybody, you son of a bitch," Miss Sissy said quite calmly. "Now, you listen to me, Jimmy. My Lollie is the only thing I have in this world. I love her with my whole heart."

"Please, Aunt Sissy," Lollie pleaded. "Don't do it. Please don't do it."

"Shhh," Destini said. "Y'all shut up, now. Lollie, you leave this to the grown folks, honey."

"That's right, Destini," Miss Sissy said. "You've got some damned sense. Leave it to the grown people."

Aside from Jimmy's heavy breathing, for a few moments there was dead silence in the room.

"Now... you want to jump on someone and hit them, then beat their ass like you're on the playground, do you?" Miss Sissy asked Jimmy. "You want to hit on Lollie and leave marks all over her body?"

"Lollie!" Jimmy yelled. "What have you been telling this woman?"

"You shut up that damned lying right now!" Miss Sissy shouted at him. "These folks wanted to have a calm intervention with you tonight. So, pull off that damned shirt you have on and take off them wool pants. You better do what I tell you, Jimmy. I know how to use this thing, and I *will* blow your brains out. This trigger is cocked and my hands ain't as steady as they used to be."

Jimmy just stared at her as if she'd gone mad. The rest of the group was quiet as could be.

"Carl Alvin, Mark, come over here and help Mr. Pill get this shit off," Miss Sissy said.

It was a few tense moments as Jimmy allowed the two men to strip him of his clothes. Then, he sat back down with only his boxer shorts and white T-shirt covering his body.

Miss Sissy picked up his garments and motioned

for Destini to come over.

"You know what to do," Miss Sissy told her.

As Destini scoured through all the pockets, she meticulously set down three prescription bottles of various pain medications and lined them up beside one another on the coffee table.

"You in a lot of pain, Jimmy?" Miss Sissy asked.

"I'm sure Lollie's told you about my accident," he said. "I hurt all the time, my leg and my feet."

"And you take these things like drinking water," Miss Sissy said as she picked up each bottle. "How many a day would you say? Do you even know?" she asked, shaking her head. "Well we're going to lock you up here and keep you locked up for three or four days, and not let you have any of these pills."

"Oh, God, no!" Jimmy yelled. "You'll kill me."

"Could be," said Miss Sissy, nodding her head. "Now, admit it, you piece of drugged up business. Lollie still loves you, and I know what it is to need something really bad. That's the reason you ain't dead yet, but admit right here and now that you hit her."

"All right, all right, I admit it," he said. "I'm sorry, oh, I'm sorry, baby," he cried, as he looked over at Lollie. "Have you told your Aunt Sissy how many times I've begged you to forgive me and asked for your forgiveness? I love you, Lollie, and I don't want to lose you."

"If you're serious about that, Jimmy, you better dial this number," Miss Sissy said, and she handed him her cell phone and a piece of paper with a phone number written on it.

"What for?" he asked.

"It's the number for the folks up at Talbot in north Georgia," Miss Sissy explained. "Carl Alvin has talked to them. He's even talked to your own personal physician. You'd be surprised how many people know about your problem, Jimmy. Now, you call this number and tell them that Sheriff Bartow Lewis of Campbell County, Florida, is driving you up there tonight. They'll be all ready for you."

"How long will I be there?" he asked.

"What does that matter?" Miss Sissy asked, beginning to get more agitated. "You are dialing that number right now or you'll sweat it out in that back bedroom. It'll be mighty bad in there with them monkeys coming after you and messing you up."

Jimmy looked over at Lollie and his eyes were filled with pain. Miss Sissy gently laid the pistol down and a collective sigh of relief was heard throughout the room.

Lollie rushed over and put her arms around Jimmy and hugged him tight.

"Baby, you're not yourself," she said. "Do you want to be this person that you've become? Everyone knows how sweet and kind you really are. That's the reason I fell in love with you, honey… your sweetness and kindness, but these pills make you somebody else, somebody I don't want to know."

Jimmy was sobbing now and holding his head in his hands.

"Will you dial the number for me, Miss Sissy?" he blubbered.

"Nope, Jimmy, I will not," she said. "I *will* hold the

phone for you, but you have to dial the number. You need to be the one to do that."

"All right," he said. "I'll do it. I don't want to lose Lollie."

"Look at me, Jimmy," Miss Sissy said. "I'm glad you love Lollie, but, honey, you need to do this for you more than anyone else. You need to do it for you."

Jimmy nodded his head and then he took the phone and dialed the number. As he spoke to the counselor, there wasn't a dry eye in the room. When he finished his conversation, he gave the phone back to Miss Sissy. Lollie gave him another hug and kissed his cheek.

"I love you, honey," she said. "I've never loved you more than I do right now. I'm so proud of you. I'll be here for you. Just as soon as they let me, I'll come see you."

Destini, who could take charge in any situation, asked everyone to form a circle and hold hands.

"What y'all witnessed here tonight is true love," she said. "That's what Christmas is all about, true love. God loved us enough, he sent his son to be born into this world, and he knew when he sent him that he was gonna suffer and die. Jimmy, honey, you're gonna suffer before you beat this thing, and you're gonna die to the old life and be born anew. You're gonna do it out of love... love for you and love for Lollie. Now, everyone say this with me. God grant me the serenity to accept the things I cannot change, the strength to change the things I can, and the wisdom to know the difference."

At the end of the prayer everyone was hugging and kissing on Jimmy, even Carl Alvin and Mark.

"Well, we'd best get going," Miss Sissy said. "The sheriff should be here any second."

"What about my clothes and all?" Jimmy asked.

"All taken care of," Carl Alvin said. "Lollie and I went to your house earlier today and packed you a bag. I'm glad you made this decision. A couple of people were getting ready to report you to the professional boards of Georgia about your pharmacy license."

"Oh, no," Jimmy said. "Really?"

"Oh, yeah," Carl Alvin told him. "You've made a few mistakes over the last few months. Your junior pharmacist, that young boy from India, has covered your ass, for the most part. You owe Gopal a sincere thank you."

"Oh, thank God," Jimmy said.

"That boy cried and cried when we told him what we had planned," Carl Alvin said. "He said no one had treated him as well as you have. He'll be riding with you and the sheriff tonight, so you can talk to him about what to do with the business while you're gone."

Just then, Sheriff Bartow Lewis knocked on the door and Miss Sissy went to answer it. She didn't say a word. She just hugged him passionately for a few moments. Meanwhile, Jimmy had finished putting his clothes back on and then he grabbed his coat and kissed Lollie goodbye.

As the sheriff and Miss Sissy stood in the doorway, Destini came up to them, holding a large brown grocery bag. She handed it to the sheriff.

"For the trip," she told him.

He just laughed and said, "Destini, you, Wanda Faye, Nadine and Dee Dee, y'all are something else. The Campbell County Four I call y'all. I'm glad you girls are my friends. Lord, I'd hate to have you for enemies," he added, laughing.

"No worries there," Destini said. "You is the High Sheriff, after all. God bless you and y'all have a Merry Christmas. You come on out to the camp next week for Christmas Eve breakfast, you hear?"

"I wouldn't miss it," he said, and he gave her a peck on the cheek.

"My man," Destini said, smiling. "Y'all saw. He's my man."

"You fast thing, you" Dee Dee joked with her. "You've got to share, you know."

Without further ado, the sheriff got a hug and kiss from everyone in the room, except for the men, that is.

As the girls stepped out onto the front porch to wave goodbye, Wanda Faye looked up at the night sky and spotted the North Star brilliantly shining. She thought about a star that led some kings to the place where the Savior lay in a manger.

"Lord, thank you for being the Lord and for your goodness," she silently prayed. "Thank you for these friends. Thank you for Christmas and Lord, mostly, thank you for love."

There was one more thing Wanda Faye was especially thankful for and that was Miss Sissy.

"Sure, she's a bit pretentious and flirty as all get out, and she's all about making money, but she has a heart of gold," Wanda Faye thought. "She proved that tonight."

Chapter 16

Daddy's Christmas wish

Inside the library at the penitentiary in Georgia, Daddy was gazing out the window at the same North Star. He had just finished listening to a Christmas story on tape and he was feeling at peace with himself.

"Would you like a peppermint candy?" Jason, the librarian asked him.

"Sho' would," Daddy said, and he stepped over to the counter.

"Well, Daddy, I hear you're leaving us tomorrow," Jason said, as he handed the peppermint to him. "You going home?"

"Yes, suh, I sho' is. I got somebody special waitin' on me down in South Georgia. I'll be spendin' Christmas down there. I sho' is lookin' forward to it. Sho' am."

"Well, I'm happy for you, Daddy. You made it through this place. I've never seen such a positive turnaround in anyone, as I've seen in you. It seems you've turned over a new leaf. You've been a model inmate the past few months."

"That's what love can do for you," Daddy said, smiling wide. "It caused those wise mens in that story I just heard to travel hundreds of miles to see that little baby Jesus. I'll be travelling soon, too. I may not be followin' the same star, but I'm followin' my own, and I know where it's leadin' me. Lord, I feels like singin'. You mind if I sing, Mr. Jason?"

"No, go ahead," Jason said. "I like good singing. How about it, officer? Is it okay if Daddy sings for us?" he asked the guard who was standing by the door.

"Sure, go ahead, inmate," the guard said. "You have a good voice."

Daddy hurried up and chewed what was left of the peppermint candy, cleared his throat, and started singing. His deep, baritone voice filled the library and all the other inmates who were there turned in their seats to watch him perform.

"Go tell it on the mountain, over the hills and everywhere.
Go tell it on the mountain, that Jesus Christ is born."

When he finished the song, he got a standing ovation. He looked so proud and even took a few bows.

"I sho' do wish y'all a Merry Christmas," Daddy said. "I'll be spendin' all my Christmases from on now with the love of my life. I'm so happy. Thank you for Christmas, Lord!" he shouted. "Thank you for Christmas and mostly, thank you for love!"

Chapter 17

Christmas Eve morning in Seraph Springs dawned cool and crisp with a heavy frost covering the flat woods in and around the Suwannee River. Out at Camp EZ, goblin-like mists hovered above all the ponds scattered throughout the thousands of acres of Brayerford property.

One large pond was surrounded by tall moss-festooned cypress trees. There was one century-old bald cypress on the northwest corner of the pond that looked as if it went on forever, as its top branches disappeared into the low hanging cloud cover.

Mr. Hamp was out for his morning ride. As he sat comfortably on the back of his dapple grey quarter horse, his hounds were barking up ahead of him, as they chased down a deer toward the river and up through the river pastures.

This one particular block of hunting land was referred to by many of the locals as the Smokehouse Block because so many deer had been hunted down and killed here.

Just up ahead of him, the low hum of an

automobile engine interrupted the quiet solitude as it wound its way along the white sand road toward the lodge.

"That looks like Nadine's big ol' van," he said, smiling, and he trotted the horse over closer to the road and paused a while. "Yep, that's her. I can see the cigarette smoke puffin' out the windows," he added, and then he shook his head and laughed. "Looks like Wanda Faye is sittin' shotgun. Yep, she's smokin', too."

As the van came closer, he could hear Elvis singing "Blue Christmas". He jumped his horse over the road ditch and waved the girls down.

"Well, Merry Christmas, ladies. Y'all are out mighty early this mornin'," he said, when Nadine pulled up beside him.

"Merry Christmas, Mr. Hamp," Nadine replied. "You're lookin' pretty good sittin' up there on that beautiful horse. We're on our way up to the lodge to help Destini, Mama, and Sister Velma. I don't know what time they got out here."

"I can tell you," he said. "I went out to saddle up ol' Major here about four this morning, and I saw your mama and Sister Velma comin' down the lane. I wondered then, do these women ever sleep?"

"They ask the same question about you, Mr. Hamp," Nadine said, laughing.

"Well, tell them the answer is no," Mr. Hamp said, laughing along with her. "The older I get, the less I sleep, and I have things that hurt I never knew was possible. I'm not gonna stay on this old boy too long or I'll pay for it later. I wanna be able to enjoy the folks comin' out here to eat breakfast."

"Well, Mr. Hamp, we better ease on down the road," Nadine said. "We got a lot to do. Folks will be comin' in before too long."

"Yes, you girls ease along. I'll be up there in a minute. Tell Destini to have me a cup of coffee ready."

"Now, Mr. Hamp, if it's past daylight out here at the camp, when have you ever known Destini not to have a pot of coffee ready?"

"You're right, Nadine, you're right. Her mama was the same way. Well, again, girls, Merry Christmas. Dink and Louie will be up after a while. They're down there on the Christmas Eve hunt."

"Great, thanks. Oh, and Essie's bringing our girls out with Mama Tee."

"Fine, fine," he said. "The more the merrier. See y'all in a bit."

"Bye, Mr. Hamp!" Wanda Faye yelled out the window as he galloped off. "You know, Nadine, I've heard what Mama Tee has said about Mr. Hamp being set in his ways and all, but he's a nice looking man, don't you think? For his age, that is, he's still a nice looking man. I wonder why he never married."

"Well, Mama said he took care of his mama, and then he helped with his sister and her husband, and Carl Alvin, and then when Dee Dee's daddy died, he looked after her. Plus, he had all this property. Maybe he didn't think he had the time. I don't know."

"Yeah, it's a shame," Wanda Faye said.

"I just know I sure do love him and I wouldn't change him a bit. If he did marry, I hope he'd marry somebody nice like Dee Dee's Aunt Hattie."

"I don't think he'll ever marry," Wanda Faye said.

"Yeah, you're probably right. He's married to this land and Camp EZ, and he loves the life he has here. He does pretty much what he wants, you know. How many people can say that?"

"Not many," Wanda Faye said. "Well, enough about Mr. Hamp. Are you and Louie ready for Christmas?"

"As ready as we're gonna get. Louie even did his part. He went and helped the kids bring home a Christmas tree, and then he sat on the couch and laughed while they made a huge mess decorating it. Guess who had to clean it up? Men, I declare. How about you? Are you ready?"

"Well, Sis, you know we're going to tell Little Chet and the children about Dink being Chet's real Daddy," Wanda Faye said. "We decided to do it right after Christmas. I'm a little nervous about it, though."

"I'm gonna tell you somethin', Wanda Faye. Either you and Dink are the most naïve people in the world or you're the stupidest."

"I beg your pardon!" Wanda Faye gasped.

"Sorry, but do you think children are stupid?" Nadine asked her. "They ain't stupid. Darlene and Charlene told me two weeks ago they were talking to Little Chet out at Mama's, and he told them that even though you and Dink ain't told him, he knows he's Dink's kid. They said he was glad about it, too. He loves Dink."

"Oh, no! How in the world?"

"Said he could tell by the way y'all was actin'," Nadine went on. "All that whisperin' and talkin' low on the phone. Then, a few weeks ago in church, he said Dink read them the story about Abraham and Isaac, and that Dink started cryin' and had to leave the room. Little Chet said that's when he knew for sure Dink was his daddy."

"Well, I'll be darned. Just like Mama says all the time, kiss me deadly," Wanda Faye said, shaking her head. "I guess I'll tell Dink when he comes in today. There's no need keeping it from him... or the other children. Geez, I should know by now that there are no secrets in this family."

"In this family," Nadine said, laughing. "Sister, you know they ain't no secrets in this family, this county or this part of the state. You may as well get it out in the open and tell your version because folks are gonna be talkin' about it for sure."

"Oh, Lord, yes, I do know it," Wanda Faye said. "There's some that won't let the truth stand in the way of a good story. They're gonna tell it the way they want it told, regardless."

As they pulled up to the lodge, Destini was standing in the kitchen doorway with a cup of coffee in her hand gazing out across the grounds. The wide expanse of lawn and pasture was all brown now, except for the winter rye that had been sown in the yard.

On either side of the walkways leading up to the front entrance stood two large, red cedar trees. They were decorated with twinkling colored lights, and they looked so enchanting in the early morning light.

"Good morning, Destini!" Wanda Faye called out, and then she and Nadine walked over to her.

"Merry Christmas, my sisters," Destini said. "I hope you got your workin' britches on, 'cause we got a good bit to do. Thank God, not as much as we would have had if your mama and Sister Velma hadn't beat me out here this morning. Those are two hard workin' women."

"Tell me about it," Nadine said. "Mama can work circles around any of us. She's in good shape for an old woman."

"Aw, she ain't that old," Destini said. "What's she about thirty-nine?"

"She wishes!" Wanda Faye said, laughing. "She's gettin' close to fifty, you know.

"Like I said, she ain't that old," Destini said. "Well, come on inside."

Aside from its usual beauty, Camp EZ was especially stunning during the Christmas holidays. Handmade baskets and antique crockery were filled with native pine, holly, and cedar all throughout the lodge. A huge red cedar tree that had been grown on the property served as the lodge's Christmas tree. It was decorated with popcorn and cranberry strings, hand crocheted doves and crosses made by the Bible Drill group, and peppermint sticks. At the top of the tree, in its place of honor, was a small angel that Jerri Faye made for Mr. Hamp last Christmas.

Another Christmas tradition at Camp EZ was red velvet ribbons and bows, and they were everywhere. Dee Dee tried her best to talk to Mr. Hamp about using different kinds of bows, perhaps a subtle tartan plaid, but he gave her an emphatic "No!" He said he didn't care what they did any other time of year, but his mama, Miss Lillian, had always loved red velvet bows at Christmas and there would be no arguing about it.

They were tied onto deer antlers, stuck in greenery arrangements, pinned on the ends of homemade pine garland, you name it. They were even draped along the front of the mantels and around all the doors.

Large bowls on tables and counters held brightly polished, fresh apples and colorful citrus fruits of every kind that were shipped to the camp by the Fernandez family from Miami.

There was always a certain unmistakable fragrance lingering around Camp EZ during the holidays. Between the pine and citrus, the brewing coffee, and the cookies and breads being baked in the oven, it was like being home at grandma's house.

The ladies were busy in the kitchen filling silver chafing dishes with pork sausage, buttered grits, homemade biscuits, and Camp EZ's signature breakfast casserole made with venison sausage.

Destini put Wanda Faye and Nadine straight to work bringing everything out to a long dining table that was set up in the main parlor, which had a perfect view of the elegant Christmas tree.

Commercial-sized urns of coffee and huge dispensers of fresh squeezed orange juice were set up on separate tables. On the east side of the great room overlooking the river, a long liquor bar was set up. Uncle Duke and two other young men were making sure it was well stocked. One could choose to have a Brayerford Bloody Mary, a Camp EZ Screwdriver, or a Mr. Hamp Mimosa. There were also plenty of bottles of Bailey's Irish Cream for those who wanted a coffee pick-me-up.

Once the crowd started pouring into the lodge, Dee Dee and Sister Mary Lee took turns playing Christmas Carols on the Steinway grand piano until all the food was ready to be served.

Brother Linton offered the blessing and Mr. Hamp welcomed everyone. Wanda Faye thought he had never looked as happy as he did today.

There were so many people in attendance that there were tables set up everywhere. Even though the weather was a bit nippy, many brave souls sat at picnic tables out on the lawn. They were surrounded by several big bonfires, though, and it seemed to be the favored spot to enjoy the feast. A lot of the guests simply held their plates in their laps while perched atop bales of hay that were even closer to the bonfires.

About forty-five minutes later, once everyone finished eating, Mr. Hamp's farm workers began driving up on the lawn in a series of old wooden buckboards. There were five of them all together.

Soon, each wagon was filled with holiday guests and the horses pulled them around the property and down by the river. This was one of the holiday traditions at Camp EZ that most of the guests looked forward to the most. Loud, off key Christmas carols were sung, and there was lots of chatter and laughter, as the wagons moved along the tram trails.

Later that morning after a lot of the guests left, Destini asked Wanda Faye and Nadine to sit with her for a while by Mama Tee's side. Mama Tee was curled up in an afghan on one of the sofas, sipping on a cup of doctored up coffee. She'd had a busy morning, enjoying herself immensely as she chatted with all the guests.

"Mama Tee, I got something to ask you," Destini said.

"Uh-oh," Mama Tee said. "This don't sound like no request for Santa Claus."

"No'm it ain't," Destini said. "This is about a dream."

"Oh, Lord have mercy, child. Well, go on and tell it. I hate to hear what you got to say, but tell it to me, baby."

"Well, in the dream, I'm here in the river field," Destini began. "I can see the river below me, and up out of the woods comes runnin' the biggest buck I ever seen. He's got huge antlers... I can't count the points, but he's running. Then, he slows down and runs right up to me. I reach out to touch him and he falls over dead. There ain't been no shot fired and there ain't a mark on him. He don't even bleed, but he's dead."

Mama Tee's body shuddered and she took another sip of her coffee while Destini took a breath.

"Keep on, girl," Mama Tee said.

"Well, his eyes are lookin' at me. They was gentle eyes, and even though he's just an animal, his eyes were full of love. I couldn't stop staring at him and then I started cryin'. That's the dream, Mama Tee. I've had this same dream several times and ever' time I wake up, my pillow's soaked with tears."

From behind Mama Tee's dark glasses, tears began to trickle down her wrinkled cheeks. She reached into her bosom and pulled out a lace-edged handkerchief and dabbed at her eyes. All the girls seemed at a loss and just sat silently waiting for her to speak, as she wiped her face.

"Destini," Mama Tee finally began. "Somebody great... somebody full of love for you is goin' leave you soon. It's somebody who ain't kin to you. Somebody who loves you more than you'll ever know and who's been trying to figure out how to show you."

"Oh, dear, Lord," Destini muttered, and she grabbed Wanda Faye's hand.

"Their life is gonna end, but there's more kindness and goodness comin' to you," Mama Tee went on. "I cain't say no more'n that. Y'all go on and leave me alone for a while. Tell Miss Jewell to come over here. I want her to sit with me for a while. Y'all go on... go on now."

The girls went back to their duties, periodically looking over to see Mama Tee and Miss Jewell with their heads together. At times, it seemed they were singing together, then praying, and then they just sat quietly for a long time, as the rest of the guests came and went around them.

A short time later, Mama Tee asked Destini to bring Mr. Hamp over to her.

"What can I do for you, Mama Tee?" Mr. Hamp asked, as he sat down beside her.

"I'll tell you what I want, Hamp Brayerford," she said. "I want you to get some of these folks to lift me. I wanna make a trip around this place with you in that wagon."

"Are you sure?" he asked. "That's a mighty bumpy ride down to the river and back."

"I know it is, but I'm goin' just the same," she adamantly told him. "I wanna smell that old river and them pine trees again. I want you sittin' right beside me. Duke! Duke, can you hear me!"

"Yes, Mama Tee, I hear you!" Uncle Duke shouted from the kitchen, and he rushed over to her.

"Duke, I want you to sit on the other side of me," Mama Tee continued. "Destini, I want you, Essie, Bunnye, Wanda Faye, Nadine, Dee Dee, Mrs. Frank, Miss Jewell, Miss Nanny and Essie. That's who I want ridin' with me in this wagon. Oh, and Brother Linton and Sister Velma. Can you get us all in one wagon, Hamp?"

"Yes, ma'am," he said. "Are you sure, Mama Tee? You think you can handle it?"

"I know I can handle it," she said. "We're all gonna handle it just fine. This is my Christmas gift from you Hamp Brayerford. You get it together for me. When you're ready, I be ready."

"All right, Mama Tee, if you're sure."

"Never been more sure. We're all goin' down to the river and back up together. That's my Christmas gift this year."

It didn't take but about ten minutes for Mr. Hamp to arrange everything. He had Louie bring up the largest buckboard, and then Louie and Dink lifted Mama Tee onto the wagon and settled her on blankets and cushions. The rest of the requested guests piled in moments later.

As soon as the horses pulled off, Mama Tee said, "Y'all sing now. I want to hear some singing. It's Christmas! Let's hear it, and Hamp! Hamp Brayerford!"

"Yes, Mama Tee."

"Hamp, did you bring us a little of that shine?"

Everyone laughed when he grabbed two bottles of homemade moonshine from a backpack, along with a bunch of Styrofoam coffee cups.

"Pour us all a drink," Mama Tee said. "We got to have the Christmas cheer."

Once the entire group were given their moonshine, they started singing Christmas carols, the first of which was "Jingle Bells".

As the trip was coming to an end, Mama Tee reached out and took Mr. Hamp by the hand.

"You got a lotta love in your heart, boy. It's been hard for you, I know. Merry Christmas, Hamp."

"Merry Christmas to you, Mama Tee," he said, and he kissed the old woman on the cheek.

"Promise me something, Hamp," she said.

"What's that, Mama Tee?"

"Promise me you won't forget this Christmas wagon ride."

"Unless I go crazy, Mama Tee, I'll never forget it."

"Take this with you, boy, wherever you go, and when you think about something special, something wonderful, think about this ride. I love you, boy. I do love you, always have."

"I love you, too, Mama Tee."

"I know you do, boy, you love other peoples, too."

Bunnye, who had been listening to the conversation, crawled over into Mr. Hamp's lap. In an instant she was sound asleep, as the group sang the final verse of "Silent Night".

"Sleep in heavenly peace,
Sleep in heavenly peace."

"Soon," Mama Tee said. "Be sleeping soon."

Chapter 18

No warning for Chester Easley

"Be sleeping wid my baby soon," Daddy said, when prison guard, Deputy Fleming, dropped him off at the Greyhound bus station on Christmas Eve morning.

"Good luck to you and Merry Christmas," Deputy Fleming said to him. "I hope you have a good life."

"Oh, I'm is," Daddy said, smiling wide. "I'm goin' down to Augusta to my auntie's house and eat a big Christmas dinner. Goin' rest for a day or two and play with my little nieces and nephews, and by New Year's Eve, I'll be wid my baby. I be sleeping wid my baby when the New Year comes in."

As the bus pulled out of the station, Deputy Fleming recalled Daddy's obsession with inmate Chester Easley. On the way back to the prison, he debated whether or not he should call former inmate Easley and apprise him of Daddy's release.

Upon entering the warden's office, he was greeted by Della, the warden's saucy secretary who always had something cheerful to say.

"How are you doing Deputy Fleming? Are you ready for some Christmas cheer?" she asked.

"I sure am," he said. "I'll be so happy to get home to my wife tonight. It's been a long day. Christmas around here seems a lot more depressing this year. Even the inmates are grumpier than usual. Is there any chance I could see the warden?" he asked.

Before she could answer, he reached into his canvas tote bag and handed her a box of chocolate covered pecans. She smiled from ear to ear and picked up the phone. Seconds later, she turned to him and nodded.

"The warden will see you now, Deputy Fleming, and Merry Christmas to you, you sweet thing. You sure know how to get to a girl's heart."

"Merry Christmas to you, Della," he said, smiling. "I hope you have a good one."

Warden Johnson was on the phone when Deputy Fleming entered his office and he had his back to him. When he heard the door open, he swung around in his big, leather swivel chair and nodded for the deputy to have a seat in front of his desk.

While he waited, Deputy Fleming glanced around the office, admiring the beautiful art work on the walls that was done for the warden by so many inmates throughout the years. Each year, the warden sponsored an art show for the inmates and it was always amazing to see the artistic talent that so many of them possessed.

Beautiful watercolors, pen and ink drawings, oils,

and even a variety of pottery pieces were displayed throughout the office. Behind the warden's desk was a beautiful watercolor of Stone Mountain done by a young man serving a life term for murdering his mother and father.

"What can I do for you Deputy Fleming?" the warden asked once he ended his call.

"Warden, thank you for seeing me," Deputy Fleming said. "I've come to ask you advice about something."

"Sure, go ahead," the warden said and he straightened up in his seat.

"I just took inmate Dexter, you know, the one known here by the inmates as Daddy."

"Ah, yes, Booker T. Washington Dexter."

"Yes sir, that's his name," Deputy Fleming said. "Well, you know how he was always fighting, cussing and causing trouble with the other inmates, and then he had that obsession with inmate Chester Easley?"

"Oh, yes, how could I forget those rumors? I heard them all, but we don't know for certain how true all those rumors were," the warden said, and then he swung around and pulled out inmate Dexter's four-inch thick file from the cabinet behind his desk.

"Well, you know how rumors go. They're usually based on fact," Deputy Fleming interjected, but all the warden did was make a grunting sound, as he flipped through the stack of papers in Daddy's file.

"Wasn't inmate Easley released not too long ago?" the warden asked, scratching his head.

"Yes, about three months ago."

"As I recall, after inmate Easley left, inmate Dexter turned himself around," the warden said, with a proud look on his face. "He became a model prisoner. Says here he even started going to our psychiatrist for his scheduled visits and then led his own self help groups."

Deputy Fleming started squirming in his seat, wondering how the warden could be so clueless as to what really went on inside his prison walls.

"He's one of our success stories," the warden went on, still grinning. "The parole board saw fit to seriously reduce his time on all those battery charges. They finally convicted him down in Augusta. Let's see... this was his second time here, but it looks like he did better this go around. First time in, he served out his full five years. This time, he was let out early on good behavior." He closed the file and looked up at Deputy Fleming. "It shows that a person can change, and it was a feather in our cap for having such a successful rehabilitation program."

"Well, sir, all he's been talking about for the last three months is being with his baby... inmate Easley, that is... and sleeping with his baby... I was wondering if you think I should call Easley and let him know that inmate Dexter is out."

"Absolutely not!" the warden emphatically shouted, as he slammed his fist down hard on the desk. "That is *not* our job. Our job is to help the inmates successfully serve their time and offer assistance for rehabilitation. Once they leave here, our responsibility to them and for them terminates, unless they break parole. In that case, they come back to us. Let's hope this won't be the case with inmates Dexter and Easley. No, Deputy Fleming, you've done your job well."

"I appreciate that, sir, but…"

"Aren't you retiring right after Christmas? I heard you were going down to Florida to do some fishing."

"Yes, sir, that's correct."

"You're taking your accumulated leave up until your retirement date, too, aren't you?"

"Yes, sir."

"So, today's your last day here," the warden said. "You've had a good career with us, Deputy Fleming. Don't mess it up now. No calls," he sternly added.

"Yes, sir, thank you, sir. I hope you and your family have a wonderful Christmas," Deputy Fleming said, and he stood up and shook the warden's hand.

"You, too, Deputy Fleming," the warden said. "On your way out, get a package of those note cards from Della and give it to your wife for Christmas with my compliments. It's the watercolor done by that young man who murdered his family. Such talent," he added, shaking his head. "To think he'll be spending the rest of his life in here. It's a shame, I tell you. A damn shame."

"Well, you have a good holiday, sir."

"You, too, and be careful on the road going home. This holiday traffic is terrible," the warden said.

As now retired, sixty-two-year-old, former Deputy Charles Fleming walked to his truck with the note cards in hand, he thought about his wife, Betty, who would be waiting at home for him with open arms. She'd have sandwich trays, dips, cookies, and everything imaginable ready for their two daughters and sons-in-law, and their three grandchildren, who were coming over for their annual Christmas Eve celebration.

He smiled wide as he thought about how much his son-in-law, Jake, loved his North Carolina style barbecue that he made each year for their Christmas Eve supper. He and the boys would also enjoy a couple of stiff cocktails of Jim Beam with a splash of water.

For only a brief moment he thought of inmate Easley again, as he drove home. His conscience kept telling him he should let Easley know that Daddy was headed his way, but then he thought of his retirement and the rustic cabin on the St. Johns River in Florida, and decided to do as the warden asked and let sleeping dogs lie.

He cranked up the radio and smiled when he heard the voice of one of his favorite country and western stars performing a holiday tune. He even sang along as he tooled down the highway toward home.

O beautiful star of Bethlehem,
Shine upon us until the glory dawns,
Give us the lamp to light the way,
Unto the land of perfect day,
O beautiful star of Bethlehem, shine on."

Chapter 19

Goodbye Grant

The same Christmas song was being played on the radio of a similar pickup truck as it made its way to a condominium on the eastern shore of Jacksonville, Florida. The young man behind the wheel had just pulled up to the guard gate.

"That was a helluva game you played over in Tallahassee a couple of weeks ago, Grant," security guard, Bob Allsworth, said after he sauntered over to the driver's side window. "You're going all the way, son. Mr. Campbell is here already and he said for you to go on up. He's got some things for you to take home to your mama. I see she didn't come with you this trip."

"No, sir, she decided to stay home. Thank you, Mr. Bob, and you have a nice Christmas."

"You do the same, son, and Happy New Year, too."

After he pulled into the parking spot Carl Alvin told him to utilize, which was close to the lobby entrance of the luxury, beachside condominium, he was a little confused. Carl Alvin's Range Rover wasn't parked in its usual spot.

"Maybe he had to run to the convenience store for something," Grant thought. "Or, maybe he's down at the mall buying that cashmere sweater he promised me."

Grant was so anxious to see his friend that he could barely contain his excitement. He snatched his tote bag from the floorboard and then ran to the lobby door, feeling on top of the world.

It was cool out, quite chilly actually, and he was ready to get up to the warmth of the condo. He knew the fireplace would be going full tilt in the luxuriously decorated living room.

"I can't wait to warm up my hands," Grant muttered. "It's so cold. Brrr," he said, shivering, as he stepped into the elevator.

When he opened the door to the condo, he was surprised to see Carl's cousin, Dee Dee Wilson, sitting in an armchair in front of the fire.

"Come on in, Grant," she said. "I'm having a drink. Do you want me to pour you one?" she asked, as she held up a bottle of A.H. Hirsch Reserve.

"Yes, ma'am, that would be nice," he said. "It's so cold outside. A shot of bourbon would warm me up right nicely."

"Good boy," she said, and she poured him a glass. "I'm not going to be here long, but you get comfortable. You can stay as long as you like."

"Where's Mr. Campbell?" Grant asked.

"Oh, come, come now, Grant. Go ahead and call him Carl or Carl Alvin. My goodness, y'all are close enough for that," Dee Dee said, grinning. "I'm afraid he won't be joining us. In fact, he won't be joining you anymore, Grant."

"Excuse me?"

"I said he won't be joining you anymore, Grant. Your Christmas presents are on the coffee table, and yes, there's a beautiful baby blue cashmere sweater in one of those boxes. Here's a little envelope for you, too," she said, and she handed it to him.

"What's this?" he asked.

"It's a paid voucher from the university. It's for the remainder of your tuition," Dee Dee told him. "Inside, you'll also find enough cash, so that if you and your mama are prudent, it'll see you through the rest of your educational needs. Oh, and there's a document in there that you're going to sign, my handsome football hero."

"I ain't signin' nothin'!" he yelled. "I ain't got to sign nothin'!"

"No, honey, you don't have to sign if you don't want to. You really don't, sugar, but look here," she said, and she grabbed another large envelope from off the coffee table.

"What is it?" he asked, as sweat began to pool on his upper lip.

Dee Dee pulled out a stack of black and white photos of Grant and Carl Alvin in various intimate and compromising positions and fanned them in his face, so he could get a good look.

"You give me those!" he shouted and he snatched

them out of her hands.

"Ohhh… bad manners, Grant," she said. "Snatching things away from people like that, but it doesn't matter because we have many more copies. It would be a shame for one of these pictures to wind up in the hands of the athletic director at the university."

"You wouldn't dare!" he shouted at her.

"Such a brilliant career ended," Dee Dee went on, as calm as a priest in prayer. "No more football hero… a fairy in a small town. Hell, they wouldn't spit on your guts if your ass was on fire. It's fundamentalist Baptist country, you know. Most of that bunch is so narrow-minded and inbred that they'd burn their own damned mama at the stake and pull her eyes out just for looking at a piece of smut. Can you imagine what they'd do if they discovered a man was having sex with another man?"

"You are a despicable woman, Dee Dee," he said, although his voice was somber and quiet.

"Really, Grant, I think you should collect your presents, get in your new pickup truck, which, by the way, is paid for now, and go on home. Consider it your big Christmas buckshot. Oh, and Grant, honey, this is from me. It's something one my friends cross stitched for you. I thought you'd like to keep it as a reminder of our little chat here."

Grant took the gift from Dee Dee's hand and tore it open. Inside was a beautifully intricate cross stitched piece inside an ornate frame, and on it was written, "It's all good."

Grant's eyes welled with tears and a few stray ones

trickled down his cheeks.

"This was one of Carl's favorite expressions," he said. "I loved him, you know."

"No you didn't, honey," Dee Dee said. "You saw opportunity knocking and you opened the door. I don't fault you for that, but the door has closed now. Nobody but you, me, Carl Alvin and the good Lord knows anything about this. My advice to you, honey, is this. If you can, go on with your life, stay in school, and make something of yourself. Do that for yourself, okay?"

"I will," he said, nodding his head as he wiped at his tears with the back of his hand.

"If Carl Alvin gave you anything, he gave you a look into another world," Dee Dee said. "It's a world in which you can participate, Grant. You're an intelligent, good looking boy, and thanks to Carl Alvin, you now speak English quite well. You have some polish to you now. You need that in the larger world."

"Yes, ma'am," he said.

"Don't go back home anymore than you have to. If someone, some nice girl or boy has a wonderful home, you go home with them for the holidays, but always, and I mean always, be good to your mama. I insisted Carl Alvin do something for her, and he has."

"Really?" he asked, seeming to have collected his composure again.

"Yes, he got her a fabulous job with the state doing employee benefits for some department... something like that, anyway, so she won't be waiting tables anymore."

Grant started crying big alligator tears now.

"How will I ever thank Carl?" he asked through his sobs. "He was good to me in so many ways, more than any man in the world. The sex was… well, just sex, but he was so good to me."

"Then, you take that with you," Dee Dee said. "Make something of yourself. You can do it. Now, look at that cross stitched picture again, honey."

'It's true, Miss Dee Dee," he said. "It's all good."

"All righty then, give me a hug and go and have a good Christmas with your mama," Dee Dee said, and she stood up and held out her arms. "Take her over to some of those lovely after Christmas sales, or maybe take her on a vacation some place nice. Give her some time, Grant. She loves you more than anyone in the world."

"I know she does," Grant said.

"One more thing," Dee Dee said, as she walked Grant to the door. "You remember Amy Wesson, the judge's granddaughter? You know, the pretty young girl you brought to Aunt Hattie's Christmas party?"

"Yes, ma'am, she's a sweet girl."

"Yes, she is. She's a wonderful girl and she likes you, Grant. In fact, she likes you a lot. You could look the world over and not find a girl as fine as Amy Elizabeth Wesson. She's a wonderful person and she's also my goddaughter. That's the reason I know how much she likes you."

"Why are you telling me this, Miss Dee Dee?"

"Because I think you're a bright boy," she said. "You know the judge is connected with folks all over the state, all over the nation really. Did you know he was offered a seat on the State Supreme Court twice and he turned it down? He turned it down because he chose to honorably serve the people right here in our little neck of the woods as a county judge, a circuit judge, and one of the best criminal defense attorneys in the state. You'll never know how many people he's helped. I'm telling you this, not to try to sell Amy to you, but to let you know that if you play your cards right, you could hook your wagon to that star. It's a bright one, too."

Dee Dee opened the door and before Grant left she had one more thing to offer him.

"Here's a bottle of her favorite perfume, all wrapped and ready for delivery," Dee Dee said, smiling. "Here's a card, too. If you're smart, and I think you are, you'll call her on the way home and go by and see her today. The two of you should go riding around and talk to each other. Wish her a Merry Christmas and then bring her out to Camp EZ on New Year's Eve."

"Won't that be a little awkward with Carl there?" Grant asked.

"No, it won't be. It doesn't ever have to be. Your weakness or silliness is the only thing that will reopen that book again, Grant. Carl won't reopen it, I can promise you. Another golden chapter is opening for you, Grant. Are you ready to open the book and turn the pages?"

"Yes, ma'am, I think I am."

"Good boy. Now, give me a kiss. I believe this is the beginning of a wonderful friendship, Grant. You'll find me to be a very, *very* good friend, but, and I hope this never happens, Grant, if you ever cross me, you'll find me to be an extremely formidable enemy. Just be kind and sweet to Amy, now, you hear?"

The two of them hugged each other and then Dee Dee patted him on the back.

"You good-looking thing," she said, smiling. "If I were just ten years younger…"

"Miss Dee Dee, you're a pretty lady… a beautiful lady, actually."

"Why, thank you, Grant. You tell Amy that same exact thing and be as sweet and kind as you are. I know that's what Carl loved about you the most, your kindness. Beauty fades, Grant, but the qualities that endure… kindness, sweetness, a sense of humor… these are the things that last, and they make people love you. Don't lose your kindness."

"That's really sweet of you, Miss Dee Dee, Thank you," he said.

"You're quite welcome, Grant… oh, and Grant…"

"Yes, ma'am?"

"Merry Christmas," Dee Dee said, and she shut the door.

Within seconds, she was on the phone, wiping her dampened eyes with a tissue as she punched in a number.

"Family will kill you graveyard dead," she said, as she waited for the party she called to answer the phone.

Chapter 20

Do you believe in Santa Claus?

Over in Jacksonville, a special Christmas Day brunch and performance was on tap at the exclusive Pink Flamingo Club. Carla Elaine, a.k.a. Carl Alvin, was in his dressing room preparing for his spotlight number, while humming the tune, "Have Yourself a Merry Little Christmas".

Every once in a while he'd take a sip of his Jingle Bell, a Christmas drink made by the staff at the Pink Flamingo that was quite tasty. Just as he set his glass down, his cell phone began ringing and he quickly answered it.

"It's all good, and Carl Alvin?"

"Yes, Dee Dee?"

"I'm sending you over a little Christmas present. I believe you're going to love it. It should be arriving any minute."

"Dee Dee, what in the world are you talking about?"

"I love you, Carl Alvin," Dee Dee said. "I'll always

love you, but this has got to be your last performance. Make it a good one."

"I will, Dee Dee. Are you coming to watch?"

"I'm leaving now, sugar. I wouldn't miss the last swan song of Miss Carla Elaine for the world, honey. You are something, cousin. Don't be sad. Remember, when one door closes another door opens. See you in a little while."

Carl Alvin hung up and began applying more of his makeup. Suddenly, there was a knock at the door.

"Who's there?" he called out.

"It's Santa's little helper," cooed a voice from the other side.

"Who? Go away!" he shouted.

"It's a long way to the North Pole and I'm so cold," the voice insisted.

"Goodness, gracious, don't people know I'm trying to get ready?" he muttered, but he went to the door anyway and cracked it open.

Before him, dressed in a long faux fur coat, a pair of fur topped Santa Claus boots and a Santa hat, was a short, tiny individual with its back to him.

"Turn around," Carl Alvin said in his most commanding voice.

"Surprise!" the voice shouted, and the person in the holiday outfit did as ordered.

"Mark?!" Calvin Alvin gasped.

"That would be me," Mark said, grinning from ear to ear.

Kissing him full on the mouth, Carl Alvin said, "You don't know how glad I am to see you. Thank you for coming over here today."

"Don't thank me, hon. Thank Dee Dee. Now, let me help you with your makeup," Mark said, as he sashayed into the dressing room. "While I'm getting this wig ready and your makeup arranged, would you be a dear and call down to the bar? I'd like that café au lait-colored Adonis wearing the Santa hat and those divine red velvet hot pants to bring us a couple of those Jingle Bell cocktails."

"Right away," Carl Alvin said, and as he dialed the number, he hummed the tune to the Christmas song, "Jingle Bells".

After ordering the drinks, he hung up the phone. Before he could let go of the receiver, it began to ring, so he answered with a cheery, "Hello, Santa Claus."

"Yep, the one and only," Dee Dee said, laughing. "I'm in my sleigh and on my way down to see one of my good children sing in a little while. Tell ol' Sol there at the club that I want one of those wonderful shrimp cocktails, and I want it chilled, not limp and lukewarm, oh, and Carl Alvin…?"

"I know," he said. "Chill you a bottle of Moet White Star because it's Christmas."

"Why, Carl Alvin, I do believe you have ESP."

"More like a lifetime of knowing you, Dee Dee," he retorted.

"Ah, yes," she said.

"Merry Christmas, Dee Dee," Carl Alvin said. "Thank you for sending Mark over."

"No problem. Mark's a good egg. He knows how to keep his mouth shut. On top of that, he's a good friend to us, a *good* friend. When your performance is over this afternoon, the two of you are coming over to my house."

"What about Uncle Hamp and Miss Hattie? Won't they be there?"

"Oh, hell, no, Carl Alvin. They're all together up at Hattie's place," Dee Dee said. "They'll eat, take a nap, ride the acres, have a few drinks and reminisce for hours. Hell, Uncle Hamp might even get lucky tonight in that gaudy mauve bedroom."

"Ohhh, don't' go there, Dee Dee. I can't imagine," Carl Alvin said, and they both had a good laugh.

"Well, you knock 'em dead, baby. I'll be there in a few minutes," Dee Dee said.

As soon as Carl Alvin hung up there was a light tapping at the dressing room door.

"It's me," a timid voice called out.

"Come on in, Doug! It's unlocked!" Carl Alvin shouted.

A muscular, young black man, dressed in red velvet hot pants and a white satin shirt, brought the Jingle Bell drinks in and he presented them in such a flamboyant manner it was almost comical.

"Doug, that's enough with the theatrics," Carl Alvin said, laughing.

"I'm sorry, my little Super Star," Doug said, blushing.

"I'd like you to meet my friend, Mark," Carl Alvin said. "Mark, this is Doug."

"Merry Christmas to you," Mark said, and he gave Doug a big hug.

"Merry Christmas to you, too," Doug said, all flustered and giddy.

"Mark, do you believe in Santa, Claus?" Carl Alvin asked.

"Actually, after all these years, I'm beginning to believe in him again," Mark said, shyly smiling before he took a sip of his Jingle Bell.

Chapter 21

About mid morning on Christmas day, after all the presents were opened and the Lowell family had devoured a delightful breakfast of sausage and pancakes that Dink had prepared, Wanda Faye called a family meeting in the living room.

Outside, it was more than crispy cold with the temperature hovering around the forty degree mark. Dink put another log on the fire, which was crackling away in the fireplacc in the corner of the living room.

With Dink by her side and her four children surrounding her, as they sat in front of the Christmas tree, it was time to announce the exciting news, not only to Little Chet, but to the other three kids, as well, that Dink was Little Chet's biological father.

Little Chet, however, didn't seem the least bit surprised at the announcement. He just shrugged his shoulders and smiled. It seemed he already knew Dink was his natural father. The public affirmation of what he had evidently known for some time wasn't the earth shattering event that Wanda Faye thought it was going to be. The other three kids didn't seem shocked, either.

It was still quite an emotional moment, especially for Dink, who shed quite a few tears as he hugged his newfound son.

The day after Christmas, Wanda Faye and Dink hosted a fish fry at their farmhouse and invited all the family, as well as many close friends. The first order of business, once everyone had arrived, was to make the same announcement to friends and family. Everyone was surprised, even Nadine and Destini, who had no idea Wanda Faye was going to make the announcement today.

While everyone was gathered in the large screened in porch on the backside of the house, Dink asked Brother Linton to bless the food. The old man, for once, finished it with some sense of brevity. Wanda Faye noticed his vigor and general health had declined dramatically since Jerri Faye's death, and she said so to her mother.

"He just ain't the same man anymore," Miss Jewell said. "It's like the starch is out of him. Even his eyes don't have the same glimmer."

Miss Jewell pulled her Bible Drill group aside, as well as their parents, and asked them all to place Brother Linton on their prayer list and to faithfully pray for him.

"Our family wants to thank all of you for coming here today," Dink said as folks began filling their plates. "We want you all to know we love you and appreciate each one of you. Me and Wanda Faye just told you the happy news about us finding out that Little Chet is my natural born son. The rest of the story, though, we ain't told a soul, not until today."

Everyone stopped what they were doing and turned to listen to Dink.

"I want you other children to come over here by me. Victor Newman, John Harrell, Little Jewell, come on over here," Dink said, as he stood in front of the large food table. "Me and Wanda Faye talked with Judge Wesson and Carl Alvin, and they've been a big help to us."

It was so quiet on the porch that you could hear a pin drop out in the woods. Everyone's eyes and ears were trained on Dink.

"Today, we want you to know that all of you children have the same daddy and mama," he said to the four kids. "You're all ours now." Then he turned to the crowd and said, "Ladies and gentlemen, I asked to adopt these four children, and they all agreed."

There was hootin', hollerin' and clapping from everyone, and then all the children, one by one, hugged and kissed both their parents. Even the starchy Miss Iris Wesson, the judge's wife, was holding a handkerchief to her face, as she dried her tears.

"You must be so proud," she said to Miss Jewell, and the two women hugged each other.

"I've always been proud," Miss Jewell said. "There's been times, and you know this being a mama yourself, when I've been prouder than others. This is one of those times that surpasses all of them."

"Well, let's eat!" Wanda Faye shouted. "Y'all come on. Brother Linton, Sister Velma, Judge and Miss Iris, Mama, Mr. Hamp, Miss Sissy, y'all come on."

Before anyone could move, Brother Linton held up his hand and asked to speak.

"Wanda Faye," he began. "You, Nadine and Destini are our children now since…" and he had to stop for a second to collect himself.

His lips were quivering and Wanda Faye hoped he wasn't going to spoil such a joyful occasion, even though she understood how much he was hurting inside. Sister Velma rushed to his side and grabbed onto his hand and then Miss Jewell hurried over to take his other hand.

"Wanda Faye," he started again. "You, Nadine and Destini are mine and Miss Velma's girls now. You're all we have in this world. That means these children are our grandchildren," he said, as he pointed to the four kids. "So, their new grandpa here says since these children are starting out fresh and new, they get to go through the food line first. Nadine and Destini, you let your children follow right after them. Jesus said unless we come to him as a little child, we won't enter his kingdom. There was never a time the Master turned a child away. So, let's let them go first."

"Oh, Brother Linton, no," Miss Jewell said. "Don't be silly."

Then, on the other side of the porch, boomed the unmistakable voice of Hamp Brayerford.

"Miss Jewell," he said. "The preacher is absolutely right. It's right for these children to go first tonight. You go behind them and fix Mama Tee a plate," he told her.

That was all he said and then he helped Essie and

Duke get Mama Tee situated in her chair. Miss Jewell merely nodded in agreement and not another word was spoken on the matter.

"I have one thing I want to say," little Chet piped up.

"Go ahead, son," Brother Linton told him.

"Well, I want to speak for all my brothers and sisters and tell you how happy we are with Mama and Daddy," Little Chet said. "I also want my Uncle Louie to know he's been like a daddy to me and my brothers and sisters all these years. Uncle Louie, this don't mean that you don't still pick us up and take us out to the camp and take us other places. We love Daddy, but we love you, too, Uncle Louie, and we won't forget how good you been to us."

"Thank you, Little Chet," Louie said, clearly emotional, as he choked back tears. "I sure do appreciate that."

"I also want to thank Aunt Destini, Uncle Duke, Aunt Essie, Mama Tee and Grandma Jewell," Little Chet went on. "We'd a been a lost ball in high weeds without y'all. Oh, and Mr. Hamp, I want to thank you for always being so good to us and to our mama. I reckon that's all I have to say. God bless you all. Now, let's eat!"

Louie and Nadine had to excuse themselves and they went inside to the kitchen for a bit to collect themselves. Destini was right on their heels. Dee Dee followed them in and she went straight to the refrigerator and opened the door.

"Well, hell, Nadine! I thought you and Destini, or

at least Louie, would have been smart enough to put a few bottles of beer in here. Damn! Here it is Christmas and y'all are bawlin' like babies and the house is dry as a bone!"

"You are one crazy woman, Dee Dee," Louie said, laughing. "Go look in that cooler on the back porch."

Dee Dee took off in a flash and came back moments later with an armful of beer bottles and then opened each one of them and handed them out.

"God Bless us all," she said, toasting the others before taking a gulp. "Let's have a good time and quit being a member of the Kleenex brigade. No more of this damned boo-hooing. This is a time for rejoicing."

"Right you are, Dee Dee Wilson," Destini said. "My Lord, girl, you are something else."

"That's what I've been told," Dee Dee said, and she winked at her. "All right, now, let's go out on that porch and get something to eat. I saw Iris was eyeing those cheese grits. She'll eat like a starved dog on the Serengeti Plain before I have a chance to get any. Let's get a move on."

Chapter 22

"Lollie!" Nadine shouted through the screen when she saw her pull up in the side yard. She rushed outside to greet her and give her a big Christmas hug. "How are you doing, honey? Wanda Faye's been looking for you."

"It's good to see you, Nadine," Lollie said. "Is Wanda Faye inside?"

"Yep, she's in helping everyone fix their plates. Come on in. Your Aunt Sissy's been here for a while already."

Once inside, Lollie waved to her aunt who was across the room chatting up Tang, Lee and Mr. Yuk.

"How considerate of Wanda Faye to invite the Yuks here," Lollie said. "That's good. I'm glad."

Tang, Lee and Mr. Yuk were all dressed to the hilt in fashionable clothes and they seemed to really be enjoying themselves.

"They brought Wanda Faye and Dink that huge floral arrangement over there," Nadine said, pointing to a magnificent poinsettia arrangement sitting in the middle of one of the dining tables.

"It's beautiful," Lollie said.

Wanda Faye happened to look up after getting Jewell Lee's plate ready, and when she spotted Lollie, she rushed over to greet her with outstretched arms.

"It's so good to see you, Lollie," she said. "How are you?"

"I'm doing so much better," Lollie said. "I was a little late getting here because Jimmy phoned me from up at Talbot. This was the first call they let him make. We didn't have long, but he seems to be getting along fine. I write to him every day."

"That's wonderful news," Wanda Faye said. "How are you really doing, though? Are you still having bad nightmares?"

Lollie made a face that seemed to beg for some alone time with her best friend.

"Dink!" Wanda Faye called out. "I'm gonna slip into the living room for a few minutes with Lollie, okay?"

Dink was preoccupied fussing over the kids and simply nodded in her direction.

"He heard you, Wanda Faye," Nadine said. "Y'all go ahead. Destini, Dee Dee and I have this under control. Take as long as you want."

The two friends went inside and sat down on the couch.

"Do you want a glass of iced tea or a cup of coffee?" Wanda Faye asked.

"No, thanks," Lollie said. "I just want to sit here for a minute and say thank you. I would never have had the strength to go through with an intervention for

Jimmy if it hadn't been for you. You mean so much to me."

"Oh, honey, don't think anything about it," Wanda Faye said. "I knew what you were going through. I know what it's like to be whipped and beat on, and to feel ashamed about it. I lived my life that way for years with Chester. It's like going through the motions. You're not living. You just go through the motions and you never escape the torment."

"Ain't that the truth?"

"A lot of women never find their way out," Wanda Faye continued. "So many women die. I've been reading a lot about why women put up with such abuse. I put up with it because I thought I had to. I had no self esteem. All those horrible things he said to me and about me, well, after a while, I started to believe it. It's just a miracle of God that they caught him making that crystal meth. I probably wouldn't be alive today otherwise."

"Thank God, you are," Lollie said.

"You know, this area needs a place like a counseling center. You know… a place where abused women can go and talk to someone. Maybe get some counseling, employment information, and maybe even a place to spend a few nights when things get out of hand at home. I asked Judge Wesson about it one day and he said there's a high rate of domestic abuse around this general area. A counseling center here would be wonderful. I'd love to be a nurse in a place like that, so I could help other women."

"Oh, Wanda Faye, you shouldn't be just a nurse.

You should be the director," Lollie said, smiling. "You know how to talk to people and make them feel at ease. Then... well, there's your own story to tell. You've been where these abused women are. You would be such an inspiration to them. You certainly have been to me."

"Oh, come now, Lollie, I just told you my story to let you know you ain't alone," Wanda Faye said, blushing. "Nobody should feel alone, but I think a lot of women do feel alone and most of their loneliness is linked to shame."

"Well, I'm gonna pray about it and ask all my friends to pray that God carves a way for this to happen in the very near future. We need a facility as a shelter, a safe oasis for women. We really do."

"I'll pray that same prayer," Wanda Faye said. "If God honors my prayer and allows me to be a part of such a thing, I know just who I'd name the center after."

"Who?" Lollie asked.

"Margot Smith, of course," Wanda Faye said, without missing a beat. "I'd name it after her if she'd let me. She inspired me so many times to go on living when I wanted to die. Yes, ma'am. The Margot Smith Women's Center for Hope."

"Oh, I love it! I believe the center will become reality," Lollie said, and the two girls hugged each other.

"Well, Miss Margot said the other day, if you can dream it, you can achieve it. I believe we'll have such a center in a year or less. I firmly believe that."

"I believe it, too," Lollie said. "The Margot Smith Women's Center for Hope... Mrs. Wanda Faye Lowell, executive director."

Chapter 23

Daddy's on his way

"Booker! Booker! Booker T. Washington Dexter!" Daddy's Aunt Minnie called out. "Bookerrrr!" she yelled louder when he didn't respond.

"Yes, ma'am," he finally answered, as he rushed into the kitchen where his aunt was standing in front of the refrigerator with the door wide open.

"Sorry, Auntie," he said. "Ain't nobody called me Booker in a long, long time."

"I knows, sugah, but I ain't callin' you Daddy," she said. "I only had one daddy and he died on a farm outside Milledgeville a long time ago. You want something to eat? I'm gonna make me a ham sandwich out of some that leftover Christmas ham. You want me to make you one? I got some sweet potato pie here, too. I know how you loves that."

"No, ma'am," Daddy said. "I ain't hungry right now. I think I'm goin' walk down to cousin Sammy's house and see what he up to."

"Up to no good or sleepin'. Since that boy got that

disability check, he don't hit a lick at a snake. Sleeps and eats, that's all. Laziest man in Georgia," she said, shaking her head.

"I see you after while, Auntie. You want me to bring you a wine cooler? One of them scrawberry flavored ones?"

"Yes, baby, that'll ease the pains in these old legs and help me get a little better rest. I tell you the tireds is done gone down on me. All that Christmas cooking. Minnie ain't as young as she used to be, Booker, but I wanted it to be a special Christmas for you chile."

"It was Auntie," Daddy said. "I loved it all. I be back in a little bit."

"All right, baby. Don't stay out too long. Ain't nothin' out there on them streets after midnight but trouble. I sho' don't want you to have no mo' trouble, baby."

"I be home before your movie's over, Auntie. I'm goin' take a piece of dis pie wid me, okay?"

"Go ahead, baby. I sho' is glad you likes it. Made it jes for you, baby."

The old woman laughed to herself, as Daddy scooted out the door.

Upon arriving at his cousin Sammy's house, Daddy spotted a half empty bottle of gin on the coffee table, a half pack of Newport cigarettes and Sammy's car keys to his vintage 1977 gold Cadillac Fleetwood.

Sammy was dead to the world on the couch and the TV was blaring with a re-run of an old game show.

At the end of the couch, neatly tucked under one corner, were Sammy's cowboy boots. He wore cowboy boots everywhere he went. Folks around town made fun of him, but he didn't care. He just told them he loved wearing cowboy boots and had been wearing them since he was a child.

Daddy picked up one of the boots and slid his hand inside, all the way to the toe area. The first boot had nothing in it, but when he felt in the second one, he found stuffed in the toe, two one hundred dollar bills and he carefully fished them out.

The next thing he grabbed was the car keys. Then, he scribbled something on a piece of paper and left it on the coffee table.

He had written, "Leaving for south Georgia for a few days. Will bring the car back soon. Cover for me with Aunt Minnie. I'll call you later tonight. Booker."

As he cranked the car, he smiled wide, and then switched on the radio. One of his favorite songs by Otis Redding was playing.

*"I've been loving you a little too long.
Can't stop now. "*

"Yes, sir," Daddy said. "Cain't stop now. On my way, Chester, baby. Cain't stop now."

Once he got onto the interstate he headed south and drove well into the night. Outside of Tifton, he pulled into a convenience store to gas up. Then, he went inside and bought himself a large Coke, a bag of pork skins, a pecan log, a humorous Christmas card with Rudolph the Red Nosed Reindeer on the front, and two quick pick Powerball tickets.

The Powerball wasn't worth as much as it had been before Christmas, but fifty million dollars was nothing to take lightly, he thought. He asked the cashier, an older black woman, if he could use her ink pen. He wrote inside the Christmas card, 'Love, Daddy.' Then, he placed the two Powerball Tickets inside and sealed the envelope.

"That sho' is sweet of you," the cashier said. "What a nice holiday gift for your baby."

"Yes ma'am," he said, smiling. "I hope my baby likes it."

"You know your baby goin' love it. Churrins always love they daddy to do sweet things for 'em. You have a safe trip wherever you goin' and a nice holiday."

"You, too," Daddy said. "God bless you, ma'am."

"God bless you, too," the woman replied.

As Daddy drove away, he felt joyous inside and out. Soon, he'd be seeing his baby and what a time they would have. Just thinking about his baby made him smile. He had so much he wanted to share. Mainly, he wanted the two of them to be together always and forever. He knew once he talked to Chester and showed him, one more time, how much he loved him, that the two of them would be together for eternity.

"That's the way true love is," he thought. "Me and my baby together forever."

Chapter 24

Chester Easley was all bundled up in a sweat shirt, wool pants and two pairs of socks trying to stay warm in his late grandma's old house that was sorely lacking proper insulation. He was sitting in a rocking chair with an afghan wrapped around his shoulders trying to shake off the cold. Just three feet in front of him, a wood burning stove was throwing out enough warmth to keep his feet from cramping up.

The night was damp and cold, and outside a light misty rain had begun to fall. The last time he checked the radio newscast, the temperature in Ludowici had dipped to near freezing.

In an attempt to warm his heart, Chester began listening to one of Brother Linton's old sermons on tape. Even though he had heard it many times before, this time it seemed to take on a new meaning. The old preacher was emphasizing the power of Satan. He spoke of Satan being the prince of the air and how he had tempted Jesus in the wilderness. He said Satan was like a roaring lion seeking those who he may devour.

"Satan will try to make you fall when you are

working the hardest to build your spiritual life with the Lord," he heard Brother Linton say.

It was Christmas and Chester had spent the entire day cooking for and feeding the poor at the shelter the church had built just down the road. As fulfilling as the work was, though, he still felt an emptiness at his very core. It was a void left by the absence of Wanda Faye and his children. He had never stopped loving them or missing them.

In his hand was the latest letter Wanda Faye had written to him about Dink's adoption of the children. When she wrote him the first time, asking if he had any objections, he didn't reply. He decided to allow her to do as she wished. After all, he had caused her enough pain, so why reply one way or the other, he thought at the time. Even though in his heart he hated giving up his children, he knew Dink would be a good father to them.

Chester was deeply hurt when he found out the oldest boy, Little Chet, actually belonged to Dink. Even though he had suspected it from the beginning when Wanda Faye told him she was pregnant, he had always held out hope that his suspicion was just that... a suspicion.

Still, it was no excuse for the way he had treated her all those years, and he honestly regretted it now.

As he stared into the fire, he came to the realization that he had so many regrets. Instead of dwelling on them, though, he decided to pick up his Bible and read the 23rd Psalm. When he finished, he popped in a peppy Southern gospel CD in an effort to lighten his somber mood. It was time to let the past be the past and not haunt him anymore.

There was so much he wanted to forget, especially the part of his life spent in prison. For just a second, when he closed his eyes, he saw Daddy's face. Then, he felt his rough, calloused hands touching and probing every inch of his body.

"Oh, Lord, help me forget," he pleaded.

Minutes later, he was in the bathroom, scouring through the medicine cabinet. He grabbed a bottle of Xanax and opened it. There were still quite a few pills left in the bottle. He hadn't taken any in a while, but tonight he felt as if he needed it.

He popped a pill in his mouth and followed it up with a swallow of water. Then, he went back to the living room, grabbed the afghan off the rocking chair and lied down on the couch, pulling the cover up around his neck. It didn't take long before he fell fast asleep.

He didn't see the bright headlights reflecting against the living room wall about an hour later, and he didn't hear the knocking at his door. As he slept, he didn't feel the moist kiss on his forehead, or hear the big man ease himself into the lounger on the other side of the room. He had no idea that, right there in his living room, a quote by a great Southern writer, William Faulkner, was being played out.

"The past is not dead. In fact, it's not even past."

At seven o'clock the next morning, Chester roused

to the aroma of freshly perked coffee. A smile crossed his lips and, for just a moment, he imagined Wanda Faye was home, and that soon he would smell bacon sizzling in the pan, as well as the delightful aroma of biscuits baking in the oven.

He was still drowsy from the Xanax he had taken and thought he was simply dreaming. When he heard a rattling noise in the bathroom, however, he knew he was wide awake. Someone was in his house.

For a moment, he thought it might be the preacher from his church coming by to check on him, until he spotted an envelope on the coffee table. The poor penmanship of his name scribbled across the front of the envelope was undeniably Daddy's.

"Oh, my God!" he thought, as his heart began to pound like a drum inside his chest.

As quietly as he could, he peeled himself off the couch and tiptoed toward the kitchen where he kept a pistol in one of the drawers by the sink. He was halfway there when he heard the bathroom door open. With his eyes tightly shut, he slowly turned around. When he opened his eyes, there, standing before him with a towel tied around his waist, was Daddy, smiling so wide Chester could see all of his teeth.

"Merry Christmas, baby!" Daddy shouted. "How's my baby gettin' along these days?"

Chester broke out in a cold sweat. He knew from past experience not to overreact in a situation like this.

"I'm doing fine," he calmly told Daddy. "How did you find me?"

"Oh, baby, now aint's dat some kind of question?

You knows I knew all de time where my baby stay. I ain't no fool. I sent you my love every night and now here I is. Did you see the card I brought you, baby? I got you a little Christmas gift, too."

"Yes, I saw the envelope," Chester said, as he continued into the kitchen. "You shouldn't have brought me a present. I feel bad because I don't have anything for you."

Daddy just smiled and walked over to the coffee table. He picked up the envelope, tore it open, and followed Chester into the kitchen.

"This is for you, baby," he said, and he handed the card to Chester. "Go on, open it."

Reluctantly, Chester opened it and inside he found two Powerball tickets. Rather than go into a diatribe about how he didn't believe in the lottery, he simply smiled, put the tickets in his pocket and said, "Thank you. I sure hope these will bring me good luck."

"Oh you ain't got to hope for dat," Daddy said. "Yo good luck is standin' right here."

With that, Daddy dropped the towel from his waist and then he took Chester's hand and placed it on his swollen, fully erect member.

"Now, turn around and drop them draws, baby," Daddy said. "You always did have somethin' I wanted. You ain't had to buy me nothin' for Christmas. You got my present right here," he added, smiling as he patted Chester on the rear end.

"Oh, God," Chester pleaded. "Please don't do this. Just let me go, and you go home, Daddy. I won't tell a soul you've been here."

"You talkin' crazy talk," Daddy said, still grinning. "You just upset 'cause you ain't had me in a while, but it'll come back to you. It's jes like ridin' a bicycle."

In one fell swoop, Daddy yanked Chester's pants and underwear down to his ankles and began rubbing his behind with his gruff hands. It was when Daddy dropped to his knees to kiss him on the rear end that Chester slowly opened the drawer. He felt around for the pistol, but couldn't find it, and wondered if he had picked the wrong drawer. Then, his hand closed in on a large butcher knife. It was one that a church member had brought over not long after he got out of prison.

Clutching the handle of the knife with a death grip, he closed his eyes. Daddy's tongue was probing him everywhere and all he could feel was rile revulsion, as his mouth filled with salty bile.

Quickly, he said a silent prayer, "Father into your hands I commit my spirit. Please take me into your kingdom."

Slowly and deliberately he pulled the knife from the drawer and then he turned around clutching it in his right hand behind his back.

"Dat's right," Daddy said. "I'll take care of my little baby for a minute. I know he want some attention."

Before Daddy could get the flaccid member in his mouth, Chester pulled away and asked, "Will you stand up, so I can kiss you? I've dreamed about kissing you for so long."

"Oh, you sweet baby," Daddy said. "Dat's the reason I loves you. I knows you feel it, too. We goin' be together forever. Me and you forever."

"Yes, forever," Chester said. "Together forever."

Daddy put his mouth on Chester's and forced his tongue halfway down his throat. Then, in one swift, fluid movement, Chester plunged the long, silver blade into Daddy's chest and forced it all the way in, as far as it would go.

Daddy fell back and grabbed his chest. Dark red blood began spurting everywhere, pooling on the floor around his feet.

"Ooh, baby, you shouldn't a done dat," he said, as if he wasn't fazed at all. "You know you cain't hurt your daddy."

As Daddy yanked the blade out of his chest, a horrible grimace spread across his face.

"You been goin' wid somebody else!" he shouted at Chester. "You been steppin' on your daddy!"

"I swear, no I haven't!" Chester screamed, feeling totally helpless now. "Oh, no! God, no!!" he screamed, but there was nobody around to hear his pleas.

It only took the big man a few seconds to do his butchering work. In a mad rage, the first slice went to Chester's throat, cutting his jugular vein. The rest of the stabs were aimed at his chest. Twenty, thirty, over forty times he stabbed and sliced until all that was left was a bloody mess as Chester slumped to the floor at his feet.

Looking down at his own blood mingling with Chester's, Daddy began to cry.

"We goin' be together forever," he said, as tears streamed down his face.

In the half opened drawer, he saw the handle of the

pistol. He picked it up, carefully examined it, and then cocked the trigger before placing it against his temple.

"We goin' be together forever," Daddy said, taking one last look at Chester's bloody body.

ঔঔঔঔঔঔঔঔঔঔঔ

Later that afternoon, the preacher from the House of Prayer came knocking at Chester's door. He'd been calling Chester's number all morning, but could never reach him. Worry got the best of him, so he decided to check in on him.

When Chester didn't respond to his incessant knocking, the preacher tried the door handle, which, surprisingly or not, was unlocked. When he walked into the kitchen and discovered the grisly scene, he called 9-1-1, and then collapsed on the floor next to the two dead, bloody bodies.

When the rescue unit arrived, the emergency medical technicians who rushed inside were clearly taken aback at what they saw. Nothing like this had ever happened in their small, rural town before. It didn't take long for sheriff's deputies, state police officers, and dozens of news crews to gather in front of the small frame house on Neighborly Lane.

Chapter 25

In Seraph Springs, the phone rang at Wanda Faye's house and Little Chet ran to the kitchen to answer it. After the caller asked to speak to Wanda Faye Easley, he laid the receiver down on the counter.

"Mama!" he called out. "You need to come to the phone! The man says it's an emergency!"

"Be right there!" Wanda Faye yelled from her bedroom where she was vacuuming the rug.

When she picked up the phone, all she did was say hello into the receiver and then she was silent for several minutes, as she listened to the caller. A few times she nodded her head and grunted inaudible sounds, as Little Chet stood and watched her facial expressions. The next thing he knew, his mama dropped the receiver as her eyes rolled back into her head, and then she fainted, hitting the floor with a big thud.

Little Chet picked up the receiver and heard a man asking, "Are you there? Are you there? Ma'am, do you understand that your ex husband Chester Easley has been brutally murdered? Can you come to up to

Valdosta right away?"

Little Chet was so distraught that he hung up the telephone and immediately called Dink on his cell phone. He was sitting in the office at Fernandez Trucking working on shipping orders.

"Daddy, you got to come home!" he shouted. "You got to come home right now! Something bad has happened!"

Then he hung up the phone and called his Aunt Nadine and told her the same thing, only in a more detail after she begged him to explain what was going on. After she hung up, she called Destini and it took less than ten minutes for the two of them to pull into Wanda Faye's driveway in separate vehicles.

They rushed inside and found Wanda Faye passed out on the kitchen floor, while Little Chet held a cold compress to his mama's head. The other three children were huddled together crying.

"Is Mama dead?" Jewell Lee asked with tears falling down her cheeks.

"No, honey, your mama's not dead," Nadine comforted her. "She just fainted, that's all."

Destini immediately whipped out a vial of smelling salts from her pocketbook. She kept one on hand at all times for the women who fell out at church. As she waved the vial of smelling salts under Wanda Faye's nose, her eyelids started blinking and seconds later she came to.

Nadine and Destini carried her to her bedroom and laid her on the bed.

"I'll be right back," Nadine said to Destini, and she

went out into the hallway and ushered the children into the living room.

"Listen to me, Little Chet," she said. "Your mama's gonna be fine. She's undergone a terrible shock. You know Chester Easley is dead, right?"

Little Chet nodded.

"Okay, now there's three things I want you children to do," Nadine continued.

"Anything, Aunt Nadine," Little Chet said.

"I want you to call your grandma and tell her what's happened. She'll want to come right over, but you tell her to wait until I call her before she comes out here, you got it?" she asked.

"Yes, ma'am," Little Chet said.

"Then, I want you to tell Grandma to call Brother Linton and Sister Velma, but remember, tell them not to come until I call them back. After you do that, fix your mama a glass of cold Coke with plenty of ice. Finally, and this is real important, Little Chet. I want you to sit by that phone, and unless it's your daddy, Carl Alvin or the sheriff, I want you to just take messages. If it's any of those three people I mentioned, you let me know and either me or Destini will talk to them."

"Yes, ma'am," Little Chet said and he went into the kitchen to make the call.

"The rest of you children can go outside and play," Nadine said. "But y'all stay close to the house, you hear? Make sure you put your jackets on, too. It's mighty chilly outside."

After a collective "Yes, ma'am" from the kids,

Nadine went into the kitchen to check on Little Chet.

"I just called Grandma," he said. "Here's Mama's Coke," he added, and he handed the glass to her.

"Thank you, sweetheart," she said, and she hurried back to Wanda Faye's bedroom where Destini was sitting beside her on the bed.

"Now, tell us, Wanda Faye, what exactly did that man on the phone say to you?" Destini asked.

"They said Chester was so badly cut up that they could hardly make out who he was," Wanda Faye began, as her body shook uncontrollably. "Since he has no brothers or sisters, I was listed as his next of kin. They've asked me to come identify his body in Valdosta. I don't think I can do it. I don't know if I'm capable of doing it."

"Now, baby, we ain't goin' worry about none of that right now," Destini said, stroking Wanda Faye's hair. "We'll cross that bridge when we get to it. Right now, I want you to rest."

Destini looked over at Nadine and made a motion with her eyes toward her purse on the nightstand. No words were spoken, but Nadine knew what she meant. Destini then held up two fingers and Nadine handed her two Xanax tablets.

"Take these, honey," Destini told Wanda Faye. "You just leave this to us right now. Everything's gonna be fine. Nadine's gonna pull down these shades now. You just go to sleep, honey," she added and then she started humming a soft tune, while continuing to stroke her hair.

Meanwhile, Nadine grabbed the phone and called

Dee Dee. After she explained what happened, Dee Dee said she was on her way to Seraph Springs from Jacksonville.

"You don't need to go to all that trouble, Dee Dee," Nadine told her.

"Gimme me that damn phone," Destini ordered her. "Thank you, Dee Dee, baby," she said. "Will you do two other things for me? Get a hold of Mr. Hamp and get a hold of Carl Alvin. Tell Carl Alvin we need him and we need him here now."

"He'll be there, sugar," Dee Dee assured her. "Y'all just hang tight."

As Wanda Faye dozed off and fell into a deep sleep, Nadine and Destini went to the kitchen to prepare a lunch for the kids. The phone rang and when Little Chet answered it, Destini heard him say, "Hi, Daddy." She immediately snatched the phone from him and in about thirty seconds flat, she explained what had happened. He told her he would be there as soon as he could.

A little over two hours later, there was a loud rapping at the front door and in burst Dee Dee and Carl Alvin, both of them looking frazzled. Mr. Hamp had just pulled up in his pickup and as soon as he opened his door he started yelling.

"Is our little girl all right? You tell her not to worry about a thing! We're gonna take care of this ugly mess!"

When he walked in the door, Dee Dee rushed over and hugged him.

"It's okay, honey," he said and then he looked at Carl Alvin. "You take care of our little girl," he told him.

"I will, Uncle Hamp," Carl Alvin said, nodding his head. "I'll call you and let you know what I find out, as I find it."

"Mr. Hamp, I'll be back over there at the camp in a few minutes," Destini said. "I got to go pick up Bunnye from Mama Tee's. She's been watchin' her all morning and Uncle Duke has to take her to the doctor's this afternoon."

"You go ahead and do what you got to do here, Destini," he said. "I'll pick up Bunnye. We'll be watching television when you get back to the lodge. We'll be fine. Don't you worry."

"Well, don't you be sugarin' her up so's I cain't get her to sleep tonight," Destini warned him.

"You just mind your business here," he said. "Me and Bunnye will mind ours."

With that, he turned on his heels and started back to his truck, giving everyone a backhanded wave as he left.

"What I'm goin' do about that man?" Destini asked, shaking her head. "He's goin' ruin my chile and I cain't fight him on it. He dotes on that chile, and young as she is, she's got his dang cell number memorized. Calls him all the time!"

"Aw, let it go," Dee Dee said, and she put her arm around Destini's shoulder. "He did me the same way and I'm not in jail yet," she added, and the two of them laughed.

"Well, let's all go sit down in the living room," Destini said. "I'll bring y'all some coffee."

"Where's Louie and the kids?" Dee Dee asked.

"Oh, I made him take them to the movies a little while ago," Nadine said. "I needed 'em all out of my hair for a bit. I'm gonna check on Wanda Faye. I'll be right back."

Once everyone was gathered in the living room sipping on their coffee, both Nadine and Destini relayed everything they knew about the situation, as well as Wanda Faye's state of mind.

"What can I do?" Carl Alvin asked.

"You can find out everything that happened," Destini said, and she handed him a piece of paper. "Here's two phone numbers. I think they're some kinda law enforcement folks up in Georgia, but I ain't familiar with all that stuff, so I didn't half understand what they was saying to me on the phone earlier."

Destini fished around in her jeans pocket and pulled out another piece of paper.

"Here's another one," she said. "This is that nosy newswoman from Jacksonville who keeps callin' here. Would you just call her and tell her something… anything, please?"

"I'll take care of it," Carl Alvin said. "You all have my number. If any of these people call you again, you tell them they'll have to talk to Mrs. Lowell's attorney, and give them my number. I'll refer them to cousin Hugh."

"Excellent," Destini said.

"I'm gonna run up to the camp and make some calls from Uncle Hamp's study. If y'all need me, I'll be there. I'll call you before I leave there and let you know where I'll be."

As Carl Alvin was getting ready to leave, Nadine went over and hugged him.

"I love you, darling," she said. "I always will. You are the sweetest thing in the world."

"He'll do," Destini said, smiling as she came up behind them.

Just then, Louie and the kids came through the door.

"Dee Dee, why don't you round up these children and take them up to the camp?" Destini suggested. "I'm sure you'll find somethin' for 'em to do. There's that big rec room with the pool table, the big screened TV, and I know there's a refrigerator full of goodies. You and Louie can play babysitter, along with Mr. Hamp. I know Bunnye would love the company."

"Sounds like a plan," Dee Dee said. "Come on, kids. Nadine, toss me your keys to the van. I'll leave my car here for y'all if you need it. Carl Alvin, you drive Destini's camp truck and take Little Chet with you," she added. Then, she whispered in his ear. "Talk to him, Carl Alvin."

"I will," he said. "He's plenty smart."

As they pulled off, Destini and Nadine waved goodbye.

"Lord have mercy," Destini said, shaking her head. "Will any of our children ever be the same? Being babysat by two of the richest folks in this county. Lord, oh, mercy me. Who in the world would believe this?"

"Nobody," Nadine said. "There ain't a soul who would believe the story of our lives. They simply wouldn't believe it."

"Well, believe it or not, I s'pose we know it's true," Destini said. "We done lived it, and we'll live through this, too, won't we, girl?"

"Yes, we will," Nadine said, and the two best friends walked back inside the house hand in hand, as they had done thousands of times in the past.

Chapter 26

The next few weeks went by so quickly, it was just a blur of intermingled scenes of chaos in Wanda Faye's mind. First, there was the heart-wrenching task of going to the morgue in Valdosta to identify Chester Easley's body. Dink and Carl Alvin had been her twin towers of strength, as they accompanied her and offered loving support to help her through the horrendous ordeal.

The press coverage of the grisly murder-suicide in the small town of Ludowici, Georgia was more than monumental. A scandal such as this made for major news in the normally sleepy town, as well as across the country.

Television stations and newspapers from all over the state of Georgia, as well as many from Florida and other nearby states, had sent reporters and camera crews to do live investigative stories to try to dig into the truth behind the killings. News vans were parked up and down the street in front of Chester's home where the scene had unfolded. They were even camped out across the street from the Ludowici House of

Prayer during the funeral, trying to get candid shots of mourners as they came and went. The fact that both men had recently been released from the state prison made the story even more shocking.

Wanda Faye was thankful that Carl Alvin, through the barrage of press inquiries he had received, never once mentioned her or her children. For that, she was eternally grateful.

After talking with Brother Linton and Sister Velma, she and Dink had agreed that Chester's funeral was no place for their children to be. With all the expected press coverage, Carl Alvin had advised Wanda Faye it was no place for her or Dink, either. In fact, the entire family was discouraged from attending the funeral or being anywhere near the town of Ludowici until after the dust settled.

Instead, Carl Alvin and Dee Dee were the only two from Seraph Springs to attend Chester's funeral service at the Ludowici House of Prayer. When it was over, Carl Alvin introduced himself to the old preacher, Brother Taylor, who had long been the pastor at the Ludowici House of Prayer.

"Would you come back to the fellowship hall and eat with us after the interment?" Brother Taylor asked Carl Alvin. "You and your pretty cousin?" he added.

"Of course, we'd be honored," Carl Alvin told him, figuring the old man wanted to either tell him something important about Chester or share something with him, or, perhaps, both.

Once Chester's body was loaded into the waiting hearse, Carl Alvin and Dee Dee followed the procession to the cemetery. There were only about two dozen people in attendance, since the majority of the parishioners at the church service had to go back to work. After Chester's coffin was lowered into the ground, Dee Dee and Carl Alvin went back to the church and on over to the fellowship hall.

Only a handful of people were there, as Chester had no family other than Wanda Faye. It was mostly the elderly members of the small congregation who had gathered to offer solace to one other.

"Well, at least they put out a nice spread," Dee Dee whispered to Carl Alvin when she saw all the food on the table.

Brother Taylor immediately greeted them at the door and invited them to join him at his table. After the meal, he asked Dee Dee and Carl Alvin to accompany him to his study over in the church. It was a short walk and they were inside his study a few minutes later seated in front of his desk.

"I want you to have this, Mr. Campbell, since you are close to the family," Brother Taylor said. "It's all legal, witnessed and everything," he added, and he handed Carl Alvin a large manila envelope. "I'm hoping you can deliver it to his ex wife."

"Do you mind if I sit down and look this over first, Brother Taylor?" Carl Alvin asked.

"Not at all, son," he said. "You and Miss Dee Dee take as long as y'all want. I'm going back to the fellowship hall to visit with some folks. Brother Chester's death has hit them pretty hard. It's been difficult for me, too. Brother Chester, with the help of the good Lord and the members of this flock, well… he made a huge turnaround in his life since he got out of prison. Praise the Lord."

The old man snatched a handkerchief from his coat pocket and began dabbing at the tears forming in his eyes. Dee Dee immediately went around to the other side of the desk to comfort him.

"Brother Taylor, let me walk you to the fellowship hall," she said, as she put her arm around his shoulder.

"That's sweet of you, honey," he said. "But I'll be okay. You go ahead and stay here with your cousin and look over the things inside that envelope," he added, and then he stood up, straightened his tie and started for the door.

Carl Alvin motioned for Dee Dee to come over to where he was sitting. He had already grabbed his wallet from his coat pocket and pulled out five hundred-dollar bills. After quickly whispering something in Dee Dee's ear, he handed her the money.

She went over to the preacher just as he was about to open the door, and then gently took his arm and placed the money in his hand.

"Honey, I couldn't…" the old man started.

"We won't hear of it," Dee Dee said, interrupting him. "You take this money, Brother Taylor. Chester's ex wife and children want you to have it, and we want you to have it. They're good people. They were advised not to come to the funeral today because of all those press folks out there. That's why they're not here. I'm sure you can understand that."

"Yes, I do understand," he said, nodding his head.

"Thank you, Miss Dee Dee, and thank you Mr. Campbell. God bless you both."

After the preacher left, Carl Alvin opened the manila envelope and pulled out Chester Easley's will. It had been duly witnessed and everything seemed to be in order, just as Brother Taylor said it would be. It was drawn up by a local attorney, E. William Leonard, Esquire, and was dated April of that year.

Within the will, it was spelled out that Chester was leaving his house, whatever cash he had, and a small life insurance policy to the Ludowici House of Prayer. His truck was to be sold, as well as all his personal items, and those proceeds would go to Brother Taylor. All other items of personal effect were to go to Wanda Faye Easley Lowell.

In a gallon-sized Ziploc bag inside the envelope were Chester's "other personal effects". There was a pearl-handled pocket knife, his wedding band, a silver wrist watch, his mama's gold wedding ring, a tie tack shaped like a cross, his Bible, and two very stained and wrinkled Powerball tickets, dated December 26th of the previous year.

"Not much for Wanda Faye and the children," Dee Dee said, making a face as if it's what she had expected.

"Well, you can't really blame him," Carl Alvin said. "Besides, they're better off this way."

Carl Alvin sat examining the two Powerball tickets for a while, as Dee Dee put the rest of the items back in the bag.

"Carl Alvin, you still with us?" Dee Dee asked, when she noticed his glazed over eyes staring off into space.

"Huh?" he asked. "Oh… yeah… you know, there's something about these Powerball tickets. I'm getting this weird vibe. Do you think they're worth anything?"

"Oh, Carl Alvin," she said, laughing. "Always the dreamer."

"I'm serious," he said. "It can't hurt to check, can it?"

"I guess not," Dee Dee said. "Actually, if it's got anything to do with the Lotto or Powerball, I can make one phone call right now and find out," she added, smiling.

"Who are you gonna call?"

"Destini," she said. "Who else? She knows more about all that stuff than the folks in charge do. That girl *knows* her Lotto games. Uncle Hamp gets on to her all the time, but she just ignores him. She doesn't spend too much money on it. Not that I know of, anyway."

Dee Dee immediately called Destini on her cell phone and, just as she thought, Destini was a wealth of information.

"That Powerball is worth 50 million dollars," she told Dee Dee, with the words rolling off her tongue without even having to think about it. "I remember there was five winners and one of the tickets was sold at a convenience store in South Georgia. Last I heard, it ain't been claimed yet. If you give me a second, I'll get you the numbers."

"Well?" Carl Alvin asked, as he paced the floor back and forth in front of where Dee Dee was standing.

"Hold your pants on, Carl Alvin," she said. "She's gone to get me the numbers. Sit down, willya? You're starting to make me nervous, now."

Carl Alvin did as he was asked and a few minutes later Destini came back to the phone. She read off the numbers 4, 14, 25, 37, 48 and 49.

"Say those numbers again," Dee Dee told her.

Destini repeated the numbers and for a moment there was dead silence. Then, all of a sudden, Dee Dee screamed so loud that Carl Alvin jumped from his seat and nearly out of his skin.

"What's wrong with you?!" Destini yelled on the other end of the line.

"Oh, my God… Destini, you stay quiet until I say so, but girl, our friend Wanda Faye Easley is now worth ten million dollars!" Dee Dee screamed. "Actually, it's probably just a little over six million after taxes."

"Six million!" Destini screamed. "Six million dollars?!" she screamed again, and it was so loud that Dee Dee had to pull the phone away from her ear. "Lord, God Almighty!" she shouted. "Who says somethin' good cain't come out of a tragic situation?"

❧❧❧❧❧❧❧❧❧❧

Inside the Lowell residence back in Seraph Springs, Dink and Wanda Faye were praying with Brother Linton, Sister Velma and Miss Jewell.

"Lord, we ask that you lift this great burden from the shoulders of our beloved daughter, Wanda Faye," Brother Linton prayed. "She's borne it like a soldier of the cross all these years. Lift this burden, Lord, and give this child the peace that passes all understanding."

When Brother Linton finished, Wanda Faye knew in her heart of hearts that everything was going to be all right. That nagging ache of emptiness that had been eating at her core for so long whenever she prayed had vanished, as if it never existed. She felt complete and whole for the first time in years. She knew beyond a shadow of a doubt that her burdens had been lifted and her prayers had finally been answered.

When she arose from her knees, she hugged Brother Linton, Sister Velma, and then her mama, who she held onto for a long time. Then she reached for Dink's hand and squeezed it tightly, as she lovingly gazed into his eyes.

"Everything is all right, now," Wanda Faye told Dink, and then she turned to look at the others. "I am at peace," she said. "Thank you, all of you."

"Praise the Lord," her mama said, as she wiped the tears from her face.

After her guests departed and Dink went out to tinker in the garage, Wanda Faye turned on the television to watch Miss Margot Smith's television program.

"Today is the first day of the rest of your life," Miss Margot said, as the show opened. "Do you believe that?" she asked the audience.

"I believe it," Wanda Faye said, as she got comfortable on the couch. "I *do* believe it."

Just then, the phone rang and she reluctantly answered it, not wanting to miss any of the show.

"Wanda Faye, this is Carl Alvin."

"Oh, no," she moaned. "I can hear it in your voice. You have bad news to tell me, don't you?"

"No," he said, suddenly sounding much too cheerful. "In fact, the news is quite the opposite. Here, talk to Dee Dee. I'm going to let her tell you."

Chapter 27

"Hello, my darling sister," Wanda Faye calmly said to Nadine when she answered the phone. "I want you to call Destini as soon as we hang up, and then the two of you get over to my house right now... and I mean right now."

"Wanda Faye, what in the world is going on? Is somebody hurt or sick? Is it one of the children? Did something happen to Dink? Is Mama okay?"

"Whoa, calm down. It's nothing like that, Nadine. I don't want to talk about it over the phone, though. Please don't ask me any more questions. Just call Destini and come now," Wanda Faye said, and she hung up the phone.

It had now been about fifteen minutes since she had spoken to Carl Alvin and Dee Dee, and Wanda Faye was still trying to wrap her head around the exciting news. As she sat on the couch, her next phone call was to Dink.

"Dink, honey, you ain't gonna believe this," she said.

Before she could tell him the entire story, Dink was

whooping and hollering so loud it was hurting her ears.

"I'm on my way home, baby!" he shouted. "I'll call Mr. Fernandez and tell him!"

"Awesome, Dink," she said, smiling from ear to ear. "You come on home, honey. I need you here with me now."

All thoughts of watching the rest of Miss Margot's show flew out the window and she turned off the TV. Then, she went into the kitchen and started a full pot of the infamous Camp EZ coffee that Destini kept stocked in her pantry.

While the coffee was percolating, she set the dining room table with coffee mugs, plates, forks, and napkins, along with half and half, sugar and artificial sweetener. There was a fresh chocolate swirl cake on the counter that her mama had just brought her. It was sitting inside a beautiful globed cake plate that Sister Velma had given her for Christmas.

"Perfect," she said, and she set it down in the middle of the dining room table.

Feeling utterly overwhelmed at the moment, she sat down at the head of the table. For the first time in days, she desperately wanted a cigarette.

"No, that's wrong. I don't want one," she said. "I need one! Now!"

Wanda Faye hoped Nadine would have a pack stashed in her pocketbook when she got there, since she had smoked her last half of a cigarette two days ago out behind the garage when nobody was around. The two girls had promised each other months ago that they would try to quit the habit, but she knew Nadine was sneaking them once in a while, just like she had been doing.

"Please have some contraband in that purse of yours when you get here, Nadine," she said, wringing her hands.

Meanwhile, her mind was still reeling from the news Dee Dee had relayed to her. Then, an awful thought flashed through her mind.

"Hmmm... I wonder if she was just playing a joke on me," she said. "Nah, she wouldn't do that to me... would she?"

She sat there scratching her head and jonesing even more for a cigarette, but finally decided to give Dee Dee the benefit of the doubt and trust that she was telling the truth. After all, she thought, a friend wouldn't do that to a friend.

It seemed to be taking forever for Nadine and Destini to arrive, but it gave Wanda Faye plenty of time to think about what she would do with the money.

She had poured herself a cup of coffee and was standing by the kitchen window when she saw two vehicles pull up outside in a cloud of dust. It was Nadine and Destini, and they both looked frazzled. Wanda Faye couldn't help but laugh as they ran to her front door.

The news she was about to tell them was going to be far from what they would expect to hear after learning of her good fortune. She figured it would be a disappointment to them, but she couldn't help it. She knew what she had to do. She had promised herself, as well as the Lord, that should she ever become financially able, she was going to do something that she knew in her heart was the right thing to do.

Not long ago, she had spoken to Carl Alvin and asked him how much a women's center like the one she and Lollie had envisioned, would cost to build. He told her then it would cost at least four million dollars.

She figured she would use the rest of the money to remodel the house, pay for her children's college educations, and pay off Dink's truck. She would also pay for the rest of her nurse's training.

"Maybe I'll get this driveway paved," she thought. "It's so bumpy and awfully muddy when it rains. Look at it now. It's so dusty during dry weather. Yeah, a paved driveway would be nice. I wonder if there'll be enough money for that."

Then, she thought she'd do something special for her mama, Nadine and Destini, although, she hadn't decided what yet. The first thing she needed to do was consult with Carl Alvin and Mr. Hamp to get their advice, since the two of them had plenty of business sense.

"First things first, though," she thought. "I have to make a trip to the lottery office in Tallahassee to cash in the winning ticket. I hope Carl Alvin will agree to go with me."

As the girls entered the house, Wanda Faye asked them to join her at the dining room table. Nadine's hair was sopping wet and she was dressed in an old pair of sweat pants, one of Louie's long-sleeved shirts, and a pair of flip flops.

"Nadine, you're gonna get sick as a dog runnin'

around like that in this weather," Wanda Faye said, laughing.

"Don't give me that crap," Nadine said. "I had just gotten out of the shower when you called. I grabbed some clothes out of the hamper and what you see is what you get. Now, what's going on?"

"Yeah, Wanda Faye, what's going on?" Destini asked, with a sly grin on her face.

Wanda Faye took her sweet time getting down to business and it was driving Nadine crazy, while Destini just kept on grinning. After she poured the two of them some coffee she sat down.

"Would you please get to it!" Nadine finally shouted.

"All right, all right," Wanda Faye said. "Well, Dee Dee and Carl Alvin called from Ludowici a short while ago. It seems the pastor from the Ludowici House of Prayer, Brother Taylor, gave them a plastic bag that contained the things Chester wanted me and the children to have."

"Are you serious?" Nadine asked. "That's why you called us over here? Shoot, what did that scumbag leave you? A pot of gold?"

Wanda Faye just chuckled and so did Destini, which made her wonder what was up with her. Normally, she'd be the one making a big fuss, as impatient as she was.

"Well, girls, it wasn't a whole lot, but in the plastic bag were two Powerball tickets. The tickets were bought up there in Georgia the day after Christmas. Well... to make a long story short, the children and me are the winners of ten million dollars!" she shouted at the top of her lungs.

"What?!" Nadine yelled.

"Who said Christmas was over?!" Destini shouted. "Whoowee! What a Christmas gift!"

With that, Destini jumped up from her chair and started dancing around the room, singing the lyrics to the "Twelve Days of Christmas". When she got to the phrase, "five golden rings", she inserted her own words, "ten million dollars!"

Meanwhile, Nadine had gone over to hug Wanda Faye.

"Lordie, lordie!" Destini shouted. "Bought by a thug in Georgia, given to old Chester the Pester, and now Wanda Faye is one rich bitch!"

"You crazy thing," Wanda Faye said, laughing. "You mean you knew and you didn't tell Nadine?"

"Nope, and it was just about to kill me," Destini said. "Dee Dee told me not to say a word, so I didn't. I haven't told a soul, but, boy, am I goin' have a good time tellin' 'em now! This calls for a party! We need to have a party! Cake, coffee and sandwiches over at the camp!"

"I haven't even told the children yet, and Dink is on his way home," Wanda Faye said. "Let's wait a while, okay?"

"I'd sure like to whip your butt, Destini, and don't think I ain't gonna remember this," Nadine said, as she wiped the tears from her face. "You keeping this from me. Shame on you." Then, she turned to Wanda Faye. "Well, all them beatin's, all that dope business, all them bad times, and now look. Mama said God never sleeps. I'm so happy for you, honey. Give me a hug."

"Louie and all the kids should be here any second," Destini said. "We might as well go ahead and tell them. They'll know somethin's going on. They ain't stupid."

"Before they get here, do you have a cigarette in your pocketbook, Nadine?"

"What?" she asked.

"Come on, girl, this ain't no time to be coy. I know you have a pack in there, and if I've ever needed a cigarette, I sure do need one now."

"Oh, hell, let's both light up," Nadine said, as she pulled the pack from her purse. "Why not? After all, we gotta celebrate, right?"

Destini shook her head and laughed at the two of them.

"Y'all crazy, both of you, so crazy," she said, shaking her head.

Later, when Wanda Faye told the children the news, it was like a bomb exploded in the house.

"Does this mean we can finally go to Disney World, Mama?" Victor Newman asked.

"And the beach?" Jewell Lee piped up.

"We'll see, kids," Wanda Faye said. "I think maybe we can manage to do both those things. For now, y'all go on back to the den and watch TV or go hang out in your bedrooms and listen to some music, okay?"

Off the kids went with Louie on their heels and then the phone rang. Nadine answered it.

"It's Dee Dee and Carl Alvin," she said to Wanda Faye.

"Gimme that phone," Destini ordered her.

"Well, excuse me," Nadine said, and she handed it to her.

"Y'all go home and change," Destini said into the mouthpiece. "Yes, ma'am, dress casual and come on out to the camp. We're gonna have a little jumped-up supper for our girl's good fortune. No, no, y'all don't bring a thing. Well, if you wanna do that, but nothin' else, Dee Dee. I know how you are. Okay, about eight o' clock. We'll see you then."

"What did she say?" Wanda Faye asked after she hung up the phone.

"Said they was stopping in Valdosta and she was bringing you a surprise," Destini said.

"Another surprise?" Wanda Faye gasped. Lord, what will that girl come up with next?"

"You never know with her," Nadine said.

"Well, there's one thing I know," Destini chimed in. "When these children are fed and sent home tonight, the four of us are stayin' at the camp. Me, you, Nadine and Dee Dee. We goin' talk deep into the night tonight."

"Any excuse for a party," Wanda Faye said, laughing.

"Honey, just give in to it," Nadine told Wanda Faye. "It's the way we do things around here. We're always together in good times and bad. We all bunch up like a covey of quail and this ain't no exception. The boys will be fine with it. I'm gonna ask Louie to get that bonfire fixed up down by the river, too."

"Well, let's get goin'," Destini said. "We got things

to do."

"Do you wanna take this cake with you?" Wanda Faye asked her. "It will help you out with the refreshments."

"Would you listen to her, Nadine? She's rich as cream now and wantin' to send a cake with me to help with the expenses. Well, honey, that's what I love about us. We are what we are. We'll always be able to have as big a time with potted meat, soda crackers and a pot of good coffee as we would with the best caviar in the world."

"Hell, we'd have a better time," Nadine said. "I tried some of that caviar when Miss Hattie had that party for Dink and Nadine. I wasn't impressed with it at all."

"I wonder if that poor man who killed Chester has any family," Wanda Faye asked out of the blue.

"What in tarnation you talkin' about?" Destini asked her. "You just won all this money..."

"I can't help it," Wanda Faye said, cutting her off. "I can tell y'all, if he has some little children or an old grandma some place, I'm gonna help them."

Destini came over and hugged her.

"Girl, you won't ever change," she said. "All the gold in Fort Knox won't ever change you. That's what I love about you, Wanda Faye. Okay, we'll see you later, baby. Come on, Nadine."

"Y'all leave the children here," Wanda Faye said. "I want them around me for a bit, at least until Dink gets home."

"Have you lost your mind?" Nadine asked.

"No, I have not," Wanda Faye said. "Just leave them here with me. They've had enough excitement for a while. I'll get them ready. They all have clothes here. I just need them around me now."

"Whatever you say, honey," Nadine said. "You sure you don't want me to stay?"

"No, you go on and help Destini. I'll be fine. I'm gonna let them play a little while and then I'll talk to Dink when he comes home. I'll get the kids ready. Go on. We'll be fine."

As the girls pulled away from the house, Wanda Faye cleared the table and turned the TV back on. She wanted to at least catch the final few minutes of Miss Margot's show.

"Lord, Miss Margot," she said. "I hope you have some pearls of wisdom for me today."

Miss Margot, she thought, looked so pretty in a white, winter outfit of slacks, a cable-knit sweater and brown leather boots. Her pearl earrings and the gorgeous gold chains spilling down the front of her sweater topped the outfit off in grand splendor.

"Today, we talked about how to deliver unfortunate or unpopular news to someone we love and hold dear," Miss Margot summarized.

"Thank you, dear, Jesus," Wanda Faye said.

From the den came Jewell Lee's voice. "Mama, we're thirsty, can we have something to drink?"

"Y'all come on in here, baby. I've got drinks, homemade cake, or fruit."

"Gee, Mama, who would want an apple when we can have a piece of Grandma Jewell's chocolate cake?"

Jewell Lee asked, as she came running with eyes as wide as saucers.

"Nobody sugar, nobody," Wanda Faye said, and she gave her a hug.

"I love you, Mama. Are we rich now?" Jewell Lee asked.

"I love you too, baby. Yes, we're rich now, but we've always been rich."

Chapter 28

The main dining area and great room of Camp EZ was something to behold that night. Wanda Faye didn't know how Nadine and Destini accomplished what they did in such a short time. It was unbelievable.

The dining room table was decorated with play money and old lottery and scratch off tickets that Destini had saved up over the years. On the wall behind the buffet table, there was a banner she and Nadine had made with the winning Powerball numbers. Underneath it the caption read, "It only takes one."

Dee Dee had downloaded an old song on her cell phone called, "We're in the Money", and when Wanda Faye entered the room, she played it full blast. She had also found old green and gold St. Patrick's Day derbies at a party shop in Valdosta. She said she bought one for each one of the girls and a gold crown for Wanda Faye. They were all decorated with play Monopoly money.

For it to be a "jumped up piece of business", as Destini had dubbed the supper, one would never have known it. There was spiral ham, smoked turkey, potato salad, sandwich fixings, baked beans, rolls, and a beautifully decorated cake with the winning lottery numbers written in green lettering, as well as, "Congratulations, Wanda Faye".

Even Miss Jewell and Sister Velma, as much against the lottery as they were, had gotten into the act. They were there to congratulate Wanda Faye. Besides that, they weren't crazy. They knew her good fortune would mean good fortune for the House of Prayer.

The two women, upon getting word of Wanda Faye's good fortune, had hurriedly fixed a huge pot of tiny acre peas, and they had roasted and salted pecan halves that were set in dishes throughout the great room.

"What a wonderful party," Wanda Faye said to Carl Alvin. "I still don't believe it. You know, I actually thought at one point that Dee Dee was just playing a joke on me when she called."

"Well, you can believe it," he said. "It's true. I've already checked, double-checked and triple-checked the numbers. We can go to Tallahassee anytime you want. I'd suggest waiting at least another day and allow me time to call over there and make arrangements."

"Whatever you say, Carl Alvin, will be fine."

Wanda Faye stood in the middle of the room and asked for everyone's attention.

"Before Brother Linton comes to say the blessing, I want to say a couple of things," she said.

Wanda Faye's meek voice could barely be heard above the noise, until Miss Sissy let out a whistle that would have stopped a locomotive.

"There, honey, they're quiet now," she said, smiling at Wanda Faye. "Go ahead and talk, sugar."

"Thank you, Miss Sissy, and thank you to all of you. I love you all. Every one of you know my story. It ain't no secret. Whether or not this money had come along, I want you to know I've been rich all my life. I had a wonderful daddy, and I am blessed with a precious, loving mama."

At this, Miss Jewell broke down and Sister Velma, as always, was there to comfort her.

"In my husband, Dink… come here, honey," she went on. Sheepishly, Dink moved closer to her and held her hand. "In my husband, Dink, I found the love of my life and in our precious children that love is magnified day after day. I love all of you, my children, my nieces and nephews who, you might as well say, are my children, too. Nadine, Destini, Louie, Dee Dee, where would my life be without you? I've loved you all my life and I'll never stop loving you. We may argue, fuss, even fight once in a while, and we may disagree."

Now, it was Nadine, who was wiping her eyes and shouting, "Amen!" after which everyone laughed.

"But I love you just the same," Wanda Faye continued. "Mr. Hamp, you've been so good to me. You've been like another daddy to me. You told me once when you had something hard to say, to tell the truth and it only hurt one time."

The old man nodded to her, winked, and said, "Go on, honey. Say what you want to say."

"Miss Sissy, is Lollie here?" Wanda Faye asked.

"She is, honey, right over here behind me, eating

these pecans and running her mouth."

Again, everyone chuckled.

"Lollie, come over here," Wanda Faye said. "Most of you in this room know about Lollie. She was being abused by her boyfriend, physically and mentally abused. She came to me, and, with the help of so many here, we were able to help her. What you may not know is that for years and years, I suffered the same kind of abuse. I was scared to talk about it. Actually, more ashamed than scared, because I felt like it was my fault. I felt I had done something wrong. Now, I fully believe, and am so thankful, that before Chester died, he made a change in his life. I thank God for that, and for him to die the way he did… well, nobody should go that way. Nobody, and I mean nobody, should feel they are alone when they're being hurt, beat and abused."

Several "Amen's" went up among the group, as Wanda Faye paused for a breath.

"So, I've prayed about this," Wanda Faye went on. "Dink, Mr. Hamp, and I talked to Carl Alvin about it… whether y'all like it or not, I prayed and vowed to the Lord that I would build a center for abused women who feel like they have no voice. Most of this lottery money will go for that purpose. If some of y'all are disappointed, I'm sorry. With my husband and children and all of you here, I'm blessed beyond compare. Now, I want to share this good fortune with others. That's all I had to say."

Mr. Hamp was the first to stand up and speak.

"Sugar, that's about the most unselfish thing I've ever witnessed," he said. "You build it, honey, and I'll leave enough in my will that it will never have to worry about funding. You see to it, Carl Alvin. Start on it right away."

"Thank you so much, Mr. Hamp," Wanda Faye said, as tears welled up in her eyes. "One last thing, I want y'all to know this center won't use up all this money. There'll be special things I'll do for each of you. I'll tell you more about that later. I just wanted you to know this part now."

Everyone clapped, while Dink and then Lollie were the first two to give Wanda Faye a hug and a kiss.

"What do you think you'll call this new center?" Nadine asked, although, Wanda Faye knew she already knew the answer.

"I'll call it the Margot Smith Women's Center for Hope, if Miss Margot will allow me, that is. Carl Alvin, you'll have to contact her about that. She is, after all, the one who gave me the inspiration to go on when I felt I couldn't put one foot ahead of the other. So, yes, I'd like to name it in her honor."

"Good girl," Destini said. "I believe Miss Margot would be proud... very proud."

The rest of the evening was full of well wishing, eating, drinking, hugging, and enough kisses to last a lifetime. Even Mama Tee had to offer her take on the situation. She took Wanda Faye's hands in hers and smiled.

"You is a winner, girl and not because of these here tickets," she said. "These tickets helped you do something for somebody else, but you'd a done it anyhow. These tickets just got you to the station quicker. I'm so proud of my baby. So very proud."

Wanda Faye leaned down and kissed the old woman's cheek. Seconds later, she watched Dee Dee and Destini head over to the grand piano.

"We got a little song we want to dedicate to our friend and I believe it will mean a lot to you, Wanda Faye," Destini announced. "It's one you've always liked. Dee Dee does pretty good on this one for a white girl playing the piano. Duke, you and Essie know this song if you y'all want to come help me sing it. The rest of you will know it, too. It's pretty easy. Well, here goes, my old friend.

> *"I don't feel no ways tired,*
> *I come too far from where I started from.*
> *Nobody told me that the road would be easy,*
> *I can't believe you brought me this far to leave me."*

As Destini, Duke and Essie sang the old song, Wanda Faye smiled.

"It's the story of my life," she thought. "I'll bet Miss Margot would love this song."

Chapter 29

The next few weeks seemed to fly by at warp speed. Carl Alvin, Wanda Faye, Dink and Mr. Hamp all made the trip to the state capitol to claim Wanda Faye's winning Powerball ticket. Mr. Hamp had recommended several avenues of investment for the money and he set up a bank account that would allow her to begin construction of the women's center. Carl Alvin helped her draft a letter to Margot Smith, advising her they would need her permission to name the center after her.

A few days after they returned to Seraph Springs, and true to her word, Wanda Faye discovered that Booker T. Washington Dexter, better known as Daddy, who had murdered Chester, had an elderly aunt named Miss Minnie, who lived in Macon, Georgia.

With Carl Alvin's assistance, she got in touch with the old woman and set up an appointment to meet her at her home. The day they drove up to her place was dark, gloomy and gray, and the trip up was a bit treacherous at times with moments of blinding rain that slowed traffic to a crawl on the interstate.

After they pulled into her driveway and got out of the car, Wanda Faye noted the temperature had dropped several more degrees. It was bitter cold and sleet was now falling across most of central Georgia.

Miss Minnie came to the door of the small wood frame house and she seemed to be struggling with the walker she was using, but she insisted she needed no help. She invited Wanda Faye and Carl Alvin to come in and sit on the couch in the living room. The room was being heated by a small portable gas heater, which was struggling to keep up with the dropping temperature. Miss Minnie sat down in a chair across from them and pulled an afghan around her shoulders and legs.

"Poor Booker," Miss Minnie said. "Lord, he was such a sweet chile. I raised him, you know. He was a star football player in high school, but he had a temper, and that temper got him in more trouble than you can imagine. I used to clean house for a judge here in Macon, and he and his wife were good to me. It was all we could do to keep that boy out of jail. Finally, they told me they had done as much as they could, and if I kept bothering them for help, they'd let me go. I needed that job, so there wasn't nothing else to do but pray and hope."

"I'm so sorry to hear that," Wanda Faye said.

"Well, he jumped on that policeman down the street from here after some of his friends were arrested at that club where he hung out all the time. He nearly beat that man to death. That's when they sent him to the pen. Like to have killed me," she said. "Never had no children of my own."

"I'm so sorry, Miss Minnie," Wanda Faye said.

"Well, it's over now," she said, and the tears began streaming down the old woman's cheeks.

"Miss Minnie, I wanted to come here and do something for you," Wanda Faye said, and she reached over to grab the old woman's hands in hers. "Your nephew gave Chester, my ex-husband, that winning Powerball ticket as a gift."

"Say what?" the old woman shrieked. "I ain't in no more trouble wid the law, am I? I done had all I can take."

"No, ma'am, it's nothing like that. You tell her, Carl Alvin."

"Well, Miss Minnie, it's like this," Carl Alvin began. "Wanda Faye has asked me to set up a trust fund for you so that you'll receive a check each month for two thousand dollars for the rest of your life."

"What?" the old woman shrieked again. "Two thousand a month? Am I hearing right? Y'all kidding with me, ain't you?"

"No, ma'am," Carl Alvin said. "In fact, here's the first installment," he added, and he handed her twenty hundred dollar bills.

"Oh, Lord Jesus, I can't believe it," Miss Minnie said, sobbing tears of joy. "Scrubbed floors and cleaned houses all my life. All I get is four-hundred and twenty dollars a month now on social security. If it wasn't for Meals on Wheels and my little church... Lord, thank you, Jesus, thank you, sir."

"Don't thank me," Carl Alvin said. "Thank Wanda

Faye here. She insisted on finding out if your nephew had any family and she wanted to do anything she could to help."

"Come here, chile," Miss Minnie said, and she held out her arms. "Lord, God, bless you, honey. You don't know what this means to me. I'll be able to heat my house and go out to eat once in a while and not have to worry about waiting in the cold at the bus stop when I need to go across town to my friend's house. I ain't seen her in three months. Can I hug you, honey?"

"Of course, you can," Wanda Faye said, and she went to her. "Here's my phone number," she added and handed her a piece of paper. I don't live that far from you, and my husband drives a truck and comes through here all the time. If you need anything or if you want to come down to Florida and stay with my family for a few days, you just give me a call."

"Lord Jesus," the old woman said, shaking her head. "I thought for sure all my family was gone and now the good Lord done brought me a new daughter. Praise the Lawd. A new daughter and new friend."

Before they left, Carl Alvin called the gas company. He arranged to have the house properly insulated, and central heat and air put in. He gave them his credit card number and told them to send the receipt to his office.

Then, the two of them took Aunt Minnie to the grocery store and loaded her cart with food. They also bought her a new 40-inch, flat screen TV and arranged to have it installed the following day. Miss Minnie was so choked up she could barely speak.

"I'll be able to watch my stories in style now," she

said, crying.

Later that afternoon, as Carl Alvin and Wanda Faye were back on the interstate heading south, Carl Alvin said to her, "Wanda Faye Lloyd, you are some lady."

"Thank you, Carl Alvin, and you are a gentleman and a good friend. Friends stick together, no matter what."

"Yes, they do. You and Nadine have always been good to me, and I know y'all know."

"Don't start that now," Wanda Faye said. "I love you for who you are, not for what I would like for you to be. Don't ever forget that."

Carl Alvin turned his face away from her for a second to regain his composure.

"I love you, too," he said, and the two of them drove on toward the Florida line.

After about an hour, Wanda Faye asked if they could stop at the next exit.

"I want to buy some of them good pecan logs to take home, and maybe some peanut brittle," she said.

Carl Alvin started laughing and shaking his head.

"What's wrong with you?" she asked.

"You and me," he said. "We can have all the money in the world, but you won't ever get the pine tar from our hands or the sand out of our shoes. We still love the things we love. I was thinking the same thing about stopping. I'm glad you suggested it."

"I hope we'll always love simple things, Carl Alvin, and I hope we don't ever get rid of all that pine tar or sand," she said, laughing.

As the two came out of Stuckey's later, Carl Alvin

reached in his pocket to grab his ringing cell phone. Wanda Faye was busy opening one of the pecan logs, anticipating the wonderful nougat and pecan taste. When she looked over at Carl Alvin, she noticed he was white as a sheet and his whole body was shaking. He looked as if he was having a heart attack or was about to faint.

"What in God's name is the matter, honey?" she asked, and she rushed to his side. "Are you okay?"

Carl Alvin dropped his cell phone on the pavement, which luckily didn't shatter into pieces thanks to its rubber casing.

"It's Uncle Hamp," he said, barely above a whisper. "He's had a massive heart attack. They've airlifted him to Gainesville, but they don't know…"

Carl Alvin fell against the car, still shaking uncontrollably and beginning to sob. Wanda Faye held onto him for a few moments until he calmed down.

"Honey, give me the keys," she said. "Give me the keys, darling. You ain't in no shape to drive."

She picked up his cell phone and then helped him get into the passenger side of the car. Once he got settled and buckled up, she handed him a Coke.

"You just rest and let me drive for a while," she said.

Carl Alvin didn't respond and she figured he was just in a state of shock. Before cranking the engine, she called Nadine, who picked up on the second ring.

"How bad?" Wanda Faye asked.

"Real bad, honey, real bad," Nadine said. "Duke and Essie are driving Destini down to Gainesville. She was the one who found him down by his deer stand. You know he's as regular as rain. When he didn't show up for supper, she went out looking for him. They don't know how long he'd been lying there, and they were surprised he was still alive. Dee Dee was at the camp with Miss Hattie, but both of them was in such bad shape, I had to call Miss Sissy. She closed up her shop, and she, Lollie and Mark are driving them down to Gainesville."

"Have you seen Dink?"

"Yes, honey, he just got here to the house and is waiting for you."

"Tell him to meet me out at the interstate in about forty-five minutes," Wanda Faye told her. "I have Carl Alvin with me and he ain't doin' so good, honey."

"Okay, me and Louie will come, too. At least I can sit in the back and hold Carl Alvin's hand. I been doing that since we were children. I love the crazy thing, you know. He's been good to me."

"Yes, I know," Wanda Faye said.

"The children are with Mama. She called the Bible Drill group, and she and Sister Velma have them baking cakes and praying 'round the clock. You know Mama. No rest, even in a time of distress."

"Well, honey, she's doing all she can, and you know nobody can circle the wagons like Mama in a time of trouble."

"Don't I know it? She's already brought enough ham sandwiches, fried chicken, potato salad, and two whole cakes in a cooler out here for us to take to the hospital. She even brought paper plates, napkins, two thermoses of coffee and drinks. How in the name of God she got all this together so fast, I'll never know."

"It's the network, I guess," Wanda Faye said.

"I told her it's not like these people don't have money to buy something to eat, but she said that ain't the thing. She said they won't be thinking about sustaining themselves, but if someone brings it to them, they're more apt to at least eat."

"Bless Mama's heart," Wanda Faye said. "I'll see y'all in a few minutes. Pray for me, honey. I ain't never driven one of these fancy Range Rovers and this thing moves like it has wings on the wheels. I hope I don't get arrested."

Forty-five minutes later, after hitting speeds of 85 and 90 miles an hour along the interstate, she pulled the car into the driveway of the Seraph Springs Truck Stop.

Dink, Louie and Nadine were sitting there in Nadine's van waiting on her. Wanda Faye asked Dink to drive, and she had Carl Alvin get in the backseat, where she sat on one side of him and Nadine on the other. That's when Carl Alvin broke down and cried like a baby. He put his head in Nadine's lap, and she stroked his hair as if he was her own child.

"You got to straighten up now, honey," she told him. "You got to pull yourself together. You can't let Dee Dee and Mrs. Hattie see you like this. They depend on you, baby. It's in God's hands now."

Louie had left the van at the truck stop and was sitting up front with Dink. The two of them were quiet and it was clear that everyone in the car was deeply concerned about Mr. Hamp. He had been like a second father to all of them, Louie, especially, who had spent so much time with him every day out at the camp.

It was a long drive down to Gainesville, especially with very little conversation going on among the group. As they pulled up to the front of the hospital, there was Dee Dee, dressed in a bright red, wool coat that went down to her ankles. Her long, dangly rhinestone earrings were glittering in the sunshine as she sat on a bench just outside the hospital entrance. As soon as Carl Alvin spotted her, he seemed to cheer up quite a bit. First he smiled and then he let out a belly laugh.

"God bless her heart," he said. "No doubt she's thinking when Uncle Hamp wakes up he'll want to see her dressed up in something bright and sparkly. Rise and shine he always said to her about how to dress. Rise and shine."

Wanda Faye and Nadine looked at each other with sideways glances, but then they, too, smiled. As soon as Dink parked the Range Rover, Carl Alvin bolted out of the car and ran over to her.

"He's awake," she told him, as the two of them hugged one another. "He woke up a little while ago. The doctor said there didn't appear to be any brain damage because Uncle Hamp is alert as ever and knows what's going on around him."

"Oh, thank God," Carl Alvin said.

"He tried to talk, but he's so doped up that nobody could understand what he was saying. The doctor said the next few hours are critical and it will let him know if he's going to pull through this or not. He did call out your name, though, Carl Alvin. We all heard that loud and clear. So, put on your game face, baby."

The entire group took the elevator up to the cardiac intensive care unit on the third floor. Only two visitors were allowed in at the same time, So Carl Alvin asked Wanda Faye to go with him, as the others stayed in the waiting room.

Wanda Faye was not prepared for what she saw lying in the bed. It wasn't just the tubes and monitors he was hooked up to that freaked her out. It was the pale grey pallor of his skin. This man she had cherished for so long, who had always looked vibrant and virile, now looked extremely weak and vulnerable. It was frightening.

For a moment, she thought she might have to leave the room to compose herself, but she toughed it out.

"Carl Alvin, is that you?" Mr. Hamp mumbled as he cracked open his eyes.

"Yes, I'm here, Uncle Hamp, and so is Wanda Faye," he said, and he reached down to take his Uncle's hand.

"Is Dee Dee here?" he asked.

"She's just outside in the waiting room," Carl Alvin replied.

"Go get her," Mr. Hamp said.

"They may not let…" Carl Alvin started, but Mr. Hamp cut him off.

"Get her," he said again, loud and clear.

As if God had been whispering in her ear, Dee Dee suddenly burst into the room and took her uncle's other hand.

"I'm here, Uncle Hamp," she said, and leaned down and kissed him on the forehead.

"Dee Dee, I love you and Carl Alvin," Mr. Hamp said, with his voice sounding weaker now. "You know how I love you both."

It was then that Carl Alvin and Dee Dee both broke down in tears.

"Oh, Uncle Hamp," Dee Dee said. "Please don't waste your breath on something we already know. Just save your strength."

"No," he firmly said. "Carl Alvin, listen to me. I've loved you mainly because you have such love in your heart. Always have. I know what people say about you. I don't give a damn about that. I know Dee Dee can keep you in line. I'm counting on that love from both of you now. Promise me something."

"Anything, Uncle Hamp," Carl Alvin said.

"Look after Nadine and Wanda Faye. They love you and they're loyal."

"We know that, Uncle Hamp," Dee Dee said, and she glanced over at Wanda Faye, who was sitting in a chair in the corner of the room weeping. "Do try to save your strength, Uncle Hamp."

"One more thing," Mr. Hamp said, barely above a whisper. "Be good to my girls, Destini and Buu Buu…"

"What?" Dee Dee asked. "Uncle Hamp, who?"

Just then, the alarm on the heart monitor started beeping. It was loud and continuous for about twenty seconds before it suddenly stopped. Then, a low, steady hum echoed throughout the room, seeming to bounce off the walls.

When two nurses bounded through his door, Dee Dee's heart-wrenching screams reached all the way down the hall and into the waiting room. It was worse than any scream Wanda Faye had ever heard. As she cowered in the corner of the room, she tried covering her ears to block out the sounds, but the screams wouldn't stop. She knew she'd be hearing them for some time to come.

The nurses eventually had to sedate both Dee Dee and Carl Alvin. Miss Hattie was in bad shape, too, but Miss Sissy was dealing with her. They were the first to leave the hospital.

About two hours later, after arrangements were made with the hospital for Mr. Hamp's burial wishes, the remaining group began the long drive back to Seraph Springs. Louie and Dink managed to get Carl Alvin and Dee Dee into the backseat of the Range Rover, while Destini's Uncle Duke loaded everyone else into his van.

"We'll be home soon, Destini," Wanda Faye comforted her friend. "We'll be home soon and you can rest."

"Mr. Hamp is already home," Destini mumbled, as tears continued trickling down her cheeks. "He's finally home."

❧❧❧❧❧❧❧❧❧❧❧

Back in Seraph Springs, Mama Tee abruptly looked over at Sister Velma and Miss Jewell, who had come by her house earlier to tell her about Mr. Hamp.

"He gone," Mama Tee blurted out. "My boy is gone, gone, gone. He done crossed over the river to rest in the shade of the trees."

"What are you saying?" Miss Jewell asked her.

"Hamp is gone, Miss Jewell. He just left me," she said, as tears streamed down her face from behind her dark glasses.

"We don't know that yet," Miss Jewell told her.

"You don't know dat, but I does," Mama Tee said, shaking her head. "Biggest foots I ever seen on a baby."

Mama Tee's phone rang seconds later and Miss Jewell answered it.

"Oh, Mama…" Nadine started.

"We know, sugar," Miss Jewell said. "God rest his soul. Oh, Lord, I'll miss him. We all will."

"How could you know, Mama? He just passed a few minutes ago."

"We just knew, honey. We just knew."

Later, when Nadine told the others about her mother's response, Destini just nodded.

"That's Mama Tee for you," Destini said. "She's always been able to sense it when somebody close to her dies. I don't know how she does it, but I've seen it happen time and time again."

Chapter 30

The private memorial service a week later was exactly as Hamp Brayerford Jr. had ordered in his will. About seventy-five of his closest friends, family members and business associates were invited out to Camp EZ for a huge breakfast feast, which would immediately lead into a simple service in the great room of the lodge.

A podium had been set up in one corner of the room, and a cloth-covered table sat in front of the floor to ceiling windows overlooking the Suwannee River. Atop it was a large brass urn containing Mr. Hamp's cremated ashes. It was draped in cream-colored roses with trailing greenery around the base. An arrangement of his prized porcelain turkeys surrounded the urn, offering just the right touch of masculinity.

As Mr. Hamp had requested in his will, his body was cremated. Wanda Faye recalled something he told her a long time ago. He said whenever he stood on the grounds at the Seraph Springs Cemetery for someone's funeral, especially if it was someone who was close to him, it was simply too heartbreaking to have to watch a coffin being lowered into the ground. He vowed then that he wanted to be cremated because he didn't want his loved ones to have to go through such anguish, especially if he died during the dead of winter.

After breakfast, Brother Linton welcomed everyone as they sat in the great room, and then he led them in an opening prayer. Dee Dee read the 121st Psalm, her uncle's favorite. Then, Carl Alvin read Longfellow's, "Psalm of Life", one of the old man's favorite poems.

Destini, who was backed up by her Aunt Essie and Uncle Duke, sang a heartfelt version of "Going Home", accompanied on the piano by Sister Mary Lee. There wasn't a dry eye in the house as Destini's angelic voice filled the room.

Dee Dee then led everyone in the first verse and chorus of "Old Folks at Home", and she hammered it out with gusto on Mr. Hamp's Steinway grand piano. Brother Linton followed her and closed the service with the Lord's Prayer.

After the service, cake, coffee and drinks were served, and everyone visited for quite a while, recalling special moments of Mr. Hamp's life and how he had blessed so many of them with his kindness and generosity.

Once the bulk of the crowd had dispersed, Judge Wesson called Carl Alvin, Dee Dee, Destini, Miss Jewell, the Lintons, Wanda Faye and Dink, Nadine and Louie, Duke and Essie, and Mama Tee into Mr. Hamp's expansive study.

"Folks, you all knew Mr. Hamp. He was a no

nonsense type of guy, and it was his request that I read this to all of you today. I can attest he was in his right mind when he asked me to prepare his will. So, if any of you wish to contest it, you go right ahead. With my reputation and testimony, it won't hold up in court, though. It is what it is."

Without further ado, he began to read.

"To my nephew, Carl Alvin Campbell, and my niece, Dee Dee Wilson, I leave ten million dollars each in trust, twenty thousand acres of land they will share between them, including Camp EZ, and seats on the executive board of Brayerford Properties, as well as on the board of trustees at all three of the banks I own in Turpricone."

Judge Wesson paused a moment and looked out at the faces staring back at him before continuing.

"To Jewell Lee, I leave $250,000, to Brother Linton and his wife, Sister Velma, I leave $250,000. To the Seraph Springs House of Prayer, I leave a trust of one million dollars."

Again, the judge paused while everyone remained silent, staring at him with blank faces.

"To Nadine and Louie, I leave a trust of $500,000, plus jobs for both of them at Camp EZ for the remainder of their lives. To Wanda Faye and Drayfuss "Dink" Lowell, I leave a trust of $500,000, plus a legacy to pay for the furnishings of Wanda Faye Lowell's proposed women's center."

"Oh, my God," Wanda Faye gasped, as she squeezed Dink's hand.

"To Hattie Wilson Campbell, I leave my interest in

the original Wilson Farm properties, a place on the bank board and controlling stock in the bank, as well as my collection of Georgian silver flatware and her choice of my china and crystal."

Wanda Faye wasn't sure, but she thought she heard Miss Hattie muffle a scream.

"To Duke and Essie Wilson," the judge went on. "I leave a trust of one million dollars to care for Mama Tee for the rest of her life, and to help with the work at Mt. Nebo for their faithful service. I also deed to them one-hundred acres of land originally owned by Mama Tee's family that borders them to the north. Lastly, I leave my log cabin on the Suwannee River to Duke and Essie Wilson. They always got more use out of it than I ever did and I know they'll take good care of it."

The biggest surprise came at the end of the reading of the will and no one was prepared for it.

"To my faithful servant and dear friend, Destini Wilson, and to my daughter, Easter Bunnye Wilson," the judge began.

At that moment, it seemed as if all of the oxygen in the room had been sucked out by a gigantic vacuum cleaner, which was followed by a collective gasp from everyone, including Destini.

"I leave the remainder of my estate, stocks, bonds and funds, consisting of approximately 35,000 acres of property and thirty million dollars," the judge continued. "An appointed committee to be named by Judge John Wesson will administer the proceeds from this portion of my estate to my daughter and her mother."

Destini fell off her chair, hit the floor with a loud thud, and fainted dead away. Nearly everyone in the room was in a state of shock after learning that Bunnye was Mr. Hamp's daughter, except for Mama Tee, who was smiling, even chuckling a bit.

Nadine and Wanda Faye, of course, had their suspicions Mr. Hamp was Bunnye's father from the time Destini got pregnant, although, it was never openly discussed. Since everyone else in the room seemed too shocked to move at the moment, the two girls rushed to Destini's side and scrambled to revive her.

Nadine grabbed the smelling salts from Destini's purse and waved the bottle under her nose. Seconds later, she began to stir.

Wanda Faye, after looking at the faces around her, figured they were all thinking the same thing. The descendants of slaves once sold on the auction block to Hamp Brayerford's maternal great-grandfather at the beginning of the twenty-first century in a backwater, north Florida timber county, had suddenly become the richest citizens in the county.

When Destini finally came around and was alert again, she scanned the room. When she found Dee Dee, she motioned for her to come over.

"Do I still have my job here at the camp, Dee Dee?" Destini asked. "Does this mean I ain't got a job no more?"

Judge Wesson heard what she said and he chuckled. He went over to help her up off the floor and then ease her down into a nearby chair.

"They ain't gonna fire me from my job, are they, Judge Wesson?" she asked again.

"Destini, do you fully understand what I just read in Mr. Hamp's will?"

"Them's just words," she said, shaking her head and making a face. "All that was words. Words that tell me my baby goin' have lots of money and lots of land. She'll have plenty of everythin'. Ain't a whole lot changed. We always had plenty of everythin', includin' love. Now, though, Bunnye will finally know who her daddy is. I loved him in life and I'll love him in death. That ain't changed, neither. I loved y'all all my life, too. I hope that ain't changin'.'"

"Oh, honey, of course that's not going to change," Dee Dee told her. She sat down beside her and placed her arm around Destini's shoulder. "But, honey, you don't have to work anymore. You don't have to do anything you don't want to do."

"Why would I wanna stop doin' somethin' I always loved? Why would I want my child not to be around people who always loved her? Why would I wanna sit home and do nothin', or turn Bunnye into one of them hip-hop hoodlums I see on TV with them bad fittin' clothes, strings of gold 'round their necks, all of 'em on drugs and actin' crazy? No, Dee Dee, my child, above everythin' else, is goin' know she's loved and wanted. That's the main thing her daddy wanted. All this other stuff don't mean nothin'.'"

When she took a breath, Dee Dee gave her a hug, but Destini wasn't finished saying her piece yet.

"I hope you, Carl Alvin and the judge will manage

this camp the way it's always been managed to bring joy to people, just the way it always has."

"We will," Dee Dee said.

"Gosh, my baby's education, thank the Lord, is goin' be paid for now," Destini went on, as the reality of the situation began to set in. "I might have the judge get me a new pickup truck every couple years, and if I leave this place, I'll just move in with Essie and Duke. I guess now we can add enough on to their new house for all of us to live. We got a good life," she added, and then she turned and looked into Wanda Faye's eyes. "This don't change nothin' between you, me and Nadine, does it?"

"Are you kidding?" Wanda Faye scoffed. "Ain't nothin' at all changing, honey. It just means we can all go to Disney World now. We can take the children in the springtime when it's warmer outside without worrying how we're gonna pay for the tickets."

"In a year or two, I wanna go to the national conference for the A.M.E. Church," Destini kept on. "Always wanted to go and hear all that good gospel singing. I wanna go to Washington D.C., too, in a few years when my baby's a little older. For now, I just want my life to move on the way it's been. Can you do that for me, Judge Wesson?"

"You are one of the smartest people I've ever met, Destini Wilson," the judge said, as he wiped the moisture that had formed on his glasses.

"Well, I know I'm happy and I know I'm loved, Judge," Destini said, smiling. "I wouldn't want it any other way. Dee Dee and Carl Alvin, I'm serious about my job."

"We know that," Dee Dee said. "If you want to stay on, by all means, please do, but don't you want us to get another girl and let you kinda supervise?"

"No, ma'am, I don't. Don't want nobody else working here but me, Nadine and Wanda Faye. This was Mr. Hamp's place. It was his house and I mean to keep it the way he left it for as long as I'm able. Keep it just the way he left it... oh, one more thing, Dee Dee."

"What's that, honey?"

"You think maybe you could fix me a cup of coffee?"

"Do what?!" Dee Dee gasped.

"A cup of coffee," Destini repeated. "I want a cup of coffee with cream and sugar."

The whole group burst out laughing.

"Are y'all crazy?" Destini asked, obviously wondering what it was that she said that could be so funny.

"We might be, honey," Dee Dee said, still laughing. "I think we all are. You are now the richest damned woman in three counties and you want to keep working here doing the cooking and cleaning. Uncle Hamp just left you millions of dollars and acres of land, and all you want right now is a cup of coffee."

"Well, yes, I do want a cup of coffee, Dee Dee, and I want a piece of that chocolate swirl cake Miss Jewell made. Then, I want y'all to fix some for yourselves and sit with me. We got to talk about Wanda Faye's project for her women's center and what we goin' do to help her."

"Well, honey, I guess we do," Dee Dee said.

"One thing's for damn sure," Carl Alvin piped up. "I don't think Margot Smith or anyone ever had a television show that would come close to capturing what our lives have been and still are."

"Oh, yeah, she's had them shows," Destini said. "And she's lived it in her own life, too."

"She has?" Carl Alvin asked, evidently not very familiar with the woman or her television show. "Well, what were they about?" he asked.

"Love," Destini said. "Unconditional love. The kind Jesus had. You don't stop lovin' folks you truly love. That's what them shows was about. Same as what I have in my heart for y'all, unconditional love. Ain't that the best kind?"

"Yes, honey, it's the best kind," Dee Dee said.

As everyone was leaving the study, Judge Wesson asked Destini to stay for a minute.

"There's one more thing I need to tell you," he said, and then he shut the door so they could have some privacy.

"Yes, sir?"

"Mr. Hamp asked that you keep his urn of ashes in a safe place for a while," Judge Wesson said. "He said once you clean out his cabin you'll know what to do."

"That might be a while," Destini said, shaking her head. "I ain't sure I'm up to that just yet."

"That's okay, honey. He said to take as long as you need."

"Yes, sir, I'll keep them ashes in a safe place,"

Destini said, as fresh tears trickled down her cheeks. "Ain't nobody goin' mess with 'em."

Later that night, after everyone left the lodge, Destini took her daughter aside and explained that Mr. Hamp was her father. It was an emotional moment for both of them, although, Bunnye said she already knew.

"Now, how could you have possibly known?" Destini asked her.

"He told me," Bunnye said. "He told me a long time ago, but said I wasn't allowed to say a word about it. It was our little secret, he said."

It was all Destini could do to keep her composure, but she did, as she always did in times such as these.

She and Bunnye went into the great room and sat together on a couch across from the still roaring fireplace. Mr. Hamp's urn was sitting on the mantelpiece with the shiny brass seeming to glow in the semi-darkness of the room.

"Well, here I am, Mr. Hamp," Destini said, as she slid her arm around her daughter. "Your little Easter Bunnye is here, too."

"I miss you, Daddy," Bunnye said. "I know I'll see you again in heaven, though. Mama said so," she added, and then she gave Destini a look that broke her heart into pieces.

The two of them sat in silence for a while and then Destini began to softly hum an old gospel song that was Mr. Hamp's favorite. Bunnye was nestled in her arms and within a few minutes she was sound asleep.

Chapter 31

The next few weeks following Mr. Hamp's death seemed to fly by like a falcon on a breezy spring afternoon. Dee Dee decided to host a Valentine's party for all the children, as well as the adults out at Camp EZ. As everyone walked through the door, she made them put on funky little headbands with wobbly antennae that had glittery pink hearts dangling from them.

She even made Carl Alvin dress up like Cupid in pink Spandex pants with a bright white diaper fashioned from an old sheet, and a skin-tight pink tank top that had fake wings attached to the back. He was sporting a large pink plastic arrow as he jumped out of a huge Valentine's box to offer folks a Valentine card as soon as they entered the great room. Everybody got a kick out of his antics, especially the children, who laughed and laughed each time another guest arrived.

One big surprise at the party was when handsome Ricardo Fernandez arrived. He was the brother of Justo Fernandez, Dink's boss. Destini told Dee Dee he was the prettiest white man she'd ever seen. He was tall, about six foot two, black, wavy hair and a beautiful South Florida suntan.

"My Cuban prince," Dee Dee said, smiling from ear to ear, as she hung on his arm throughout the festivities.

Later in the day, Nadine decided to be bold and pose a question to Dee Dee. Destini and Wanda Faye were right beside her.

"Okay, girl, you know you can't keep a secret from us," she said. "How long has this been going on?"

"Oh, since about Thanksgiving when he came up here to hunt with his brother and Uncle Hamp," Dee Dee explained. "I accidentally bumped into him in the bathroom that adjoins mine here at the lodge."

"Accidentally?" Nadine asked, raising her eyebrows.

"Yes, accidentally," she retorted. "He had a face full of shaving cream and a towel wrapped around his waist, and when he turned toward me and smiled, well, I couldn't move or speak. I just stood there staring at him. Anyway, I figured I better do something about it, since he had such an effect on me, so we got together right after Thanksgiving."

"Girl, you better hang on to that pretty man," Destini told her. "I know you cain't cook, but you better start tryin' out some o'them flan recipes, oh, and some of them black beans and rice dishes. You better lift them puppies of yours, too. You know how them Cuban men love a curvy woman."

"Here's a question for you, Dee Dee," Nadine said, with a sly grin on her face. "I know them Latin guys love the mambo. Have the two of you done the mattress mambo yet?"

Dee Dee's face turned blood red with embarrassment.

"Uh-huh," Destini said. "Somebody we know has been gettin' some and she's in love. You know, if you get hitched to this Señor Fernandez, Mr. Hamp's legacy will be just like the United Nations. Every color of the rainbow," she added, laughing.

"I do like him a lot," Dee Dee admitted. "He's the sweetest, kindest thing. I'm supposed to go down and meet more of his family in Miami next week and I'm so nervous."

"Well, don't be," Wanda Faye said. "Just be yourself and they'll love you."

"And if they don't, and he kicks you to the curb, invite him back hunting up here," Nadine suggested. "Once he gets lost in that river swamp a few days, he'll wish he'd treated you better. I bet that boy ain't never been snipe hunting."

"Nadine, you're plum crazy," Dee Dee said, laughing. "I'll keep it in mind, though."

Just then, Ricardo walked over and put his arm around Dee Dee's shoulder, after which he looked at Destini, who had just winked at him.

He smiled at her and asked, "What does that mean?"

"It means we know some news, Señor," Destini whispered. "You treat our girl right. That Bay of Pigs won't be nothin' compared to what we can put you through."

"Don't worry," he said. "Dee Dee had my heart from the first moment I saw her. I just have to convince her I'm perfect for her."

"If you use the right tactics, you can do it, Señor," Destini told him. "But if you ever lie to her, your black beans will be burned, and I mean burned up. So, just be yourself, be honest, and treat her right. That heart of hers is as true a one as I've ever known."

"I will," he said. "I promise I will."

Chapter 32

Easter Sunday arrived and with it Essie and Duke's annual community Easter egg hunt. Instead of having it at Mama Tee's place, they decided to hold it at the local park, so the kids could play on the new playground equipment that had just been installed.

Everyone went to church at the House of Prayer Sunday morning and then around two in the afternoon they gathered at a picnic shelter in the local park, bringing with them a variety of covered dishes to go along with the barbecued chickens, beef, and pork that Duke was preparing for the occasion.

Nadine, Destini and Wanda Faye lost count of how many eggs they had colored for the Easter egg hunt. After boiling and coloring twenty-five dozen eggs, they gave up counting. Between their eggs and the ones other folks brought, there were well over one-hundred dozen colored eggs that needed to be hidden throughout the park before all the children arrived.

Dee Dee had an extra special birthday cake made for Easter Bunnye in her favorite colors of hot pink, purple and bright green. Miss Jewell and Sister Velma made a large pound cake, and a friend of theirs from Pittstown decorated it with an Easter motif.

Once everyone arrived at the park, the first order of business was to sing "Happy Birthday" to Bunnye after she blew out the candles on her cake. After all the clapping and well wishes, but before Bunnye had a chance to open all her presents, Dee Dee let out her signature wolf whistle, which quieted everyone down.

Carl Alvin had climbed atop one of the picnic tables and everyone turned to listen to what he had to say.

"Friends and family members, we are happy today to celebrate the sixth birthday of my cousin, Easter Bunnye, and to wish her many, many more happy birthdays."

Everyone applauded again, as Bunnye took a bow and smiled wide with joy.

"We are also pleased to announce that I am in receipt of a letter," Carl Alvin continued. "I'd like to read it to you all now," he added, and so he did.

Dear Mr. Campbell, it is a great pleasure and honor for me to know that my name will be honored as the name of the women's center in your area. As you know, one of my major aims in life is to offer hope to individuals. I am proof that with hope, dreams do come true, and so, it is with great pleasure that I agree to lend my name to this center funded by one who knows and believes in dreams, Mrs. Wanda Faye Lowell.

Please apprise Mrs. Lowell that if she and her Board of Trustees for the Margot Smith Center of Hope for Women so desire, I will be happy and honored to attend the dedication of the center over the upcoming Memorial Day weekend. I don't know when I have been more pleased about the possibility of meeting such a unique and wonderful group of women as those described in your letter. With sincere appreciation, Margot Smith.

When he finished reading the letter, loud applause filled the air, as well as shouts of joy. Dink gave Wanda Faye a big, sloppy kiss, and then she broke down in tears.

"I can't believe it," she said, wiping her eyes. "It's a dream come true. Margot Smith is coming here! Can y'all believe it? When is she coming, Carl Alvin?"

"Well, her schedule executive says she plans on coming in on Friday afternoon and she wants a slumber party with you girls out at Camp EZ," he told her. "She said her friend Deborah might be coming with her, but she doesn't want y'all going to all kinds of trouble for her. Just whatever you all would have for one of your slumber parties, she said, is fine with her."

"Lord, I hope she likes hamburgers, home fries, baked beans, a salad and fudge for dessert like we usually have," Dee Dee said.

"No, no, hell no!" Destini shouted. "Beggin' your pardon, Miss Dee Dee, but no, honey. This Mississippi gal ain't goin' come down here to north Florida and visit without knowing us gals can cook some darn good soul food. No, ma'am, we goin' fry up some of our famous Suwannee River catfish, make cheese grits, hushpuppies, a pot of greens, maybe some collards or mustards, and some macaroni and cheese."

"Here, here!" Nadine shouted. "Now, you're

talkin'!"

"Let's not forget coleslaw, cornbread, sweet potato pie and some of Mama's chocolate swirl cake," Wanda Faye added.

"I'll tell you somethin' else," Destini went on. "Remember that man who used to be her chef and won all of them cookin' competitions with his fried chicken? Well, Miss Margot's gonna see he ain't the only one who can put a good scald on a chicken, no ma'am. That girl is goin' know she's come home when she comes to visit. We'll make some of our Camp EZ coffee, too, and Miss Jewell, you can make us that fudge. We got to have your fudge. We just goin' be our crazy selves. She ain't no different just 'cause she's on TV. That lady is real. Y'all hear me? She's the real deal."

"You're right, Destini," Dee Dee said. "We do have to show her what we can do with some of our own regional dishes. I'll leave that to you, honey. You know I can't cook a thing but Hawaiian Bundle Bake and butterscotch candy made with Chinese noodles," she added, and everyone laughed.

"Mainly, we goin' show her our own special craziness," Destini said.

"Especially that," Dee Dee agreed.

"Just like you said, you goin' leave the cookin' to me," Destini said. "I'm goin' leave the crazy to you, Dee Dee, 'cause, honey, you are the queen of crazy, but we'll march right along with you, you know that."

"Miss Margot might do a show on the value of laughter after leaving us," Wanda Faye interjected.

"She will," Nadine said. "She'll be giggling just thinking about us, and when she hears "Suwannee River" or even thinks of it, she'll say, 'Lord them was some crazy girls, but I had a good time.'"

"Like Miss Sissy often says, she ain't here for a long time, she's here for a good time," Wanda Faye summed it up.

Chapter 33

The day of Margot Smith's arrival was a major event in the small town of Seraph Springs, especially for the girls. Destini, Wanda Faye and Nadine made sure everything at Camp EZ was cleaned to perfection and could pass the white glove test. Louie, Dink and the older children did a magnificent job manicuring the lawns and shrubs around the lodge, and it looked as regal as it ever did when Mr. Hamp was alive.

Carl Alvin and Dee Dee had a contractor come over from Turpricone to repaint the eaves all around the roof of the lodge in a soft emerald green color, as well as touch up all the window facings.

Dee Dee, along with her aunts, made flower arrangements from Miss Hattie's gardens, along with freshly picked wildflowers in various shades of purple and gold. The arrangements were placed at specific vantage points throughout the lodge and on the porches. In many of the arrangements, they used wild honeysuckle and its light fragrance seemed to tell its own story of the region.

In one crystal dish, Dee Dee even floated some

exquisite magnolia blossoms that she and the younger girls had picked down near the river. Their pristine whiteness and lemony fragrance was heavenly.

Meanwhile, construction of the women's center was moving along briskly. The great room was already completed, as well as the foyer, but the therapy rooms and classrooms were not quite ready yet. Still, Wanda Faye and her governing board, which consisted of Destini, Lollie, Miss Sissy, Judge Wesson and Essie, decided to go ahead with the dedication.

Carl Alvin hired two limousines in Jacksonville to pick up Miss Margot and her friend, Deborah, along with her public relations manager, Emily Burns, so they could be transported in style over to Camp EZ.

Bunnye, Jewell Lee, and the twins, Charlene and Darlene, had posted themselves at the main gate that turned off from the paved road and onto the dirt road leading to the lodge. Louie had made sure the road was freshly graded so that the limousines would have a smooth ride up to the lodge.

The four young girls wanted to be the first ones to catch a glimpse of the limousines when they arrived. Last night, they constructed two large cardboard signs on which was written, "Welcome Miss Margot." The twins had their brand new cell phones with them and were given strict orders by Destini to call the lodge as soon as the limousines were in sight.

While they waited on the procession to arrive, the girls immersed themselves in a fun card game of Old Maid to keep themselves occupied. As they sat in a circle on the freshly mown lawn, Bunnye happened to look up and saw the first limousine approaching.

"Here they come!" she screamed. "Here they come!"

She started jumping up and down, waving one of the welcome signs over her head, while little Jewell Lee waved the other sign. Meanwhile, Charlene dialed the number at the lodge.

"Aunt Destini!" she yelled. "She's on her way! They just rounded the curve!"

Destini, Wanda Faye, Nadine, and Dee Dee all rushed into the bathroom to touch up their hair and check their makeup one last time. They were all wearing casual cotton knee-length dresses that Dee Dee had picked out for them from the department store where she worked as a buyer.

Minutes later, when Miss Margot stepped out of the limo, she was greeted first by Wanda Faye, who handed her a bouquet of spring flowers.

"Welcome to Camp EZ, Miss Margot, and welcome to Seraph Springs and Campbell County, Florida. This is a dream come true for me. I've loved you ever since I turned on the TV years ago and watched your first show. It is such an honor to finally meet you in person."

"Wanda Faye," Margot said, blushing. "The honor is all mine, and you can drop the Miss. I want us all to be on a first name basis. This is my friend Deborah and this is my favorite PR lady, Emily."

"Pleased to meet you both," Wanda Faye said, and everyone shook hands. "I'd like to introduce my sister, Nadine Lloyd, and my two best friends in the whole world, Destini Wilson and Dee Dee Wilson."

'Well it's nice to meet all of you," Margot said, shaking hands with each one of them.

"Well, these boys will bring in your bags and stuff," Destini said, and she gave the kids a little shove toward the open trunk. "Margot, you, Deborah and Emily come on in and let me show you to your rooms. Then, we're gonna have some lunch. You notice I didn't say a little lunch, because there ain't nothin' little about this lunch."

"I'm afraid Emily won't be staying with us," Margot said. "She has to head back to New York for an emergency called meeting."

"Yes, I do," Emily said. "I wish I could stay, but duty calls. Margot, I'll see you when you get back," she added, and she got back into the limousine to head back to the airport.

Margot and Deborah, it seemed to Wanda Faye, were thoroughly fascinated by the elegance of the lodge. She offered them a brief tour of the downstairs area and both of them kept commenting on how beautiful the wood paneling was, and how utterly magnificent the furnishings and wall prints blended together. Margot was fascinated with all the flower arrangements and Wanda Faye said she could take any one of them she wished back to New York with her when she left.

"If you'll follow me, I'll show you to your rooms upstairs," Wanda Faye said.

Once Margot and Deborah settled in, they both changed into comfortable jeans and cotton T-shirts.

When they came back downstairs, Margot complimented all the girls on their stylish cotton dresses.

"Now, ladies, show time is over," Margot said. "You all made a good impression with your pretty spring outfits, but I want y'all to get comfortable, too."

"See, I told y'all," Destini said, glaring at the other three girls. "Excuse us just a few minutes, Miss Margot," she added. "Why don't you ladies have a seat and try some of our signature Camp EZ coffee."

Destini quickly rounded up the other three girls and they hurried up the stairs to change. They emerged from Destini's bedroom five minutes later wearing faded cut-off jeans and Camp EZ T-shirts.

"Much better," Margot commented, when the three girls waltzed into the great room.

She and Deborah were admiring the river through the big picture window as they sipped on their coffee.

"By the way," Margot said. "This is the best coffee I think I've ever had."

"We think so, too," Destini said, smiling from ear to ear.

"Now, y'all remember that movie I was in, *The Faded Orange*?" Margot asked.

"Lord, yes!" Destini said. "Who could forget it?"

"Well, I'm going to use a line from one of the scenes in that movie where my character, Alene Jones, and her new boyfriend, Amos, went to visit the mayor and his wife... 'What's for supper?!'"

"Oh, Miss Margot, you crack me up!" Destini shouted, laughing until tears were running down her face. "You just sit yourself right down over there at the dining room table with your coffee. Come on… you, too Miss Deborah."

Dee Dee, Nadine and Wanda Faye were already removing the covers from all the chafing dishes on the buffet table. A few minutes later, Destini invited the two special guests to go first down the buffet line.

"Come on, ladies, grab a plate and see if you think this might suit your fancy," Destini said.

"Oh, my, Lord, girl, I'm glad these jeans have elastic in the waistband," Margot said, as she eyed all the food laid out in front of her. "What a feast y'all have prepared. It reminds me of my grandma's house on Sunday afternoons when I was a young girl. Lord have mercy. I told y'all not to go to any trouble."

"The thing is, Miss Margot, this wasn't no trouble," Wanda Faye said. "Never is when you're doing for a friend, and we know you're our friend."

"Yes, I am," Margot said. "I feel like I've been y'all's friend forever."

"I do, too," Deborah chimed in. "Thank you all so much."

"By the way, I told y'all to drop the Miss," Margot said, as she filled her plate to overflowing.

"We cain't help it, Miss Margot," Destini said. "That's just the way us folks treat each other 'round here."

Once everyone, including all the kids and the rest of the family were seated around the huge dining table, Dee Dee asked Wanda Faye if she would say the blessing.

"I'd be happy to," Wanda Faye said. "Let's hold hands, shall we?"

Wanda Faye closed her eyes, inhaled a deep breath, and began.

"Lord, we thank you for this day and for these good friends gathered around us. We thank you, Lord, for bringing Miss Margot and Miss Deborah here. We thank you for the interest Miss Margot takes in the lives of so many, and I do thank you, Heavenly Father, that when my life was at its lowest ebb, Miss Margot was there for me. She was my star then and she still is today, leading and guiding me as your earthly witness. How I thank you for her and her testimony. My life has been blessed in so many ways, too numerous to mention. I love everyone here, Lord, and I thank you for your love and for theirs. Bless this food now, Father, and bless the hands that prepared it. Bless it to the nourishment of our bodies, and our bodies to your service. In the name of Jesus, we pray, Amen."

"And Amen," Margot said.

"Now, dig in!" Destini added.

For the next two hours, lively conversation and laughter filled the dining room, as the ladies enjoyed a long, leisurely lunch. It felt like old home week to Wanda Faye, as they all became better acquainted with one another.

Both Margot and Deborah said they had never eaten such a fine meal before, which made Destini's face glow like the setting sun.

Throughout the rest of the afternoon and well into the evening, everyone at the lodge was having a wonderful time visiting with Margot and Deborah. Just after five o'clock, Duke, Louie and Dink had hooked the horses up to Mr. Hamp's old wagon and took Miss Margot, Deborah and all the girls for a ride down by the river.

Memorial Day weekend was off to a rousing start. The weather was cooperating nicely, too, with lots of sunshine during the day and a cool seventy-six degree temperature as the sun began its descent.

When the group returned from the river and pulled up to the front of the lodge, there was Mama Tee in all her glory, sitting in a rocker on the screened porch.

"Destini!" she called out.

"Yes, ma'am!" Destini shouted back.

"Is she here? Is Margot Smith here?"

Destini didn't respond, but Margot did, as she came up onto the porch.

"I'm here, Mama Tee," Margot said. "Destini has told me so much about you. I'm so pleased you were able to come by."

'Would you come here, so I can touch you, chile?" Mama Tee asked.

Margot drew close to the old woman and took her hands in hers.

"Praise the Lawd, yes, praise the Lawd," Mama Tee said, shaking her head. "I am so overjoyed you came to see us. You is a sweet, good girl. Do you mind if I touch your face?"

"No, ma'am, you go right ahead."

"I want to remember you... what your face felt like."

Slowly and gently, the old woman moved her fingers over Margot's face.

"Face of an angel," Mama Tee said. "Hug me, angel baby."

Margot had tears running down her face, as she hugged Mama Tee.

"Now, now," Mama Tee said. "I know I'm old and ugly, but I ain't worth cryin' over."

"Oh, yes, you are," Margot told her. "Of all the things I'll remember from this visit, I'll carry this memory of you with me always."

"Enough of this crying now," said Mama Tee, who never could handle it when people fussed over her. "Dee Dee, do you or Destini know where Hamp Brayerford kept his private shine? I know he made it out here and kept it just for his closest friends."

"I know where it is," Destini said.

"Well, let's serve us a little drink and toast Miss Margot… and Miss Deborah, too," Mama Tee said. "Not a whole lot, but just enough to wake everybody up good."

Everyone had a good laugh, as did Mama Tee. Meanwhile, Nadine and Wanda Faye brought out more chairs to the porch, so that everybody could have a seat. Moments later, Destini returned with a big, brown antique jug. She poured everyone a small amount in short, crystal cocktail glasses.

"May I propose a toast?" Margot asked, but she didn't wait for a response. "To some of the most remarkable women I've ever met. You had a dream, Wanda Faye, and you, along with all these wonderful women, made that dream come true. Tomorrow, as wonderful as it will be, and as extraordinary as the women's center will be for women throughout this region, it will only serve to perpetuate the strength, the beauty, and the love I feel here today. So, here's to dreams and dreamers, and to dreams that come true."

As Wanda Faye looked around at the faces of her friends, both old and new, and her family, she realized most of her dreams had already come true. It was all around here, right here and right now.

She wasn't thinking about Margot Smith or the dedication of the women's center tomorrow. Instead, her heart felt full of blessings for having such a loving family, as well as friends who stuck together through thick and thin.

Her mind drifted back to her childhood days when she, Nadine, Dee Dee and Destini were lying on a braided rug at her mama's house watching *The Wizard of Oz* on TV. That one inimitable line spoken by Dorothy at the end of the movie still, to this day, brought tears to her eyes.

"If I ever go looking for my dreams, I won't look any further than my own backyard, because there's no place like home."

Chapter 34

The dedication ceremony for the Margot Smith Women's Center for Hope went off without a hitch and the entire town of Seraph Springs, as well as folks from the three adjoining counties, turned out for the event. Wanda Faye estimated nearly five thousand people came and went throughout the day, which was filled with exciting activities for the children, and enough food to feed an army, all of it generously donated, even the three bounce houses that kept the kids entertained for hours.

All day long, Margot signed copies of her latest book, "Memories of a Lifetime", for thousands of her loyal fans. The book was an intimate glimpse inside her life as a celebrity, as well as her humble upbringing.

Meanwhile, Wanda Faye was in her glory as she led tours throughout the new center, explaining all the programs and services that would be available to abused women who desperately needed help.

The remainder of the construction project, she advised everyone, would be completed by month's end, at which time there would be a grand opening ribbon cutting ceremony.

When Miss Sissy arrived just after the noon hour on the arm of Sheriff Bartow Lewis, all the nosy rumor mongers in town, who had been speculating about their relationship for the last two years, were huddled in groups all over the grounds around the women's center, fully engaged in their gossip circles.

"Well, I'll be," Nadine said to Destini. "Did you know those two were having an affair?"

"Well, o'course, I did," Destini said, rolling her eyes. "Been goin' on for a while."

"And you never told us?"

"Weren't my place to do that," Destini said. "Now that the sheriff's divorce is final, though, I guess I can tell you."

"Well, shoot, Destini. What's to tell? I can see now that the two of them are doin' the down and dirty. I mean, look at the way he's holdin' onto her, like she's the pistol in his holster."

"You sho' got a way with words, sister," Destini said, laughing. "There's a whole lot more to tell about them two, though. I'll fill you in later after our company leaves."

"You'd better!" Nadine chastised her. "And don't leave out any juicy details."

As the day was winding down, Wanda Faye started to feel a bit nauseous. She wondered if she had perhaps eaten too much, or if she was coming down with a bug, or maybe it was just all the excitement of the past few days.

"Well, allergy season just kicked in, you know,"

Nadine told her later, as they were cleaning up. "I'm sure that's all it is."

"Don't you worry, baby," Destini said. "I'll fix you up good when we get back to the lodge. There ain't no bug alive that can survive my medicine tea. Ain't that right, Dee Dee?"

"That's right, honey," Dee Dee assured Wanda Faye. "It sure brought me out of that bad flu I caught last spring."

"I hope so," Wanda Faye said. "I'm sure not feeling good right now. By the way, did Dink leave yet to take Margot and Deborah back to the lodge?"

"Yeah, they left about thirty minutes ago," Nadine said. "Miss Margot said she wanted to turn in early tonight. She and Deborah are leaving at five in the morning, you know, so they can get back to Jacksonville in time to catch their flight back to New York."

"Speaking of which, we need to get you back to the lodge so you can lie down and rest, Wanda Faye," Dee Dee said. "You're starting to look a little green around the…"

Before she could finish her sentence, Wanda Faye put her hand over her mouth and ran over to one of the garbage cans on the other side of the lobby. She upchucked everything she had eaten earlier, as the other girls watched in horror.

"Ewww, gross," Nadine said, covering her mouth, as if she was going to be the next one puking.

"Okay, that does it. Come on, girls," Destini said. "Nadine, you get her in the back of Dee Dee's car and take this plastic bag with you in case she hurls again. Dee Dee, you drive slow and take it easy back to the lodge."

"What about all this mess?" Nadine asked, as she looked around the lobby of the women's center.

"It can wait," Destini said. "Tomorrow's another day. I'll tell Louie to take all the kids back to your place and I'll get Mama Tee home. Then, I'll be right behind y'all. Go on, now, git!" she ordered them.

Later that night, after everyone had gone to bed, Destini went in to check on Wanda Faye, who was sitting in a chair by the window, sipping on the medicine tea Destini had made for her.

"You feelin' better, baby?" she asked.

"Much better, Destini. Thank you so much for fussing over me. You're a good friend."

The next morning, Wanda Faye felt like herself again. She even managed to get up in time to have breakfast with Miss Margot and Miss Deborah before they left to catch their flight back to New York.

Destini, in her usual grand style, had prepared a full southern breakfast of sausage, eggs, grits and home fries, as well as her signature biscuits. Wanda Faye could tell Miss Margot was definitely impressed, judging by how much she ate and the satisfied smile on her face when she swallowed the last bite of her meal.

"Miss Margot, I know I've said it a hundred times already, but thank you ever so much for coming here to Seraph Springs. I know how busy your schedule must be," Wanda Faye said, as they walked out onto the front porch.

"It was my pleasure, sweetheart," Miss Margot said. "Now, you keep me posted on the date of the grand opening. I will definitely be back to share in the excitement. You have my word on that."

"Oh, thank you," Wanda Faye said, smiling wide as she hugged her. "I look forward to seeing you again."

"Now, Destini, you take good care of our girl, you hear? She's gonna be a busy woman over the next few weeks," Miss Margot said, as she and Deborah walked toward the waiting limousine in the driveway.

"She's in good hands, Miss Margot," Destini told her. "Don't you worry 'bout a thing."

Chapter 35

Throughout the days before and after Margot Smith's visit and the dedication of the women's center, Wanda Faye began noticing that she was struggling to keep up with all the activity, although, she never let on to anyone. Normally, she was full of energy with another ounce for good measure. This past week, however, she had been feeling completely exhausted by the end of the day. There were also a couple times lately that she couldn't keep certain foods down, especially eggs and milk products. It wasn't all the time, just every now and then.

"It's just exhaustion, plain and simple," she told herself. "There's been so much going on around here for so long, is it any wonder I'm so worn out?"

She dared not say anything to anyone, as she didn't want people fussing over her, especially Destini, who would feel she had to dote on her hand and foot.

About a week after the dedication ceremony, Dee Dee decided to host an impromptu brunch out at Camp EZ on Saturday morning. When asked what the occasion was, all she said was, "Just because," which was typical of her.

"Any reason for a party," she told Wanda Faye when she called to invite her.

The morning of the brunch, when the breakfast casserole was being passed around the table, Wanda Faye abruptly, but quietly, excused herself from the table. She rushed up the stairs and into the bathroom at the end of the hallway. This time it was just the dry heaves as she bent over the toilet bowl.

"God, what is wrong with me?" she wondered, and then she looked at her face in the mirror.

With the dark circles underneath her bloodshot eyes, she looked as if she'd been on a three-day bender, although, she hadn't had a drop of alcohol since that moonshine on the front porch with Miss Margot. Even then, she only took a few sips and gave the rest to Nadine.

"Lord, I can't get sick now," she said, as she wiped her forehead with a cool washcloth. "I have too much to do. The grand opening is coming up and…"

Before she could finish that thought, she was leaning over the toilet again. Since she hadn't eaten anything yet, it was just yellow bile coming up.

"Well, I guess this is it. I really do have the flu," she said, as a cold shiver went up and down her spine.

Just then, Destini opened the door and came inside.

"Are you okay, Wanda Faye?" she asked.

"Do I look okay?" Wanda Faye snidely asked her.

"Actually, no, you look like crap," Destini shot back.

"I'm sorry," Wanda Faye said. "I didn't mean to snap at you. I just don't feel good."

"Do you want me to take you to the doctor?"

"No, no... I'm sure it's just the flu. I can't believe this. I have so many things to do."

"Well, come on, girl," Destini said, and she put her arm around Wanda Faye's waist. "You just hold onto me and we'll get you laid down on my bed. Then, I'll bring you up some more of my medicine tea."

"Thanks, honey. Will you let the others know?"

"Don't you worry 'bout a thing. Ain't nobody goin' be botherin' you."

Wanda Faye lied in bed all day and into the night. When she woke up at two in the morning, she recalled that at some point, Dink had come in, but she was so groggy she couldn't remember anything he said, other than Nadine had offered to take care of the kids, so that he and Louie could work on restoring the antique truck they'd been slaving over every weekend for the past few months.

All through the night, Wanda Faye was haunted by one nightmare after the next that kept her on edge. Each nightmare had something to do with her health. All she kept thinking was that she had contracted some dreadful, incurable disease or worse yet, cancer.

When dawn broke the next morning, it was hot and humid in the room and she was sweating profusely. As soon as she opened her eyes, a feeling of nausea swept over her. She didn't make it to the bathroom this time. Instead she puked up more yellow bile in the trash basket beside the bed that she assumed Destini had placed there at some point during the night.

Around seven o'clock, just as the sunlight began streaming in through the window shades, Destini bounded into the room, bringing with her more medicine tea, which seemed to be the only thing she could keep down.

"I'm so sorry about this, Destini. I know you have plenty to do, but here you are making a big fuss over me."

"That's what friends are for," Destini told her, as she stroked her hair.

"Oh, yes," Wanda Faye said with a big sigh. "You are my very best friend."

"You may change your mind about that after I give you this," Destini said.

She pulled out a small, brown paper bag from the pocket of her robe and handed it to Wanda Faye.

"Are you serious? Are you crazy?!" Wanda Faye gasped when she looked inside the bag.

"Never been more serious, and you know I'm crazy," Destini said. "I'll be waitin' right here for you when you get back."

Reluctantly, and still shaking her head, Wanda Faye stumbled out of the bedroom and tiptoed as quietly as she could down the hallway, so as not to awaken Dee Dee, who would undoubtedly be sleeping in until noon. About twenty minutes later, she came back into the bedroom and sat down on the bed beside Destini.

"I told you so, didn't I?" Destini said, smiling from ear to ear.

"How did you get to be so smart?" Wanda Faye

asked her.

"I guess some of Mama Tee's genes done rub off on me," she said, and she put her arm around Wanda Faye's shoulder.

"I guess so," Wanda Faye said, shaking her head. "What are we gonna do?"

"We'll figure it out, baby. We'll figure it out."

Chapter 36

The following Saturday, Wanda Faye, who had been feeling much better, decided to drive out to Camp EZ, while Dink and Louie continued their work in the garage. Nadine had offered to take all the kids to an early morning cartoon matinee, in order to give Wanda Faye some time to relax and get back into her usual happy groove.

Just after eleven o'clock, after discussing things with Destini, Wanda Faye called Dink and asked him to round up Louie, Nadine and all the kids and bring them out to the camp.

"What's wrong, Wanda Faye?" Dink asked. "You sound really strange."

"There's something I need to tell y'all," she said. "See if you can't get my mama and the Lintons to come, too."

Dink tried his best to worm it out of her, but Wanda Faye wouldn't budge. She wouldn't tell him anything other than to have everyone there by one o'clock for a lunch feast.

"We've got so much food left over from Dee Dee's

party, and Destini's been cooking up a storm for some reason. We need to start eating it up before it all goes bad," she told Dink. "Don't be late, honey. I love you."

"I love you, too, Wanda Faye," he said. "See you soon."

After everyone arrived and seated themselves around the dining room table, Destini asked Brother Linton to say the blessing. He graciously obliged and even kept it short, knowing how everyone was anxious to find out what the big secret was that Wanda Faye had to announce.

Destini, being her usual self, then said, "Okay, folks, dig in! There's plenty of food here for everybody. You can even have seconds if you want."

"I thought you had something to announce, Wanda Faye," Dink said.

"I do," she said, smiling. "Let's eat first, though, okay? Would you pass me some of those cheese grits, please?"

Dink just shook his head and did as she asked. All throughout the meal, everyone kept speculating on what it was that was so important that a family meeting had to be called. By the time dessert was served, the chatter had become so loud that Destini had to shush everyone.

"Y'all ain't never gonna figure it out, so stop buggin' this poor girl," Destini said. "She'll tell you when she's good and ready."

Wanda Faye smiled at her and reached for her hand.

"Thank you, Destini," she said. "I think I'm ready

now, though."

"Well, then, go for it, girl," Destini said, and then she turned toward Dink. "You need to come over here and stand beside your wife, Mr. Lowell."

"Whoa, so proper, Destini," Dink said. "This must be some kind of breaking news," he added, and then he came and stood behind Wanda Faye's chair.

Wanda Faye stood up, too, and grabbed Dink's hands. As she looked lovingly into his steel blue eyes, she calmly said, "Looks like you're gonna be a daddy again."

You could have heard a pin drop in the room. Everyone was stunned and speechless, especially Dink, whose eyes grew so wide that Wanda Faye thought they were going to pop out of his skull.

"Well?!" Destini finally shouted. "Don't anybody got anythin' to say?"

"Is it true, Wanda Faye?" Dink asked. "Is it really true?"

"Well, as far as I can tell from the last four home pregnancy tests I took, and after a visit to Dr. Sullivan's office over in Turpricone the other day, yeah, it's true. We're gonna have a baby," she said.

"Yee haw!!" Dink shouted, and then he picked Wanda Faye up by the waist and swung her around the room.

"Oh, honey, you'd better put me down unless you want today's lunch all over your head," Wanda Faye said.

"Oops, sorry, baby," he said. "I guess I got some learnin' to do about pregnant women."

"You ain't got no clue what you're in for, Dink," Destini said, laughing.

"That's okay," Dink said, and he gently kissed Wanda Faye on the lips, and then lightly patted her belly. "That's perfectly okay. I missed out on all that excitement the first time with Little Chet. Now, I get to experience the whole nine yards with my beautiful wife."

Within seconds, everyone else in the room was gathered around the happy couple and hugs and kisses were flying everywhere.

"How far along are you?" Nadine asked.

"About three months, according to Doc Sullivan," Wanda Faye answered.

"And how long have you known about this, Destini?" Nadine asked, with her hands on her hips, as if she was ready for a fight.

"Oh, I dunno. Probably since that first time when Wanda Faye puked up her guts at the dedication ceremony."

"And you never told me?"

"Weren't my place to tell you," Destini said.

"I asked her not to say anything, Nadine," Wanda Faye explained. "I wanted to be absolutely positive before saying anything to anybody."

"Well, you told Destini," Nadine countered.

"No, actually, she told me," Wanda Faye said. "You know how she is about these sorts of things."

After Nadine quit fuming, she asked when the baby was due.

"Our best guess is right before Thanksgiving,"

Wanda Faye said.

"I'm so happy for y'all," Dee Dee said. "Nadine, aren't you happy for them?"

"Aww, I guess so," Nadine said, looking a bit sheepish. "Come here, Sis, and give me a hug."

"I love you," Wanda Faye told her, as she held her tight.

"I love you, too," Nadine said, as tears welled up in her eyes.

"So, have you picked out any names yet?" Dee Dee asked.

"Goodness, I haven't thought that far ahead yet," Wanda Faye said.

"Well, you best be concentratin' on a boy's name 'cause that's what you're havin'," Destini said.

"How do you know that?" Dink asked.

"A little stork told me," she said, smiling.

"Well, assuming it is a boy, how about Drayfuss Hamp Lowell?" Wanda Faye asked.

"Oh, that's perfect!" Dee Dee shouted.

"Yeah, we can nickname him Little Hamp," Nadine suggested.

"Or Little Dink," Destini piped up, with a stupid grin on her face.

"That might not go over too well with his buddies on the playground," Dink said, laughing.

"Yeah, I guess you're right," Destini said. "Little Hamp it is!"

Chapter 37

It was Saturday morning, the first day of autumn that same year, and it had been several months since Mr. Hamp's passing. The weather was more than picture perfect and Nadine and Louie had offered to take all the children to a carnival over in Pittstown. Wanda Faye and Dink were busy at the women's center making sure everything was running smooth as a well-oiled machine.

The grand opening ribbon cutting ceremony last weekend was a sight to behold. Margot Smith, as she had promised, was on hand to congratulate Wanda Faye, and even more of a crowd had shown up than were at the dedication ceremony.

Mr. Hamp's will had just gone through the probate process and all the paperwork had been finalized and filed with the court.

Meanwhile, his last request was still weighing heavy on Destini's mind. She had been putting it off and putting it off, but the time had come for her to honor his wishes. She got into her brand new pickup and followed the dirt road out to his cabin on the north end of his property, crying the entire way.

"I don't want to do this," she kept saying over and over, but she pressed on.

Once inside the cabin, she felt completely alone, but it was the way she wanted it. It was the way she needed it to be. She could still smell his odors throughout the old cabin, even his favorite aftershave lotion. It felt to her as if he was still there, still lingering, still watching over her.

"You know I hate this, Mr. Hamp," she mumbled, as she went from room to room.

She had only been inside the cabin a few times before and it was always at his request. He was a private man and rarely allowed anyone inside other than Carl Alvin and Dee Dee. Surprisingly, or not, the place was immaculate. Everything in the kitchen was spotless. Even his bed was made.

Mr. Hamp had always been a saver of things, but he was a tidy saver, which was something Destini was well aware of after spending so many years at Camp EZ with him. He not only saved money and pricey antiques, but he also saved old letters and mementos, especially items that were near and dear to his heart, which she found in one of the bedrooms. The entire room was filled with boxes of this, that and the other.

Hours later, after going through each box, she still hadn't discovered anything that would give her a clue about what to do with his ashes.

"Well, Mr. Hamp, it looks like you goin' be sittin' on that mantle for a while," she said, laughing.

As she was about to leave, she decided to take one

last look in his bedroom. On a whim, she looked underneath the bed.

"Well, I'll be…" she said, shaking her head, as she pulled out an old wooden box about four foot square.

Inside, were yellowed copies of obituaries from the *Turpricone News* for his father, mother, and his sister Bessie, as well as old birthday cards from Carl Alvin and Dee Dee. When she came across hand drawn pictures Bunnye had made for him, she broke down in tears again.

The first one she picked up was one where she had written her name the very first time. The letters were all over the paper, but they definitely spelled out B-U-N-N-Y-E in a rainbow of colors.

There were a ton of photos in the box, too. One that caught her eye was a photo of him, his sister Bessie and Miss Hattie when they were young. They were all dressed in formal attire. Miss Hattie had on a long, white evening gown, and in faded ink across the front was written "Hattie's Debut Party 1946".

When she got to the bottom of the box, she found another small, rough and worn cypress box with a gold clasp keeping the lid secure. Inside was a sealed envelope with her name written on the front in Mr. Hamp's undeniably sloppy penmanship.

"I guess this is it," she said.

She stuffed the letter in her pants pocket, walked out of the room, out of the cabin, and then got into her truck to head back to the lodge.

The first thing she did was call both Wanda Faye and Nadine, and asked them to come out to the lodge after dinner.

"I just need the two of you here," she said. "Don't ask me no more questions. It shouldn't take long."

When the girls arrived at eight that night, Destini didn't waste any time. She asked them to join her in the great room where she had Camp EZ coffee ready and waiting for them, as well as a plate of freshly baked cookies. A fire was burning in the fireplace and Mr. Hamp's urn was still atop the mantle, only it had been freshly polished just a few minutes ago.

"I'm goin' read somethin' to y'all and if you start cryin' I'm goin' stop," Destini warned the girls. "Just keep that in mind," she added, and she began.

"Dear Destini, if you are reading this note, I am dead. I want you to take my ashes and spread them in the field here beside my cabin. I kept the long leaf pines well tended here. My daddy and I planted these pines when I was just a boy in 1939. Through the years, some of them have toppled down from the wind or lightning, but I kept replanting with old longleaf pines that have been here since the first white man came to this land.

There's a big field here, about 80 acres, and a road that leads down to the river. I want you to see to it that my ashes are scattered among the pine trees and down by the river. Hook up the mules, Sal and Buster, to the old buckboard and take Carl Alvin, Dee Dee, Nadine, Wanda Faye, yourself, Buck and Essie, and if she's able, take Mama Tee with you. I want her to be the one to say something, if anything is said about me. She won't make a long to do out of it. I can promise you that.

Destini, I hope my ashes don't kill any of the pine trees. There's a lot of piss and vinegar in those ashes, girl, and some folks would say there's just about as much poison in them as there is in deadly Nightshade. Love, Hamp."

"Can we cry now?" Wanda Faye asked, as she held Nadine's hand.

"Yes, you can cry now," Destini said. "I think I'm goin' join y'all, too."

Chapter 38

Destini was up bright and early Sunday morning with a mission to accomplish. She, Wanda Faye and Nadine had decided last night that today would be the day to put Mr. Hamp in his final resting place, just as he had asked her to do. As soon as she finished preparing breakfast for a group of hunting guests out at the camp, she made a phone call to her brother.

"Buck, see if Mama Tee is up to ridin' about a mile in Mr. Hamp's old wagon this afternoon," she said to him.

After she explained why, he said he would make certain Mama Tee was there right before sundown.

That evening, as the north Florida sun, in all its orange and red glory, began to descend behind the moss-festooned pines and oaks and dissolve into the majestic Suwannee River, Mr. Hamp's final journey began.

Invited to share in the journey, as Mr. Hamp had requested, was Dee Dee, Carl Alvin, Buck, Essie, Mama Tee, Wanda Faye and Nadine, along with Destini and Bunnye.

Buck had the wagon spit-shined and polished, and looking like a royal chariot. Wanda Faye thought the two animals pulling the wagon looked more like regal Clydesdales than mules, as they made their way toward the tall pines down by the river.

Buck was doing a good job keeping them on the trail and offering everyone a comfortable ride. Mama Tee was sitting quietly beside Buck with the urn clutched tightly to her chest. It took about twenty minutes before they arrived at a clearing alongside the river.

Destini and Buck helped Mama Tee down from the wagon, which was no easy task, considering how frail she was.

"Mama Tee, would you like to say something?" Destini asked.

"Yes, I would," she said. "Just a little something."

Mama Tee waited for everyone to gather around her and then she smiled and cleared her throat.

"It was an early mawnin' in nineteen and twenty-seven when I went with my mama up to the big house in Seraph Springs," Mama Tee began. "This boy's daddy came driving a pickup at full speed, pulled up to Mama's house and screamed from the window. He said, 'Minnie, you and Tee come go wid me! Miz Lillian's bad off! Bring yo bag!' We knew she wuz deliverin' and ol' Doc Campbell wuz with her. He wuz old, close to eighty, and his eyes were goin'. Miz Lillian was laborin' hard, real hard. Had been for a long time. Doc Campbell told Mama that if things didn't change, he didn't hold out much hope. Mama told Miss Sukie,

Miz Lillian's maid, to have a note sent over to the Brayerford house right away, and then have someone go over to Nebo to tell the pastor to ring the bell and call the peoples in to pray."

Mama Tee started to choke up and asked for a few moments to compose herself. After she chewed on some snuff for a few seconds, she continued.

"Mama told Doc Campbell she was goin' try somethin' and he said okay," Mama Tee said. "Then, she looked at me and told me to put my hands inside Miz Lillian and try to turn that baby's head around toward Miz Lillian's feet. My hands wuz small. I was only about fifteen years old at the time, so I reached in, but I was scared to death. I was scared 'cause other than combin' Miz Lillian's hair from time to time, I never put a hand on a white person, but I did like Mama told me. I turned Hamp Brayerford Jr. around and he come into this world," she said, grinning from ear to ear, and proud as could be.

The smile on her face didn't stay long, though. As she stood holding the urn to her bosom, tears began to stream down her cheeks, but she wasn't quite finished talking.

"I'm blind," she said. "Have been for years, but I can still see dat boy's face and dem feet. Biggest feet I ever seen on a newborn baby. Mama and I laughed about them feet. When his daddy came in to hold him, he said the boy had a good understandin' and he gave Mama and me both a twenty dollar gold piece. I wear mine around my neck to this day," she added, and she showed it to everyone.

Meanwhile, the rest of the group was fighting back their emotions, but it soon became a losing battle, as buckets of tears began to flow.

"That gold piece was minted in 1873," Mama Tee went on. "That was the year Miz Lillian's daddy acquired this piece of property we're standing on. Sho' did. Bought it outright from her mama's people, the Jarrellsons. It had been a part of the Jarrellson Plantation back during slavery times. This piece of property where these tall pines grow has heard the misery of them pickin' cotton and dippin' turpentine, and it heard the spirituals being sung. It also heard the laughter of my boy Hamp when his daddy and sister was fishin' here. Oh, lawdy, how Hamp laughed when he was younger and makin' google eyes at Miss Hattie before she married. This land has seen happiness and sorrow and yet, this land has stayed put."

Mama Tee motioned for Buck to hold the urn while she opened it. When she looked down at the ashes and placed her withered hand inside, her tears began to flow freely.

"Sorta soft and smooth, Destini," she said, as she let the ashes run through her fingers. "Just like when he came into dis world, soft and smooth. Not like my Hamp later on. He wuz an outdoorsman, never wearing shoes, and me havin' to get on to him, even in winter about goin' 'round wid no shoes. You coulda braided briars with the bottoms of his feets. Hated wearin' shoes. I'd see him walkin' toward my house with a string of catfish and a bunch of quail he'd shot, and sayin', 'Mama Tee, heat up the grease! Me and

Junior and Buck are gonna clean these and we'll have a feast!' And eat, my Lord, that boy could eat. Eat the most hoppin' john in one sittin' of any human I ever seen," she added, even managing a lighthearted laugh.

With that, she held the ashes in the palm of her hand, turned to the east, and then tossed them into the north Florida breeze. Everyone watched as they drifted across the sandy soil and the land covered with palmettos and tall, long leaf pine trees.

"Farewell, ol' boy, farewell!" Mama Tee shouted. "We'll see you soon, my baby, my friend. See you in duh mawnin."

One by one, everyone else reached into the urn, scooped out some of Mr. Hamp's ashes, and scattered them on the ground. Buck took a handful and walked down to the river, with Essie and Destini right behind him. Just as they were about to release the ashes, there was a rumbling sound coming from the other side of the river.

"Goodness," Essie said. "Sounds like some wild animal, don't it?"

"Looks more like Miss Aberdeen Jackson and the choir from Mt. Nebo," Destini said, as she gazed across the river, smiling a great big smile.

The choir was clad in white robes as they walked along the sandy bank to the river's edge. They were singing one of Mr. Hamp's favorite spirituals, "Wade in the Water".

"Wade in the water,
Wade in the water, children,

Wade in the water,
God's gonna trouble the water,
God's gonna trouble the water.
See that host all dressed in white,
God's gonna trouble the water,
Looks to me like the Israelite,
God's gonna trouble the water,
See that host all dressed in red,
God's gonna trouble the water,
Looks like the children that Moses led,
God's gonna trouble the water,
Wade in the water,
Wade in the water, children,
Wade in the water,
God's gonna trouble the water."

As the mortal remains of Hamp Brayerford drifted down the dark, tannic waters of the Suwannee River, Wanda Faye realized a truth. The dust from which this man was made was now his memorial, for it was the land that he loved. That was never a secret to anyone who knew him.

When the choir finished singing, Destini shouted across the river and invited them up to the lodge for refreshments. Miss Jewell, Sister Velma and the Bible Drill group had prepared a spread of food that was fit for a king.

That evening, everyone recounted stories about Mr. Hamp and they were all delightful.

"You know, stories are really what helps folks go on livin'," Destini said to Wanda Faye.

"Yes, so many stories," Wanda Faye said, as she put her arm around her best friend. "I'm so thankful we come from a place where so many gifted storytellers will keep Mr. Hamp's memory alive."

"Me, too," Destini said. "Not just for me, Carl Alvin and Dee Dee, but for my little Easter Bunnye, who will now know everything about her father, Mr. Hamp Brayerford. He was a good man."

৵৵৵৵৵৵৵৵৵৵৵

When Thanksgiving arrived, Camp EZ held their usual feast at the lodge and, as usual, quite a crowd of folks gathered to celebrate the event.

After dinner was served and not long after the first piece of pie was cut, Wanda Faye's water broke and she went straight into labor. There was no time to get her to the hospital, so Destini took charge, as she always did during any crisis.

Right there on the couch in front of the roaring fireplace in the great room of the lodge, Destini delivered Drayfuss Hamp Lowell, a six-pound, blue-eyed, bouncing baby boy.

"Welcome to the world, Little Hamp," Wanda Faye cooed, as she cradled her son in her arms.

"Yes, welcome to our world, Little Hamp," Destini said, as tears welled up in her eyes. "You will be loved."

About the author

White Springs native Johnny Bullard was born in a place where two cities and two counties interconnect on the banks of the historic Suwannee River. His family roots run about seven generations deep into the sandy soil of north central Florida, a place he dearly loves and where his entire life has been spent as an educator, public servant, musical performer and writer.

Born into a family of prolific storytellers, Bullard absorbed all the tales that were told aloud, as well as the ones whispered quietly inside screened porches and around the dining room table when family and close friends gathered together.

Bullard's grasp of the culture and life of this region is expressed by one who has not only lived it, but who loves it and is a part of it. He offers a humorous, poignant and honest voice of a South that is still colorful, vibrant, rich and real. Bullard is as much a part of the region as the historic Suwannee River, immortalized by Stephen C. Foster in the unforgettable tune, "Old Folks at Home".

An old turpentine distillery at the Eight Mile Still on the Woodpecker Route north of White Springs is where Bullard calls home. He boasts four college degrees from Valdosta State University in Georgia, including a B.A. in English. He also did post graduate work at Florida State University in Tallahassee, Florida, and was privileged to be selected to attend the prestigious Harvard Principal's Center at Harvard University in Cambridge, Massachusetts in 1993.

Bullard writes a weekly column, "Around the Banks of the Suwannee", which is published in the *Jasper News* and *Suwannee Democrat* newspapers. He has also written magazine articles for several well known publications including *Forum*, a quarterly publication of the Florida Humanities Council.

His weekly newspaper column always ends with his signature message to all his readers, friends and relatives throughout the region. He writes, "From the Eight Mile Still on the Woodpecker Route north of White Springs, I wish you all a day filled with joy, peace, and above all, lots of love and laughter."

Johnny Bullard

❧ ❧ ❧ ❧ ❧

Made in the USA
Lexington, KY
02 June 2016